Was he suggesting they take up where they left off eighteen years ago?

"Are you asking me on a date, Daniel?"

He grinned. "And if I were, what would you say?"

I would say that my racing heart couldn't take an entire evening with you. She cleared her throat. "Considering the recent events in my life—" *and a few significant ones from the past* "—I'd have to say no."

He leaned his forearm on the roof of her car. "Okay, then. I'm not asking you on a date. We'd just be two friends going out for the evening to catch up on lost time. What would you say to that? See if some of the magic still exists?"

Dear Reader,

Sisters. What a mountain of complexities in that one word. I suppose a sister can be a best friend one moment and a worst enemy the next. I lost my sister to disease many years ago when we were both still children. Perhaps that's why I've always longed for that special family member and gal pal to see me through the tough spots.

And maybe that explains why this miniseries for Harlequin Heartwarming, The Daughters of Dancing Falls, is so dear to my heart. The settings for the love stories of these three sisters is northeast Ohio, where I grew up. Each story is as unique as the heroine, but all share one vital commonality. Alexis, Jude and Carrie wouldn't have found their true loves without the love and support of the other two.

I hope you will enjoy this first story, *A Boy to Remember*, about Alexis, the oldest. Maybe you'll finish reading the book and call your own sister just to say I love you.

I love to hear from readers. You can contact me at cynthoma@aol.com.

Sincerely,

Cynthia

HEARTWARMING

A Boy to Remember

———

Cynthia Thomason

Recycling programs
for this product may
not exist in your area.

ISBN-13: 978-0-373-36772-6

A Boy to Remember

Printed in U.S.A.

Cynthia Thomason inherited her love of writing from her ancestors. Her father and grandmother both loved to write, and she aspired to continue the legacy. Cynthia studied English and journalism in college, and after a career as a high school English teacher, she began writing novels. She discovered ideas for stories while searching through antiques stores and flea markets and as an auctioneer and estate buyer. Cynthia says every cast-off item from someone's life can ignite the idea for a plot. She writes about small towns, big hearts and happy endings that are earned and not taken for granted. And as far as the legacy is concerned, just ask her son, the magazine journalist, if he believes.

To Amanda Sue Brackett, my sister,
and to all the sisters out there who mean
so much to each of us.

PROLOGUE

THE LUCKIEST GIRL in Ohio. How many times had Alexis Pope heard people refer to her this way? And today, driving through the lush, green pastureland that carpeted the mini ranches of Fox Creek, she could almost agree with them. Who wouldn't feel lucky to be returning to this magical, beautiful place of grace and charm?

And yet, in truth, Alex had never really believed in luck. Yes, she was lucky enough to be raised by loving parents in this town, with its top schools and clubs. But for the most part, she had made her own destiny.

The high grades she'd achieved throughout her schooling were not handed out to a *lucky* student. She'd worked hard for every A. Luck hadn't landed her in the National Honor Society. Luck hadn't rewarded her with first chair in the high school orchestra. Years of violin study, cramped and callused fingers, had put her in that chair.

And luck hadn't brought her back home today. No one would say "Oh, my, it's Alexis Foster…what a lucky girl." Especially not when they realized that she was only thirty-five years old and had recently buried her husband.

"It's so pretty here, Mom," her daughter said from the passenger seat. "I'm glad we came, but I hope we didn't leave Chicago just for me. I hope you wanted to come, too."

Those were the first words Lizzie had spoken in many miles. The silence had caused Alex to worry that her daughter, grieving over the loss of her father, would rather not have made this trip. She covered Lizzie's hand with hers and smiled. "Of course I wanted to come, sweetheart. I think the change of scenery will do us both good. And you know how happy Grandpa will be to see you."

"Auntie Jude will be here, won't she?" Lizzie asked.

"You know your auntie Jude. She is as much a part of this acreage as the trees and the grass."

"And Aunt Carrie?"

"The last I heard, Carrie was out west taking forestry classes. Unless she surprises us with a visit, I doubt we'll see her."

Dr. Martin Foster's three daughters were as different as could be. But one thing they all had in common. Each of them knew she was loved by her generous and supportive father. Each one knew she could always come home.

Alex turned into the drive, which led to a tall iron gate with the words *Dancing Falls* stamped in gray steel across the rails. With a touch of whimsy, a metal medallion showing a frothy waterfall lent authenticity to the name her father had chosen for his patch of heaven.

"The gate is open," she said. "Grandpa is expecting us."

They drove a quarter mile under ancient oak and maple trees before the house came into view. As stately as ever, its white brick walls and ebony shutters gave a majestic feel to the Georgian structure. Alex pulled around the circular drive and turned off her engine. Martin Foster, looking young for his sixty-four years, was dressed in tan chinos, a light blue golf shirt and boat shoes, his thick gray hair catching an Ohio breeze. He came down the front steps before Alex had opened her car door.

"You made it," he called, opening his arms to his daughter and granddaughter. He managed to fold them both into a hug at the same time. "I'm so glad you've come. I'm going to do my darndest to see that we make the most of this summer before Lizzie goes off to college."

Alex kissed her father's cheek. He meant that promise. But could a bottomless well of paternal caring erase the grieving of the past months? Alex stole a glance at Lizzie and found her bravely trying to smile, exactly what she had done during the funeral five months ago, exactly what she had been doing since. How Alex wished she could see a genuine smile on her daughter's face again. But the girl had adored Teddy Pope, and she missed him with an unquenchable ache.

"I guess it's all been said a million times, Lizzie." Martin's voice was gentle. "I know I said it at the funeral, but I'm so sorry about your father. I miss him, too. He was a good friend as well as a colleague."

"I know, Grandpa. Thanks." Grabbing her

backpack from the car, Lizzie walked into the house.

Martin put his arm around Alex's shoulders. "She'll be all right, darling. She just needs time."

Right. *And she needs to keep living the lie*, Alex thought. The lie that Teddy Pope was her father.

CHAPTER ONE

AT SEVEN O'CLOCK PRECISELY, Dr. Foster's house-keeper announced that dinner was served. Alex, Lizzie and Martin headed for the family dining room but were interrupted when the back door slammed.

"That must be Jude," Alex said.

"Of course it's Jude," Martin replied. "She may live in that apartment above the tack room, but at least she has the good sense to come here for her meals. Your sister has never been accomplished in domestic arts."

Jude Foster O'Leary, wearing what was obviously a hastily put-together outfit consisting of a belted aqua T-shirt over a long madras skirt, bounded into the dining room just behind her adorable five-year-old son, Wesley. The child still wore what Dr. Foster called his "barn clothes"—jeans, a button-down shirt and scuffed cowboy boots—but his hands looked clean and his hair had been combed. Alex couldn't say the same for her sister. Humidity-frizzed strands of blond hair refused to be tamed like the rest of her mane in the long braid down her back.

"Hey, you two," Jude said, hugging her sister first. "It seems like an age since I was in Chicago for Teddy's…" Realizing her niece might not be prepared to relive those memories, Jude glanced guiltily at Lizzie before kissing her cheek. "Yup, it's been too long, and I've missed you both. How are you doing, honey?"

"I'm okay, Auntie Jude," Lizzie said. She reached for her cousin and wrapped her arms around him. "You look like a real cowboy, Wes," she said. "A really hunky one."

The boy giggled. He had a little-boy crush on his cute big cousin.

"Glad you made it for dinner," Dr. Foster said.

"Are you kidding? I knew my sister was due today, so I wouldn't have missed it." She smiled at Alex. "Besides, I could smell Rosie's chicken enchiladas from the barn."

Jude was the first to admit that she was much more comfortable in jeans and a work shirt than a dress. But to her credit, she managed to fluff her long skirt gracefully over the seat of one of Martin's reproduction twentieth-century Chippendale chairs.

Jude had been Alex's rock during Teddy's funeral. Sadly, her sister understood all too well what the family was going through. She'd lost her own husband five years before when he was serving in Afghanistan. Now she managed the Paul O'Leary Foundation she'd established in his honor. Paul had possessed a heart as generous as his willingness to serve his country, and the money that came into the foundation was used for several philanthropic endeavors.

"Still not giving up your rooms over the barn to come back to the house, I see," Alex said.

Dr. Foster chuckled as he passed the platter of enchiladas and Spanish rice. "I've tried everything I can think of to get her to move in with her mother and me, but she insists on staying out there with the animals."

"I'm here when you need me," Jude said. "Besides, the barn is barely two-tenths of a mile from the house, Daddy. It's not like I'm living in a foreign country."

"But I still worry. You're remote out there…"

"When *don't* you worry, Daddy?" Jude said with a hint of impatience. "Wes and I are perfectly safe. If anyone comes near the barn, Mutt barks like the world is coming to an end."

Alex smiled to herself. Mutt was hardly a mongrel as his name suggested. He was a purebred Bernese mountain dog that Jude had come across in her work with animal rescue. She'd bonded with the friendly black-and-white dog immediately and brought him into her living quarters as the family mutt. The name just stuck.

"How about you, Wesley?" Alex said. "Do you like living above the barn?"

The child shrugged. "Sure. It's okay."

Conversation strayed to matters of gossip and local news until Jude asked the customary question. "How's Mama doing tonight, Daddy?"

"She's resting comfortably," he said. "The nurse told me she didn't have one of her anxiety attacks today."

"I went up earlier," Alex said. "I think she might have recognized me. At least I hope so."

"I'll go up and see her later," Jude said.

Her offer was met with pretended enthusiasm. Everyone knew that Maggie Foster, suffering from late-stage Alzheimer's disease, wouldn't know if her daughter came into the room or not. A good day was when Maggie's eyes focused long enough to bring hope to one of her family. Unfortunately, any hint of recognition had been rare the past year.

Once dinner was finished and the dishes had been cleared, Lizzie took Wesley into the family room for a game of War with Grandpa's worn deck of cards.

"So how is my niece really doing?" Jude asked after a moment.

Alex tried to convince her that things were not so bad. "She's improving all the time. In the last weeks she's even gone out with her friends, but I think she's been looking forward to the end of her senior year and the opportunity to come here. An apartment, no matter how spacious, doesn't offer the same healing benefits as this farm."

"She looks thin," Jude said. "And I agree with you. After a few months here, she'll get some color back in her cheeks and be more like her old self."

"We'll have to keep her busy," Martin said.

"Maybe she can volunteer at the hospital a couple of days a week. We can always use more teens."

"I'm not sure a hospital environment is what she needs right now," Alex said.

Martin agreed. "Who's got another idea?"

"She can help out at the barn," Jude offered. "I can definitely use a hand with feeding and grooming."

Alex remained silent for a few moments as she considered these suggestions. "Maybe," she finally said. "But I'm hoping to find an activity that is more in line with Lizzie's interests. Remember, she joined the drama club at school and scored the lead in the senior class play. I thought perhaps I could contact Glen Spenser." She focused on her father. "Does he still head up the summer stock theater?"

"He sure does. That's a great idea. Spenser's group is supposed to be getting ready for several performances of *The Music Man*. If Lizzie could get a role, rehearsing, learning lines—all of that will take up a lot of her time."

"If Lizzie gets a part, I'll have to make sure Glen understands her situation," Alex said.

"You don't really want her treated differently because she lost her father, do you?" Martin asked.

"No. But I need to be assured that she'll be in a healing, supportive environment."

When both Martin and Jude stared at her, she added, "I guess I've become an overprotective mother."

She felt her eyes well with tears, and her father got up, came around the table and sat beside her. "What about you, Alexis? How are you doing? Losing Teddy, worrying about Lizzie. I can see this is all taking its toll on you."

Alex leaned her head against her father's shoulder. Along with Teddy, her mother and father were the only people in the world who knew the truth about Lizzie's birth, everything but the biological father's name. As far as everyone else was aware—her sisters, and Lizzie herself—Teddy Pope was her dad. Through the years Jude had asked leading questions. But Alex had dodged all of them and believed that no one, not even Lizzie's biological father, whom Alex hadn't seen in almost eighteen years, could have been a better parent than Teddy.

"Tomorrow will be a better day, baby,"

Martin said. "Rest up the remainder of the weekend and see Glen on Monday. I have a hunch that the bright lights of Fox Creek's summer theater will be exactly what the doctor ordered for our Lizzie."

Alex sighed. If only she could count on that.

MONDAY, USING THE pretense of going to the rural farmers' market, Alex drove with her daughter past the Red Barn Theater. "Oh, look, it's still in business," she said, glancing at Lizzie to gauge her interest.

Lizzie leaned forward in her seat. "I wonder what production they'll put on this summer." She pointed to a sign near the road. "It's *The Music Man*. And they're announcing auditions. I love that musical."

Alex slowed the car. "Me, too. Why don't we turn around and go inside to check out what parts haven't been filled."

Lizzie shrugged, showing less enthusiasm than Alex had hoped for. "Mom, I didn't know you were interested in theater," she said.

Alex raised her eyebrows in an incredulous stare. "I was thinking about you, honey. You're the actress in this family."

The use of the word *family* seemed to leave a pall hanging over the car. As Alex pulled next to the renovated barn, Lizzie just said, "Oh."

Once they were inside the theater, Lizzie's demeanor changed. Her gaze darted around the interior, seeming to take in everything at once—the red velvet chairs, the rough-hewn rafters, the elevated stage with lights above and below. The stage lights weren't illuminated now, but one could just imagine... And Lizzie obviously was.

A man a couple of decades older than Alex called from the stage. "Can I help you?"

Glen Spenser was eighteen years older than the last time Alex had seen him at the Birch Shore Resort on Lake Erie. He had been their guru back then, both for the actors, like talented Daniel Chandler, and for the set builders and extras, like Alexis Foster.

Glen shielded his eyes from the glare of the overhead lights and came slowly down the steps at the side of the platform. "We're having tryouts today," he said. "If you'd like to audition..."

He stopped midway down the aisle. "Oh, my gosh, Alexis Foster!" He quickened his pace and took Alex's hand. "You haven't changed a bit. Still that gorgeous strawberry blond hair and a dazzling height of... What are you, five foot nine?" He chuckled. "I can still remember needing a prop from the top shelf and calling for you to come get it for me."

Alex smiled. "Hi, Glen. You haven't changed, either."

"Oh, honey," Glen said. "It's been almost twenty years, hasn't it?" He smoothed his hand over the sparse hair at his crown and smiled. "I think I'm even shorter now. Old age does that to a guy."

"How have you been?" Alex asked.

"Busy. Doing some graphic art work for local businesses and still puttering around theaters. Can't seem to get it out of my blood."

"Nor should you," Alex said. She took Lizzie's arm. "This is my daughter, Lizzie. We're going to be here for the summer."

"Wonderful. Staying out at the farm, are you?"

Alex nodded. Everyone in the area knew about Dancing Falls. Most everyone had been to barbecues there or knew the medical skills of Martin Foster.

Glen cupped his hand under his chin and appraised Lizzie. "You're as pretty as your mother," he said. "But your dark hair suits your olive complexion. You didn't get that from the Foster girls."

Lizzie smiled. "I guess not, but my dad was fair, too. So who knows? Genetics is a mystery to me."

Alex quickly jumped into the conversation. "I thought Lizzie might want to audition. Do you have any parts left?"

"You bet. One very important part. Zaneeta Shinn, the mayor's daughter. It's not a big role, but it's vital to the production." Glen took Lizzie's hand and began walking her to the stage. "Read for me now, honey. I know it's a cold reading, but you can take a script home and practice and come back tomorrow for a retry if you want."

Lizzie shot her mother a perplexed look as she was more or less propelled toward the stage. But she was smiling. Just like Alex was almost always smiling during that summer eighteen years ago.

Just like she was smiling now—until she

heard the door open behind her and turned to see who'd come into the theater.

Later, when she had time to think about it, she would have to admit that recognizing Daniel after eighteen years from thirty yards away down a long aisle was as natural as breathing. Only she wasn't breathing now. She felt light-headed and dizzy, fighting an urge to flee and a struggle to draw air into her lungs.

Alex was aware of noise around her though she felt as if she were in a vacuum. Someone on stage, working on the set, pounded a hammer. Overhead a fluorescent light buzzed and pulsed. And Glen hollered, "Hey, Danny. You're just in time, buddy. We've got a new audition for Zaneeta, and Larry needs a hand building the bridge."

"I came as soon as I could," Daniel responded, walking down the aisle toward Alex. His voice was as familiar as the sound of the waves on shore that summer, or the soft beat of rock and roll coming from a window in the summer staff's dormitory. Alex trembled, almost as if his words had been whispered into her ear.

Of course he was nowhere near enough to

whisper anything into her ear. But she could see he hadn't changed. The years had been good to Greenfield's native son, the young man who'd risen from humble roots to succeed in college and become the youngest state senator ever sent to Columbus from their district.

He slowed his pace when he got to Alex, gave her a brief smile as he walked past, and said, "Morning."

Then he refocused his attention on the stage. A hint of silver threaded the dark, wavy hair at his temples. Hair the same color as Lizzie's. He moved with the purposeful gait of a politician, each step determined and powerful. There had been nothing subtle about Daniel back then. There wasn't now.

And all the self-esteem and confidence Alex had acquired during her marriage to Teddy vanished in that one awful moment. Daniel Chandler didn't have the faintest idea who she was.

Eighteen years earlier

"So what do you think, Alexis? Does Birch Shore Resort look any different now that you're going to be working here? You used to love coming here when you were a kid."

Martin followed the signs leading to the employees' dormitory, keeping his large SUV within the twenty-mile speed limit.

Alex's anxiety had reached new heights in the last five miles. Granted, she was only seventy-five miles from Dancing Falls, but this home away from home seemed remote and alien, while at the same time exciting.

Martin pulled up in front of Pelican House, a two-story wooden structure built for Birch Shore employees. "Remember, Alexis, the first floor is for girls only. The second is for the boys. No wandering around in the middle of the night."

Martin's smile took the sting from his words. "Stop teasing, Daddy," Alex said. "I'm here to earn money for college."

"And don't I appreciate it!"

Martin and Alex got out of the car, and he opened the back cargo door. She'd managed to cram her most necessary possessions and three months of clothes into two suitcases and three large boxes, but getting them to her room wouldn't be such an easy task.

"I don't want you carrying this stuff," she said. "We need a cart or something."

As if by divine miracle, one appeared, an old grocery basket steered by a tall, incredibly good-looking boy. Alex swallowed, blinked her eyes. Actually, he wasn't a boy at all. She'd left all the boys behind in Fox Creek. This guy had to be two or three years beyond boy. Mature, handsome, smiling. Oh, my.

"Hi," he said. "Need some help?"

"Thank you, son," Martin said, giving the young man a thorough scrutiny. "You look familiar."

"I'm Daniel Chandler," he said, shaking Martin's hand. "I'm from Greenfield. I'll be working here this summer."

"Aren't you Gus Chandler's kid? I've seen you at the hardware store."

"I am."

"Small world. My daughter Alexis will be working here, too. This is her first extended stay away from home." Alex wished she had worn something much more fashionable than cutoffs and a T-shirt. She was mortified because her father made her sound like such a kid. Martin had told her this would be her

chance for adventure, freedom, independence, and already he'd pegged her as an inexperienced child. And to this mature man!

Daniel's grin spread, showing remarkably cute dimples. "Sounds good," he said. "Follow me."

The trio and their wobbly cart headed up the sidewalk to Pelican House. Daniel asked Alex for her room number and steered her belongings to a cramped bedroom for two at the end of the hall. The only furnishings were twin beds, two small dressers and one drying rack for towels and such. But to Alex it represented a whole new life, one where this wonderful boy would be living just upstairs.

Once the boxes were unloaded onto Alex's bed, Daniel wished her good luck and said he'd see her later.

Alex wanted to say something clever to ensure that he would, but nothing cute or flirty or even intelligible came to mind. She didn't know how to flirt, a skill she wished she'd perfected before this.

She walked outside with her father, hugged him and assured him she would be fine. When she went back inside Pelican House, Daniel was in the small lobby. Was he waiting for her? She could barely breathe.

"We've got a busy day tomorrow with orientation," he said. "How about if I pick you up at your room this evening at five thirty and show you where the employee cafeteria is?"

"Thanks. That would be nice."

She raced into her room and set her clock.

CHAPTER TWO

HAD THERE BEEN a place to hide, Alex would have run for it, but all the nonpublic places were backstage, and to get to them, she would have had to approach the three people on the stage. So, until the flare-up in her cheeks returned to normal—darn the curse of women with fair complexions—she sank into the audience seat and waited until Lizzie had auditioned.

How ironic that Daniel, the guy who had suggested she join the musical revue at the Birch Shore Resort, the man who'd dazzled her and changed her life, was now about to offer an opinion on Lizzie's immediate future. She couldn't trap a sigh as more memories of that magical summer flooded her mind. Her father had been right. Working at Birch Shore had given her opportunities. She'd met new people and shown off her talents. But Martin hadn't known that three days into her summer she fell in love with a charismatic Greenfield boy.

Alex sat forward in the theater seat, trying to hear her daughter's read for the part of Zaneeta. When Lizzie squealed her character's famous line, Alex couldn't help smiling. When Lizzie argued with Glen, who was playing her father, Alex felt proud. Lizzie had never argued with Teddy. Within reason, he'd given her everything she'd ever wanted, as if he was compensating for the family secret, the fact that he wasn't her real father.

She heard Daniel's booming baritone. "I can't see any reason to audition another girl. This one is perfect." He grinned at Lizzie. "Great read."

"So what do you think?" Glen said. "Do you want the part? You realize we have three weeks of rehearsal before the run of the musical begins. Then it's a full week of performances, a total of eight shows. Are you up to the challenge?"

Lizzie glanced into the theater. "I'll have to talk to my mother, but yes, I can do it."

Daniel moved to the edge of the stage. "Is that your mother out there?"

Lizzie nodded and Alex involuntarily sank farther into the chair.

"Hi, Mom," Daniel called. "We need to talk." He strode to the steps at the side of the stage and came down the aisle.

This was it. If he didn't recognize her now, she could maybe pull off anonymity until the summer was over. The only other choice was to deny Lizzie the opportunity to be part of the play, and Alex wasn't about to do that. This was the first time in months Lizzie had shown such enthusiasm.

Standing next to her, Daniel offered his hand. "Daniel Chandler. Among other things, I am an amateur actor—sort of."

Daniel had never been an amateur anything.

"May I join you?"

Alex took the hand that had felt as natural as a glove during that summer. "Hello, Mr. Chandler." She moved over a seat so he could sit next to her. What else could she do?

He did, giving her the same friendly smile that had won her over years before, a smile that was as genuine as it was memorable. "Daniel, please. I don't even get called Mr. Chandler at the statehouse."

Alex didn't comment, not wanting him to realize that she knew anything about him. As far as he was concerned, this was a first—and hopefully a last—meeting. After all, Glen was in charge of directing and producing. With any luck, Alex wouldn't even see Daniel again.

Daniel stared at the stage. "Your daughter gave a good read," he said before turning his attention to Alex. "We want her in the production."

Alex's gaze was caught in the warm beam of deep olive green eyes she'd never forgotten. She wanted to look away, look down, anything to keep him from scrutinizing her so closely. But his stare only became more intense.

And then his eyes widened. His brow furrowed. Another grin, slight, but just as charming as she remembered, tilted his full mouth. "Wait a minute," he said. "I know you."

She shook her head. "Well…perhaps…"

"Alex? Alex Foster?"

"No longer Foster now," she stammered. "Alexis Pope."

The grin spread. "So some lucky guy caught you. I'm not surprised. Do you remember me?

If you don't, it's okay. There were lots of guys after you that summer."

And she'd agreed to go out with a couple of them. But that was before Daniel became the best part of her stay at Birch Shore. The rest of her summer had been just Daniel.

"We were at the Birch Shore Resort together. I was going into my junior year of college at OSU and you were going to Wittenberg, I think, as a freshman."

She never made it to Wittenberg. Instead, she enrolled in art history classes as Alexis Pope at the University of Chicago, where Teddy took her to live.

"I seem to recall having to talk you into joining the revue that summer," Daniel continued. "It was the best way I could think of to get to know you better."

And it worked. Daniel was unlike any of the boys she'd gone out with in high school. He was experienced in ways they weren't. And he was nice. From the first day she'd met him, he'd treated her as if she was truly someone special.

Alex drew a long breath. She could hardly confess to not remembering the boy who'd… But then again, she couldn't admit what they'd meant to each other that summer. Daniel might have forgotten her once he was back at school, once she told him she'd moved on.

"Oh, right," she said. "I do remember you, though I don't recall too much about that summer…" If lying was a sin, she was doomed.

His eyes narrowed with a flash of doubt. "You don't remember spending time together, just you and me?"

"Well, yes, some," she said. "But there were other kids around most of the time."

He seemed to accept her answer. "It was a great summer, living in dorms, eating in the cafeteria, wearing those goofy uniforms."

"Yes, it was."

"Funny I've never run into you before now," he said. "You still live in Fox Creek?"

At least she didn't have to lie about that. "No. After I married, I went to live in Chicago. I'm just here visiting my father."

"I hope you'll be around long enough for Lizzie to have her chance on stage."

"Yes, we plan to stay awhile."

"Great. She's a minor, right? So Glen will have to get your signature on some papers, but we'll treat her with kid gloves."

"How involved are you, Daniel? Will you have an acting part in the play?"

"Nothing as glamorous as that. While I'm on hiatus from my real job, I'm helping with the sets. And since I've had some acting experience, I may try my hand at coaching some of the newer players. It's just a diversion for me really, and I've known Glen for a long time."

He was being modest. He had been the star of the resort revue. Audiences had loved his singing and dancing. All the girls had confessed to having crushes on him. The resort guests asked for him personally when they needed a favor during the day. That summer he had cleaned up on tips, stashing away every cent to pay for college.

"So this has your stamp of approval for Lizzie, Alex?" he asked. "I hope so. She's a natural."

"Sure. Whatever she wants."

He stood and called toward the stage. "Come on down, Lizzie. Your mom is on board."

Lizzie bounded down to the main floor. She scurried up to her mother and Daniel. "It's okay with you, Mom? I can drive myself whenever you don't want to bring me. You won't have to operate a taxi the whole summer."

"Yes, honey, I think it's a great idea."

Lizzie gave her a hug.

"It's settled, then," Daniel said. "Take a copy of the script home and start learning the lines. We'll have to get your dress size and shoe size so we can alert the costume designer that we have our Zaneeta. This was the last major role we had to fill."

Having heard the exchange, Glen joined the others. "I'd say this calls for a celebration, not just because we have our Zaneeta, but because old friends have met in this theater today. We need to catch up with each other. What do you say, Alex? All of us, dinner on me at the Jug and Boar?"

Alex ran a hand through her shoulder-length hair. "I don't know, Glen. I have obligations…"

"You can bring your husband," Daniel said. "And Lizzie can bring a friend…"

"I don't have friends here," Lizzie said. "And my father died…"

Alex felt the cold rush of guilt creep into her cheeks. There had been no reason for her to tell Daniel she was a widow, and yet she somehow felt as if she'd withheld that information from him.

Daniel stepped back. "I'm so sorry. How long ago?"

"It was January," Alex said. "We're still adjusting."

"Of course you are. Wow, that's tough. If there's anything I can do…"

"There isn't. I'm with my family."

"Okay, but if you think of something…"

Glen covered the awkward silence. "I think that dinner is even more important now," he said. "What do you say, Alex? Is tomorrow night good for you?"

Alex stood and maneuvered her way to the aisle. "I couldn't. You understand. Lizzie and I have to go now."

"Sure," Glen said. "We start rehearsals on Wednesday, kid. We'll see you at nine o'clock."

"I'll be here."

Alex and Lizzie walked to the exit, and only when she'd opened the door did Alex take a normal breath. She'd felt Daniel's gaze on her the entire way up the aisle and now had to convince her knees to quit trembling.

"Why didn't you want to go to dinner, Mom?" Lizzie asked. "Those guys are so nice. I wanted to go."

"Maybe some other time, honey. We've just arrived here. Grandpa wants time with you."

"Okay, but if they ask again, say yes."

Alex nodded. *You got away with this*, she told herself. No harm done. Surely she could manage a short summer season without Daniel Chandler knowing the truth about his daughter.

"HEY, WE'VE STILL got a bridge to build. Can we get some work done today?"

Daniel hadn't realized he'd been staring at a closed door until Richie Parker's voice echoed off the theater walls. Beside him, Glen chuckled. "Guess Richie doesn't realize we got something important done today that didn't include the bridge."

"Yeah," Daniel agreed. "Hiring Lizzie was a stroke of luck."

Both men turned and headed toward the stage, where construction of the romantic bridge had halted. "I don't know about luck," Glen said. "I remember Alex having a good bit of talent that summer at the resort. Maybe it runs in the family. At any rate, you and Alex made my job as choreographer run smoothly."

Daniel had thought of Alex Foster many times in the past few years. Because of her, that summer was the best he'd ever spent at Birch Shore. He had noticed her right away. In fact, he clearly recalled rushing up to the SUV her father drove and offering to transport Alex's bags into the dormitory. And it hadn't been ten minutes after her dad left that Daniel had invited her to go with him to the cafeteria for supper. And so began a relationship that seemed to have been built on days of grinding rehearsals, subpar meals and, what made it all worthwhile, moonlit walks on the beach that led to his eventually making love to Alex.

Oh, yeah, he'd had it bad for Alex that summer. Unfortunately, she seemed to have developed something equally as bad for another guy as soon as the season ended. The resort closed, the kids left, and except for a few phone calls, Daniel never made contact with her again. He'd searched his brain for reasons to explain her sudden surprising behavior. When logical explanations didn't come to him, he tried to forget her, to move on with other girls. But he'd ended the best summer of his life with a broken heart.

Eighteen years earlier

DANIEL RETURNED TO Ohio State believing that he'd met the girl of his dreams, the one who would make all his hard work and sacrifice worth it. Someday I'm going to marry Alex Foster, *he'd told his friends at Ohio State.*

The first phone calls had been exciting, fun, sprinkled with sweet words, and them sharing their dreams. They planned when they would get together again. And then, the last time she spoke to him, everything changed.

"You shouldn't call me anymore, Daniel," she said.

"Why? What's wrong? Are you ill?" If there was something wrong with Alex, Daniel made up his mind to leave campus and go to her immediately.

"No, I'm fine. But I'm moving on."

"Moving on? What does that mean?"

"I never meant to hurt you," she said. "But I've met someone else. Actually, he's a man

I've known for quite some time, and we've just discovered we're in love."

"I don't believe you, Alex. Something's wrong. We don't have to wait for Thanksgiving. I'll come to Wittenberg to see you. I can leave tonight."

"No, I don't want you to do that." She paused for torturously long moments. "I won't be at Wittenberg. I'm getting married."

"So it's over, just like that? We're through?" He hated the petulant tone of his voice, but it was so difficult to get the words out.

"I'm sorry. Really, I am." Her voice hitched. He wanted to reach out and grab her, shake her, find out what was wrong. "I have to go now."

The line went dead, and he held on to the phone even after her voice had faded. It took a long time for him to accept what had happened. That the girl he'd fallen so hard for had joined the insular world of the married, while he became part of the blur of a summer soon forgotten. But Daniel didn't forget. His grades suffered. His friendships became almost meaningless. No, Daniel hadn't forgotten.

"You're awfully quiet," Glen said.

His friend's voice brought Daniel back from a heartache he'd carried for a long time.

"Something wrong?"

Daniel shook his head. "No. I was just thinking…it's a shame that Alex is a widow at such a young age. Must have been hard."

"I'm sure it was, but maybe not all that surprising."

"Why? What do you mean?"

"I heard that she married someone her father's age, another doctor. That would make him even older than I am." Glen smoothed a few strands of thinning blond hair from his forehead. "If you can imagine that."

Daniel halted, stared at Glen. "Wow, I almost can't." Truly, he couldn't put the young, sweet Alex Foster with a man her father's age. "Why would she do that?" he asked.

"Love works in mysterious ways, my friend," Glen said. "I'm just sayin'…the guy could have died from old age."

Daniel didn't believe that, but still, it was strange. "Incredible," he said under his breath.

"Maybe she'll get another chance with someone her own age," Glen said, echoing Daniel's thoughts. "In the meantime, our pal Richie up there is getting grumpier by the minute. Hope you've got some time left in your busy day, Senator."

"I do. I told my dad I'd be at the hardware store by 3:00. That gives me five hours, minus a few minutes to eat the lunch you're going to treat me to."

Glen laughed, slapped a hand on Daniel's back. "You got it. Isn't it nice to have a hiatus from the state capital, Danny? You have all this time to sit around and contemplate the meaning of life."

"Right. Between working for you and my father, I haven't had time to contemplate the headlines in the *Greenfield Gazette*."

Only now he found himself contemplating relationships, especially one from his past.

CHAPTER THREE

WEDNESDAY MORNING JUDE breezed in the back door of the house, followed by an energetic Mutt. She grabbed a piece of toast from the platter left from breakfast, poured a cup of coffee and sat in the nearest chair. "Hi, sis. I talked to Dad before he left for the office, and he says you're going into Greenfield today."

Jude moved so fast and with such an economy of effort that Alex's head was about to spin. "I am, just as soon as I take Lizzie to the Red Barn Theater. Rehearsals start today."

Jude munched on the dry toast, alternating taking a bite for herself and offering bits to Mutt. "She excited?"

"She is. I think this activity is going to be great for her." *Minus the fact that she might be working with her biological father.* "And just exactly why are you interested in my trip to Greenfield? I need a few things at the drugstore, so I shouldn't be long."

Dusting crumbs from her hands onto the table, Jude reached into her back jeans pocket. "I thought maybe you could pick up some stuff for me at the hardware store."

No way. The only hardware store close by was Chandler's, owned for years by Daniel's father, Gus. Alex intended to steer clear of that location. Not that the junior state senator would be there, but why take the chance?

"I don't know anything about hardware, Jude," Alex said. "I live in a maintained condo in the middle of Chicago. I've never fixed so much as a loose lightbulb."

"You don't have to know in order to buy," Jude said. "Just show the list to Gus, and he'll gather everything. Anyway, it's just a slide bolt for the hay bin, some pegs for the board in the tack room, a galvanized bucket..."

"Whoa. This sounds confusing."

"No, it doesn't. Why are you acting like stopping at Chandler's is such a big deal?"

Jude's ability to see through any ploy had often been irritating, but never more so than this morning. Jude had a sixth sense for sniffing out the truth, and she was right. Going to a hardware store shouldn't be a big deal. Unless a woman's old boyfriend, one who barely remembered her and was the key to a life-altering secret, might happen to be there.

Alex couldn't think of a reason to avoid Jude's errand. Besides, rehearsals started this morning. Daniel had said he wanted to coach, so if he was anywhere close, he'd be at the theater. And even if he wasn't, what were the chances he'd be at the store? Didn't he have civic duties to perform?

"Fine. Give me your list," she said.

"You'll be back by 2:30, won't you?"

"Sure, but why?"

"I have to pick Wesley up at the bus stop, and I want to be at the barn when you come by. Thought you might like to see some of the improvements I've made to the property."

"I would. Lizzie enjoyed her tour yesterday, and she's even less of a horse person than I am."

Jude stood suddenly. "Gotta go. Got a dozen goats waiting for breakfast." She left by the back door, trailed by a tail-wagging Mutt, and hollered over her shoulder. "Thanks, Alliebelle!"

Alex smiled. Despite the tension of knowing Daniel was nearby, coming home had its advantages. Like being with her mother and father, and hearing the nickname she'd almost forgotten in the past few years. The Foster sisters were a tight group, each different from the other, yet loving in her own way. Alex missed Carrie. They talked two or three times a week, but even so, her absence felt as if a piece of the puzzle was missing.

"Mom, I'm ready!" Lizzie came into the kitchen, her backpack over her shoulder, the script she'd been studying in her hand, and her dark hair fastened into two braids. "It's 8:30. I don't want to be late."

"Let's go, then."

The drive on the rural road to the Red Barn was peaceful. A few farm trucks gave a pastoral feel to the mix of BMWs and other classy cars of Fox Creek neighbors. On the way, Lizzie went over her lines. "I don't have that big a part, but I want to do a good job. This is my first real acting gig."

"And your last before you head off to Bryn Mawr," Alex said. The two women had carefully considered all the top schools in the east where Lizzie could study literature, and they'd decided on the all-female Pennsylvania college. At first Lizzie had protested the absence of men, but when she discovered she could take classes at the University of Pennsylvania, which was coed, she readily accepted Bryn Mawr's offer.

"I wonder if Daniel Chandler will be here today," Lizzie said as they approached the theater. "I hope he is."

Alex took a deep breath. "I don't know, honey. He didn't sound as if he'd be terribly involved when I talked to him."

"He's really good-looking, isn't he?"

"Ah…" What would be the point of denying what was so obviously true. "I suppose."

"Did you notice his arms and hands? He has lots of muscles for a guy who normally wears a suit."

Alex didn't answer, but she definitely remembered those strong, athletic arms.

"I mentioned him to Grandpa, and he told me that Daniel was elected to the state senate two years ago. He's really popular with everyone in this district. Grandpa voted for him."

"I would imagine that he's kept busy with his duties. I wouldn't count on seeing too much of him at the theater."

Lizzie sighed with a typical teenage dreaminess. "He'd make a hunky Henry Hill, don't you think?"

Determined not to focus on the fact that Lizzie was talking so openly about her *father*, Alex made light of the question. "I'm sure a state senator doesn't have time to be the lead in a small-town summer production."

"You're probably right."

They pulled into the lot and got out of the car. Lizzie entered the theater first and went right to the stage, where Glen and several other people were milling about. Thank goodness Daniel wasn't one of them.

"Hey there, Zaneeta!" Glen called. "Now we're all here for the first day's rehearsal." He smiled at Alex. "You want to stay, Alex? I'm sure we can put you to work."

She laughed. "I've already been given an assignment from my sister. I'm on my way into Greenfield."

"Okay. We'll probably wrap up around three. But I'll have Lizzie call you."

Glen was introducing Lizzie to the other cast members as Alex left the theater. Okay, so their first meeting was just a temporary snag. Chances were, Lizzie wouldn't see much of

Daniel for the rest of the summer. And Alex wouldn't, either. Crisis averted.

Once she'd finished paying for her purchases at the drugstore, Alex drove down Main Street to Chandler's Hardware. She'd run in, hand the list to Gus and be out in five minutes, tops. She angle-parked in front of the century-old brick building and went inside. Familiar smells made her remember trips to this store with her dad when she was a very little girl, before her studies kept her busy. The scent of freshly cut lumber, the rusty tang of old nails, the smell of tanned leather. All good memories, until she met the owner's son and hadn't returned since.

Gus Chandler was behind the cash register. His gray hair was thinner than she remembered, and his skin had the pallor of an Ohio winter. But in his flannel shirt, loose-fitting denim pants and carpenter's apron, he looked as if he was dressed for a business he loved. There was something comforting about the perseverance of small-town icons. They stuck it out, didn't cut and run, like she had.

Gus gave her a welcoming grin. "Well, well…look who's here. I haven't seen you in a month of Sundays."

"It has been a while. You're looking good, Mr. Chandler."

"You, too. Pretty as I remember. My son told me he ran into you the other day. Said you lost your husband."

Alex nodded. Daniel had mentioned her to his father?

"Sad thing, that," Gus said. "You're too young to be a widow."

Alex handed him Jude's list. "My sister needs some things at the barn. Since I don't know what any of this is, I'm trusting you to get them for me."

"No problem." He moved a few steps from the register and that was when Alex saw the cane leaning against the counter. And the noticeable limp in Gus's right leg. "I don't get around like I used to," he said. "But I've got good help here today."

He cupped his hands around his mouth and called, "Danny, can you come in here a minute?"

Alex's mouth went dry. She'd thought she might see Daniel at the theater, but she hadn't expected to find him at the store. She quickly glanced around, nervously seeking an exit.

But leaving was ridiculous and would call more attention to herself than staying.

Dusting off his hands on a rag, Daniel came from the back storeroom. His eyes lit up, and a smile spread across his face when he saw her. An honest reaction or a politician's gimmick?

"Hey, Alex! Imagine seeing you twice in— what? Four days. Must be my lucky week."

"Hello, Daniel. Lizzie was hoping you'd be at the theater today."

"Nope. Not today. I'm helping Pop with inventory. I expect Glen will have me working a few hours tonight, though. The sets are pretty complicated for this musical."

He removed a Cleveland Indians ball cap long enough to smooth a lock of dark hair from his forehead before replacing the hat and tugging the brim low. "How is Lizzie this morning?"

"Excited. I dropped her off at the theater."

"She'll love working with Glen. He makes it fun." Tucking the rag into the back pocket of his jeans, Daniel crossed his arms over an Ohio State T-shirt. His gaze, however, never left Alex's face. She suddenly felt small and vulnerable. "What can I do for you?" he asked.

"She's got a list of things," Gus said from behind the counter. "If you don't mind…"

"Happy to." Daniel took the list, grabbed an empty box from the floor and said, "Follow me."

With the expertise of someone familiar with every nook and cranny of a hardware store warehouse, Daniel went about selecting the items from Jude's list. When he filled the box and had seemingly exhausted every bit of small talk about Greenfield town life, he turned to Alex and said, "So how's your stay in Ohio going?"

"It's all good. This is home, so you know."

"You bet I do. I spend most of my time in Columbus these days, but it's always nice to come back to Greenfield."

Unable to pretend any longer that she knew nothing about Daniel's career, Alex said, "I heard you were elected to the state senate. That's quite an accomplishment."

"I don't know about that. I like to think I connected with voters on a basic level of honesty and caring."

"I guess you did. Sorry I wasn't here to vote for you." As if he needed her one measly vote.

He smiled. "I would have gotten your vote, Alex? That means a lot to me."

Her face grew warm. "I must admit I didn't know your opponent, but yes, I'm pretty sure I would have voted for you."

He made a quick check through the box and set the list inside with the items.

When the silence became uncomfortable, Alex said, "So, do you have aspirations beyond the state senate?"

"We all have aspirations, don't we? But for now I'm content. I'm working on a few projects that I believe will benefit both the citizens of Fox Creek and the Greenfielders. Just need to acquire more funding."

"Well, I'm sure you'll succeed." Alex nodded at the box. "I have to be on my way now. Can I carry this?"

"Probably, but why should you? I'm the jack-of-all-trades around here. Is your car out front?"

"Yes, but I think I'd better stop and pay."

"Oh, sure. Pop would appreciate that."

Alex reached out a hand almost as if she would touch Daniel's arm, but immediately pulled back. "He's okay, isn't he? Your dad, I mean. He seems a bit frail."

Daniel's face clouded with an emotion that could only be pain. "I don't suppose there's any reason not to tell you, at least not now that certain decisions have been made. Pop's ill, Alex. He has bone cancer. Even a bone marrow transplant won't help him now."

Her heart clutched in her chest. "I'm sorry, Daniel. This must be so hard."

"It is. He's got some time left. A few months, so the doctors tell him. That's why I'm here and why I took hiatus from my senate job this month. I'm helping him clear out inventory so the building can be put up for sale. Once that's done I figure he might take a short trip, see some of America he never had a chance to visit before."

"Will you go with him?"

"I can't. I wish Mom were still alive, but his sister has agreed to go. They get along well. And I'll stay in touch with them every day."

"Why doesn't he try to sell the business?" Realizing she might be crossing a line between concern and poking her nose into someone else's family matters, Alex amended, "What I'm trying to say is, this store has been here for decades. It's a shame to see it close and the building be turned over to some other establishment. This town would miss Chandler's Hardware."

"You just said it, Alex. This store is *Chandler's*. That's why people keep coming back. If it changed hands, I think the big-box stores around Cleveland would get our local customers." Daniel sighed. "I think Pop's right. It's been a good run, but it's time to close it up." He picked up the box. "You stop at the register and I'll meet you outside."

Alex paid her bill. She tried to keep her voice cheerful, but she could no longer ignore the lines etched in Gus's face, the signs of the pain he must be enduring every day. And that cane, propped against the counter like some bleak reminder that everyone's future had an ending.

"You have a great day now, sweetheart," Gus said when she was ready to leave. "It was great seeing you again."

"Same here, Gus. I'm sure I'll be back a time or two before I return to Chicago."

Marveling at the way Gus kept his spirits up around other people, she went outside, motioned to her Honda CR-V and beeped the hatch open in back.

Daniel slid the box into the cargo area. "Nice seeing you," he said when he'd closed the door.

"Again, Daniel, I'm so sorry."

"Thanks." He paused while she went to the driver's side and got in. "Oh, Alex, before you go…"

"Yes?"

"Would you like to get together while you're in town? Maybe take in a movie?"

Was she reading his question correctly? Was he suggesting they take up where they left off eighteen years ago? Didn't he remember she was a widow? "Are you asking me on a date, Daniel?"

He grinned. "And if I were, what would you say?"

I would say that my racing heart couldn't take an entire evening with you. She cleared her throat. "Considering the recent events in my life…" *and a few significant ones from the past* "…I'd have to say no."

He leaned his forearm on the top of her car. "Okay, then. I'm not asking you on a date. We'd just be two friends going out for the evening to catch up on time lost. What would you say to that?"

She smiled. "Still no, but thanks anyway."

"You know where I am if you change your mind. Either here, at Pop's house or at the theater. People can always use friends, Alex, and you and I were tight once, as I recall."

That was the way he remembered that night under the dock, the last night of the summer? They'd been two hormone-driven teenagers who couldn't keep their hands to themselves. He'd had a few beers. She'd had one powerful one. And to inexperienced Alexis Foster, Daniel had been much more than a friend. He'd been the brightest star in her summer, maybe in her entire life, and he'd just reduced the most important emotions she'd ever experienced to the word *tight*. He might have been talking about teammates on a sports roster.

She put her car in gear before she said something much too meaningful for this moment. "Maybe I'll see you around, Daniel."

"That would suit me fine. I'll be looking for you."

"Wow, COULD YOU have made it sound any worse?"

Daniel didn't even realize he was speaking

out loud until his father said, "What's that, son? Couldn't quite get that."

He tried to put his asinine comment about being *tight* with Alex from his mind as he walked to the counter. He hadn't been talking to his best friend from high school, for heaven's sake. He'd been crazy about Alex.

"Nothing important, Pop," he said. "I was just giving myself a personal evaluation."

Gus chuckled. "How'd you do?"

"I failed."

"I doubt that." Gus continued flipping through the day's invoices. "She's a pretty one, that Alexis Foster," he said.

"It's Alexis Pope," Daniel said.

"Oh, of course. I always remember her coming in here with her daddy. I don't usually keep up with the social news around here, but her marriage was something of a surprise. She married a colleague of her father's, much older man. And I remember your mother commented that they didn't have a big hullabaloo of a wedding like you'd think for a Foster girl."

"Strange you or Mom never mentioned that marriage to me. I even asked about Alex a couple of times."

"I guess it slipped our minds," Gus said. "Or we didn't think you'd be interested. Besides, the wedding seemed downplayed to me."

That was odd, Daniel thought. Most girls wanted big weddings, didn't they? Why did Alex make up her mind and tie the knot within weeks?

"What else did you hear, Pop?"

"Not much, but a few months back, a customer mentioned that the doctor had died. A shame. That pretty lady won't wither long on the vine, though. Some lucky man will snap her up."

Daniel thought of one man who had tried and failed. Back then he'd been a struggling college kid who earned tip money by catering to the people who had it. Maybe Alex had appreciated his charm, but she sure tossed him aside when something better came along. All the charm in the world couldn't compete with a successful doctor on his way up the ladder.

Going back to his inventory of the warehouse, Daniel continued on this train of thought. Besides having his heart ripped out and stomped on, he had been disappointed in Alex. He hadn't pegged her as the kind of girl who would marry for money or prestige. Meeting her again after so long, she still didn't seem that way. Sure, she was classy and cultured and could hold her own in any crowd, but there was still some of that shy, eager small-town girl who had shown up at Birch Shore that day. So why had she married the much older doctor?

Maybe Daniel had pegged Alex wrong. Maybe he'd pegged himself wrong, too. Maybe he hadn't been as charming as he'd thought back then. Maybe she'd seen something in him that summer that made her rethink her interest after they parted.

He shrugged his shoulders, trying to shake off his memories of Alex. Did it really matter why she broke up with him? His father was probably right. Soon enough, some lucky man would snap her up. Maybe another doctor.

CHAPTER FOUR

ON THURSDAY MORNING Alex quietly entered her mother's cheerful, serene room and padded across the plum-colored carpet, past the single bed where her father had slept every night for over four years. Pulling up a delicate, petit point French armchair, she settled next to the large double bed where Maggie Foster lay peacefully.

"Good morning, Mama," Alex said. "Daddy's gone to the office, Rosie's out doing the marketing and your nurse won't be here for another hour, so it looks like you're stuck with me."

The heavy lids over Maggie's dull blue eyes lowered for a moment, and Alex could almost convince herself that her mother was trying to clear her vision to see her better. "That's right, Mama. It's me, Alexis."

She cradled her mother's palm in hers and imagined a smile curving the rosy lips that had kissed her forehead so many times in the past. Alex stared at her mother's hand. Heavily veined now, the skin was still subtle and smooth, the fingers delicately bent at slender knuckles. If only those fingers could contract and grab hold of Alex's hand like they used to.

If Maggie's mind hadn't started to fail her, slowly and deliberately beginning six years ago, she would probably still be the vibrant, energetic and caring woman who had stood by her husband's side and raised three daughters. Today her heart was strong, her vital signs healthy. But her mind, once merely confused, was now mostly dormant, like a pond that once rippled in a breeze but now remained still as a mirror.

"I'm kind of in a pickle, Mama," Alex said. "It's about what happened eighteen years ago, the thing I told you and Daddy about." Alex sighed, gathered her thoughts as if the words she was about to say really mattered to the person hearing them. "You and Daddy were both so caring when I came to you with my problem. You didn't pressure me to tell you the name of my baby's father. You let me keep my secret. And you didn't argue when I said I wanted the baby.

"I loved you for your understanding then, and I still love you for it today." Drawing a deep breath, Alex continued. "But I saw him, Mama. I saw Lizzie's father. I never expected to, and now I don't know what to do. He's a decent man. He's accomplished and well liked and—" Alex let a small smile precede her next words "—I have to say he's quite good-looking in that tall, dark and handsome way we Foster women have always been drawn to."

Alex leaned closer to the bed and lowered her voice. "The thing is, Mama, Lizzie has met him, too, and she likes him. So you can see what a muddle this all is. Lizzie misses Teddy so much, which is why this is so hard. If only things were different. This man could never take Teddy's place. No one can fill the void left by Teddy in Lizzie's life. And even if it were possible, I can never tell her. Not now. Not ever. Lizzie would never forgive me."

Alex scrubbed away a tear she realized had spilled onto her cheek. "I thought I was doing the right thing all those years ago. This man…and I still won't tell you his name…" Alex chuckled at the absurdity of her words.

"He wasn't a Fox Creek boy, not that it

would have mattered to you and Daddy. He came from a good middle-class family. His parents both worked and he had a job at his father's place from the age of thirteen on. He was his family's pride, their hope for the future. Circumstances weren't as easy for him as you and Daddy made them for me. He scrimped and saved for college and now has made a name for himself. He couldn't have done that if I'd saddled him with a baby, and I have a pretty strong hunch that he wouldn't have allowed Daddy to support him."

She gently squeezed her mother's hand. "He wouldn't be where he is today if I'd made him marry me, Mama. In fact…and this is what hurt the most at the time… I don't believe he even loved me, at least not the way you and Daddy taught us about love. Oh, he liked me well enough. He even called a few times. But the bottom line is, I screwed up, Mama. One time, but I'll never be sorry. Not as long as I have Lizzie. I would do anything to keep my daughter's love and respect."

She bent over the mattress and kissed her mother's cheek. "Thanks for listening, Mama. You always do, and even if you don't know it, it always helps. I know I can never make this right, not with Lizzie, not with Dan…" She stopped herself. "I would lose too much, more than I already have, and I can't risk it."

As if hearing her words for the first time, Alex paused before saying, "Does this seem selfish to you, Mama? Maybe it is, but Lizzie is all I have left." She thought of Daniel and realized that he would probably never be more to her than a faded memory from her past. "And all I'll ever have," she added.

Alex stood and went to the window. "Jude is riding this morning," she said. "She is beautiful on that horse, Mama, just like you were. I think of the three of us, Jude is most like you, and I'm thankful every day that your light still shines through her."

She sat again in the chair, picked up a book and began to read aloud until the nurse arrived.

AT FOUR O'CLOCK Alex drove to the Red Barn Theater to pick up Lizzie. She no longer thought about avoiding Daniel. In the past week she'd realized that he could be anywhere, doing who-knew-what good deeds for the community and his father. He was on a monthlong hiatus from the senate, and she would have to adjust to seeing him around the area.

Like she did when she entered the theater.

Her breath caught. In faded jeans and a T-shirt, he looked so like the boy she once knew. Only today he wasn't wearing the ball cap, and his hair, slightly long for a politician with *aspirations*, reached to his crew neck and fell over his brow. Maybe this was his idea of "hiatus hair." Whatever, it worked, and Alex reminded herself to remain aloof.

"Hi, Mom!" Lizzie called from the stage, where she was stapling material to a backdrop. Alex never knew her daughter was adept with a staple gun, but then, Lizzie probably never knew that herself until now.

Alex stayed at the back of the theater and waved. Daniel looked up from a project he was working on, smiled and continued with his job. He didn't call out to her. Maybe he'd gotten the message yesterday. That was good, wasn't it? So why was Alex disappointed?

Lizzie put down the stapler and came off the stage. "I tried to call you," she said when she reached Alex. "I wanted to ask you if I could stay later today. We're all sort of in a groove here with the set. I'd like to help out."

Alex took her phone from her pocket and checked the screen. Yes, Lizzie had tried to call and somehow Alex had missed it. "How much longer do you want to stay?" she asked.

"Probably nine or so."

"So long? But dinner…"

"It's no problem. Glen is going to order pizza." She leaned close. "And besides, Daniel just got here a few minutes ago, and he's promised to give me some acting lessons later."

Alex couldn't keep her attention from darting to the stage again. Daniel was deep into his work and didn't look up. She might not even have been there.

"Isn't he just the coolest guy?" Lizzie said. "So handsome."

Alex forced her gaze back to her daughter. Lizzie and Daniel together another five hours? So not a good idea. "I wouldn't know about that. What I do know is that I'm not too keen on going home for five hours and then coming back out on these dark roads to pick you up."

"Oh, please, Mom. Glen says Daniel is the best. He can really help me with my part. You have to let me stay." Lizzie smiled in that little-girl way that always earned her mother's sympathy. "Can't Auntie Jude ride out here with you later so you won't be alone?"

Now Alex felt like a simpering weakling. "I won't need Jude. I'll come back. But be outside at nine. I don't want to have to come in after you."

"I'll be ready. And thanks. Can you imagine? A former actor and a state senator helping me? It's way cooler than anything!"

It's downright scary, Alex thought. Introducing Lizzie to Glen had seemed such a good idea. She didn't know she'd also be introducing her little girl to her fa— *Don't go there, Alex.*

Thankfully, Lizzie had always had a good head on her shoulders, but Alex felt she had to say something now. "Just don't lose sight of your future, young lady," she said. "When the summer is over, it's over. No more acting gigs, no more hanging out in theaters. It's college time."

"I know that!" Lizzie darted away, heading back to the stage. "See you later, Mom."

Alex returned to her car. A sinking feeling settled in her stomach as she started the engine. Her daughter had just called her bi-

ological father *the coolest guy*. Hadn't Alex
thought that herself about Daniel some years
ago? This was going to be a long five hours
and an even longer few weeks.

AT NINE O'CLOCK Alex pulled into the theater
parking lot. Her daughter and Daniel were
sitting on a flower box next to the front door.
A single light illuminated their faces. The
only other car in the lot was a Ford SUV,
probably Daniel's. Glen and the other volunteers had obviously gone home. Alex stared
at the two of them a moment while trying to
control the pounding of her heart.

   The similarities astounded her. Both dark-
haired and with almost olive complexions.
Both with strong, wide shoulders as if they
could build sets for the world. Both with those
incredibly deep green eyes. Both of them
good-natured, helpful, charismatic. And each
of them could be deeply hurt if they knew the
truth about each other. The sight of them on
that flower box, their heads together, their
hands animated in conversation, was enough
to make a lying mother spin out of control.

   Not now, Alex, she told herself, opening the
car door. No spinning allowed.

She walked up to the flower box and was greeted by both her daughter and Daniel.

"We were just talking about ways to make the Wells Fargo Wagon scene more authentic," Lizzie said. "Daniel has such wonderful ideas."

"Don't give me too much credit," he said, chuckling. "I'm just enjoying using my hands again and not having to decide policy for a few weeks. Besides…" He smiled fondly at Lizzie before switching his attention to Alex. "Your kid here is the one with the hammer skills. If she doesn't pursue a career in acting, she can join a set-building crew."

Alex appreciated the genuineness of Daniel's compliments, but she couldn't allow the false impression to go on. "I'm afraid acting and building aren't in Lizzie's future," she said. "She's going to Bryn Mawr to study literature." Alex almost cringed. Even to herself she sounded like a stodgy old mom.

"Wow, Bryn Mawr," Daniel said. "Very nice."

"I guess," Lizzie said. "But this is so much fun."

"Let's go, Lizzie," Alex said. "It's getting

late." Turning to Daniel, she added, "Thanks for keeping an eye on her."

Daniel stood. "No problem. I never get tired of talking shop. In fact, I was wondering if you ladies would like to grab some ice cream. Sounds like a perfect topper to a productive day."

Alex tried to convince herself that this wasn't a second date invitation. This was simply a small kindness from a charming man on a warm summer night. Still, there was no way this threesome could be pals, even over ice cream.

"Oh, please, Mom," Lizzie said. "Let's go for ice cream, just the three of us."

She struggled to keep her tone light as if this suggestion was no big deal. "Not tonight, honey. Grandpa is waiting for you to play a game of chess with him."

Before Lizzie could protest, Daniel said, "Another time, then. I have a hunch we'll have a lot to celebrate by the end of the summer." He walked to his car and opened the door. "Rain check, ladies, okay?"

"Sure," Lizzie answered for both of them.

He waited until Alex had pulled out of the parking lot before he followed. Alex wondered where he lived in Greenfield. Probably with his father now. He had a lot farther to go than she and Lizzie did.

After a short distance, Lizzie said, "Daniel is so great, Mom. He's smart and funny, and he's helped me with my acting. I really like him."

Alex's brow furrowed in alarm. "You do realize that this production is just a diversion for you, right? Your sights are still set on Bryn Mawr and later on a teaching position."

"Well, sure. But it's not every day a girl gets to work with someone as talented as Daniel. And a state senator! You've got to admit, Mom, he's a really great guy."

Alex was not a bit comfortable about the direction this conversation was taking. Lizzie had so recently suffered a terrible loss. She was young and impressionable. And she was obviously vulnerable to the same Chandler charms that had influenced her mother. Alex could only envision a nightmare of problems ahead for all of them if Lizzie developed a crush on her mentor.

"Yes, he is all that, I suppose," she said, "but Lizzie, don't get any ideas about you and Daniel…"

"What do you mean *ideas*?"

Alex cleared her throat, glanced at Lizzie. All at once her daughter's eyes widened in shock and her jaw dropped. "Mom! Are you kidding me? You think I like Daniel *that way*?"

Alex swallowed. Yes, that was exactly what she'd thought. "I'm not jumping to conclusions, honey…"

"Yes, you are. How gross! I like him, yeah, but he's old enough to be my father!"

A sharp pang sliced into Alex's chest.

"You couldn't be further from the truth, Mom," Lizzie said. "I was considering Daniel as date material, sure, but not for me. I was thinking he'd be perfect for you!"

ALEX COULDN'T FIND any words to respond. She was grateful the road was nearly deserted or she might have wiped out, taking a farm truck with her. Her hands gripped the steering wheel and she focused her gaze on the ribbon of blacktop. *Just drive, Alex*, she said to herself. *Don't say anything that could get you in trouble.*

After a mile or so, Lizzie said, "Mom, did you hear me? I said you and Daniel would be so good together. And I think he might be interested in you."

Alex exhaled a deep breath. "Yes, I heard you."

"Well, doesn't it make you feel better that I'm not interested in him for myself? Good grief, Mom, he has gray hairs! And since you married Daddy, you obviously like gray-haired men."

Alex felt her temper, the one she rarely showed, flare inside. Her cheeks felt hot. She could almost sense a rise in her blood pressure from the pounding in her head. "I didn't choose your father for the color of his hair, Lizzie. That was very unkind of you."

"I'm sorry. I'm only trying to be helpful."

"Well, you're not being helpful at all. I don't need my daughter to arrange dates for me or to interfere in my social life."

"No offense, Mom, but what social life?"

Alex gave her daughter a sharp look. "It's only been five months. What did you think? That I'd start looking for dates the first chance I got?"

"No, of course not, but this wonderful man, Daniel, has just about fallen into your lap.

Would it have hurt you to go out for some stupid ice cream?"

"I'm not going to discuss this with you any more, Lizzie. This whole conversation is inappropriate." *And uncomfortable. And frightening.* "I'm your mother, for heaven's sake!"

"And I love you, so I want you to know that I don't expect you to live like a nun. You're still young."

Alex's shoulders relaxed and she loosened her hands on the steering wheel. In a calm voice, she said, "How I choose to live my life is my business, Lizzie. Right about now, life in a convent doesn't look so bad."

Lizzie giggled, erasing the remaining tension from the car. "Have you looked at Daniel, Mom? I mean really looked? He's your age. He's single. He's successful. And he's gorgeous. Any woman would be happy to share a hot fudge sundae with him!"

"Enough, Lizzie!" Alex caught a quick glimpse of her daughter, who was smacking her lips. "You're impossible."

"I'm only having fun, Mom, and I want the same for you. Haven't we been sad long enough? Loosen up, maybe give Daniel a try."

Oh, my poor, sweet, blissfully ignorant daughter. If only Lizzie knew that her virtuous mother had already given Daniel a try, and that it was coming back to haunt her in the worst possible way.

CHAPTER FIVE

AT SIXTY-FOUR, Martin Foster knew he could retire. He'd been healing hearts for decades. He'd saved many lives and lost very few. He paused to consider the vow he'd made when he'd first become a doctor. That the ones he'd lost would always remain in his memory.

Yes, he could retire, maintain his lifestyle, help his daughters if they needed him and continue the care his Maggie so desperately needed. But he liked being a doctor. He was good at it, so he decided to practice for two more years and retire when he was sixty-six.

He worked five days a week and rested on the weekends. He loved his Saturdays. He could play golf in the summer, take his grandson, Wesley, to a ball game or do what he was doing this particular Saturday morning, sitting on his back patio with the newspaper and a cup of coffee. Ah, bliss…

Until a knock at his front door disturbed

his solitude. Rosie had taken the day off. Alex and Lizzie were out shopping, and Maggie's nurse never left her bedside. So that meant there was no one to see who it was but him.

He folded the newspaper with a gentle curse and went to the door. He opened it to a petite woman he couldn't remember ever seeing before. She had a soft cotton rope in her hand. On the other end of the rope was none other than Mutt. Behind the woman, parked in his circular drive, was a rusty red pickup truck at least half as old as he was.

"Ah, hello," Martin said, his attention switching from the woman to the dog.

"Hello. I won't take up much of your time," the woman said. Her voice was stronger than he would have expected from a lady no taller than five feet three inches. Maybe her attire should have clued him in to an inner strength. Her blue jeans were loose-fitting and practical. The sleeveless plaid shirt tucked into the jeans was frayed at the shoulders. One of those trendy outfitter labels over the pocket indicated she might have once paid a pretty penny for her clothes, but nature and a washing machine had taken their toll.

"No problem," he said. "I believe you have my daughter's dog."

"Good. I was hoping he came from this direction. I don't have a lot of time to track down a stray dog's owners."

"I assure you, he's not a stray," Martin said.

Since Mutt was pulling on the rope, trying to get to Martin, the lady removed the make-shift collar from around his neck. Mutt immediately lifted his front paws to Martin's Dockers and nuzzled a large furry head into Martin's chest.

"This fella still has a lot to learn about manners," Martin teased. "But I'd say he's glad to be home."

"He has a lot to learn about boundaries, too," the woman said. "Or at least his owners do."

"I beg your pardon?" Was the woman indicating that Mutt had somehow run off and was wandering the roads? He'd never done that before. At least Jude had never complained that he had. Good grief, the canine had at least fifteen acres to satisfy his desire to sniff.

"He came onto my property, right into my backyard. I had my parrot in the screened room, and Bully started up such a ruckus, I thought a gorilla was trying to get to him."

Anticipating where this was going, Martin reached for his wallet. Perhaps the parrot had had a stroke and Martin would have to pay a vet bill. Or, if he was lucky, he'd only have to reimburse this woman for a torn screen. "Were there any damages?"

"I don't want your money," the woman said, scowling at his wallet. "I want you to control your animal."

Martin slipped the wallet back into his pocket. "Understandable. I apologize for any inconvenience. It's not like Mutt to run off."

The woman almost smiled but stopped herself in time. "That's his name? Mutt?"

"That's what my daughter called him when she rescued him. It stuck."

"He's not, you know."

"Not what?"

"A mutt."

"Yes. I've heard he's some sort of mountain dog, and believe me when I tell you I've never known him to attack birds at sea level."

"He's a Bernese," she said. "A valuable animal, which is another reason to watch him more closely. Dognapping is a serious problem, you know."

He didn't. "I'll do that, or at least have

my daughter pay more attention." Martin snapped his fingers to bring Mutt all the way into the house, and put out his hand. "My name is Martin Foster. I don't think we've met before." He would have remembered that haphazardly cut auburn hair with streaks of gray that didn't age her in the least, but were somehow appealing as a framework for her blue eyes and animated face.

"Just moved in a week ago." She shook his hand. "I'm Aurora Spindell."

"Aurora. A lovely name." Now he remembered. Several months ago his neighbor to the west had put his large home on the market and moved to Florida. The place had stood empty since then, which explained why Martin never gave it much thought. So, it finally sold. But probably not for the enormous price tag Jamison wanted. "You're in the Jamison house, right?"

"I am. It's the Spindell house now."

"Welcome to the neighborhood."

A strong breeze blew strands of hair across her face. She gathered the whole patchwork mess of it into a bun thing and wrapped it in some sort of elastic band she pulled from her wrist. For some reason Martin was fascinated with her practiced movements. In two seconds the hair was bound, leaving only a few wispy strands over her forehead.

"I want to be a good neighbor," she said. "But I can't have a big dog like this coming into my yard. I'll be having guests starting in about a month, and a dog this size can be intimidating."

"I'll do my best."

"You might have to do better than that," she said. "Obviously, your best so far has been to allow your animal to traipse wherever he wants."

The criticism made Martin back up a step. "Now, just a minute, Aurora… I may call you Aurora?"

"Makes sense. That's my name."

"Yes, of course. Please call me Martin. My family and I weren't aware of any problems with Mutt. But now that we are, we'll be more vigilant. I appreciate your bringing him home."

"Thank you. That concludes my business, then. By the way, I don't believe in creatures being tied up. It's not natural. But you might consider mending your fence. Your dog obviously knows his way through the holes." With that, she strode back to her truck, climbed inside with ease and sped around his drive.

Martin had thought about repairing the fence around Jude's space before. Now, as he watched Aurora Spindell leave, he guessed he'd have to do it. But he couldn't help wondering what guests she would be having. So far, her clothes, her frank way of speaking, her beat-up truck were the only clues he had. Was she a throwback to the hippie era and starting some kind of commune? Did she have a large, raucous family? Was the neighborhood going to seed?

He only had to wait until Monday to find out. When he went into city hall to pick up a permit to add more fencing to his property, he ran into Aurora. He was tempted to avoid her and not admit that he was acquiescing to her demand, but instead, he waved the paperwork in front of her face.

"You know the old saying, Martin. Good fences make good neighbors." She smiled.

"Sound advice then. Still is."

"Seems wanting to me. What about a few other qualifications," Martin said. "Like civility."

"Here's your permit, Ms. Spindell," the clerk at the counter said. "Best of luck to you."

Martin couldn't resist taking a quick look as the paper was passed across the counter. It read "Aurora's Attic, an authentic English bed-and-breakfast."

He left shaking his head. How was that little ball of fire going to pull off a pinkie-raising tea party?

By Wednesday night at dinnertime, the existing fence had been repaired and stakes laid out for new sections, and Jude had been properly warned about keeping an eye on her dog.

"I don't see what the big deal is," Jude said, taking a large helping of Rosie's stew. "Mutt wouldn't hurt a flea."

Martin frowned, though he agreed. Mutt was a tongue-lapping, lap-climbing canine, whose only interest was pleasing everyone in Fox Creek. "You and I may know that, but our new neighbor thinks he could seriously damage the peace and calm of a certain parrot."

Alex laughed. "Mutt versus a parrot. That I'd like to see. Something tells me the bird would come away unharmed, and Mutt would be covered in bites."

Lizzie darted a glance underneath the table. "Shh, he'll hear you, and all this talk might hurt his self-esteem. He thinks he's a miniature grizzly."

They talked a bit more about the mysterious lady who'd moved into the Jamison house and intended to open a bed-and-breakfast. Alex noted that she'd seen workmen at the location. Jude mentioned seeing landscapers on the lawn. Martin was silent. Alex wondered what was going on in her father's head. He'd brought up the subject of Aurora Spindell a few times in the past four days. Strange behavior for a man who was dedicated to three things in his life—his practice, his family and his ailing wife.

"I think I saw her at the feed store yesterday," Jude said.

Martin leaned forward in his chair. "Really? What was she buying?"

"Bales of hay," Jude said.

"Why would she want hay?" Martin asked.

Jude shrugged. "And now that I think about it, she also bought birdseed."

"That's for her parrot," Wesley said, obviously proud of his powers of deduction.

"You know, I'll bet you've got something there," Martin said.

Conversation switched from Aurora to Lizzie's rehearsals. As usual, she praised her mentor, Daniel Chandler. And as usual, Alex refrained from joining the praise fest.

"He offered to take Mom and me for ice cream," Lizzie said. "Mom wouldn't go."

Jude dropped her fork on her plate. "Really, Allie-belle? From what I remember of his campaign posters, he was ice creamy delicious-looking."

"That's what I told her," Lizzie said. "I said he was just being friendly and maybe even a little bit interested in her."

Alex did a quick mental count to ten before speaking. No one at this table needed to know that she agreed about Daniel's looks. Or that he'd asked her on a date. "I didn't come home to find a man," she said. "And in case anyone has forgotten, I'm just getting over a very stressful time."

"No one has forgotten, honey," Martin said. "You take all the time you need. Just thought I'd remind you that I voted for Daniel."

What was this? Another spokesperson for the Daniel Chandler fan club. "So I heard," she snapped back.

"And no one accused you of looking for

a man," Jude said. "But if one as dreamy as Daniel lands at your feet, I'd think you'd at least take notice."

She was planning a retort when Rosie came into the dining room. "A phone call for you, Alex. Shall I tell him to call back?"

"Him?" Jude said.

Alex sent her a scathing look. "No, Rosie, thank you. I'll take the call." She appreciated an excuse to get away from all these well-meaning, interfering people!

She went into her father's study and picked up the receiver. "This is Alex."

"Hi, Alex. Daniel Chandler."

She blushed just thinking about how they had all been discussing him only moments before.

She gripped the phone tightly. "What can I do for you, Daniel?"

"I'm calling with an invitation," he said. "But I thought it only fair to give you a heads-up since this concerns Lizzie."

"Lizzie? You're inviting my daughter some-where?" She instantly began to come up with reasons why she wouldn't allow such a thing. "Daniel, I don't think…"

"No, no. You misunderstand, Alex. I'm not inviting Lizzie to go somewhere just the two of us. I have tickets to *Les Mis* at the Cleveland Auditorium. I thought Lizzie would enjoy it."

"Well, yes, but still…"

"Alex, let me finish. I have three tickets. I'm inviting both of you to go along with me. The performance is Friday night. It's the perfect break for all of us who have been working at the Red Barn. What do you say? I can pick you ladies up at Dancing Falls."

The three of them out on the town together? It was unthinkable. Alex couldn't allow it. They would be attending the theater almost like a family… Alex concentrated on drawing a deep breath so that her next words wouldn't come out sounding rushed and panicky.

"Alex? You there?"

"Yes, I'm here. It's a nice idea, Daniel, but I'm afraid we can't make it Friday night. We have plans." Her brain scrambled to come up with a reasonable excuse if he asked.

"Can't you change your plans? I'd hate for Lizzie to miss out. The reviews of *Les Mis* have been spectacular. This is the Broadway performance."

What kind of a mother was she to prevent her daughter from attending a special theatrical event? Alex quickly pushed the guilty thought from her consciousness. A careful, protective mother—that was what kind. One who wouldn't play games with fate by putting the three of them in a social situation. A slip of the tongue, a chance remembrance of past encounters, the uncanny resemblance between father and daughter…

"No, Daniel, we can't change our plans. I appreciate your offer, but it's just not possible." She sucked in a breath between her teeth. Even after keeping this secret for eighteen years, she was a terrible liar. And, at times, an awful mother.

"Okay, if you're sure…" Daniel said.

"Mom, what's wrong?" Lizzie's voice permeated the charged air of Martin's study. "You're as white as a sheet." Lizzie came into the room. "Who's on the phone?"

"It's Daniel Chandler, Lizzie," Alex replied. "But we're done talking. I was about to hang up. Go on back to the dining room and I'll be there shortly."

Daniel's subtle accusation came over the line. "You're not going to tell her, Alex?"

Lizzie reached for the phone. "Can I speak to him, please? I want to ask him something about tomorrow's work schedule."

"No, now's not a good time," Alex said. "Daniel is busy."

"No, I'm not," he said.

"Daniel, please, I'm talking to my daughter," Alex said.

Lizzie grinned and mouthed the words, "Did he ask you out? I knew it!"

"I'm hanging up now, Daniel."

"Then I suppose I am, too. If you change your mind—"

"I won't."

Alex replaced the receiver on the cradle. The walk back to the dining room seemed to take forever as she dodged Lizzie's questions.

"What did he want?"

"Where did he ask you to go?"

"You said yes, didn't you?"

"Mom, talk to me!"

"What's going on?" Martin asked when they'd returned. He took a large helping of peach cobbler. "Who was on the phone?"

"It was Daniel Chandler," Lizzie said. "And Mom won't tell me what he wanted. I think he called to ask her on a date."

"He did not," Alex protested, though she couldn't come up with any other reason why Daniel would call. And since her daughter saw him nearly every day, she would probably hear about the invitation to *Les Mis* anyway.

"A date?" Jude said. "How exciting. You're going, aren't you?"

"There's no date!" Alex said again.

"Then what did he want?" Lizzie asked.

Alex let out a long, defeated sigh. "All right, I'll tell you. He has three tickets to *Les Misérables* at the Cleveland Auditorium for Friday night. He asked us to go. Both of us," she said with a pointed stare at her daughter.

"Oh, my gosh, *Les Mis*!" Lizzie clasped her hands together. "How great is this!"

"I told him no," Alex said, pretending not to notice the look of shock on Lizzie's face. "You and I had talked about going to dinner and a movie on Friday, honey, remember? I thought you wanted to do that."

"Instead of *Les Mis*? Are you kidding, Mom? Call him back. Tell him we'll go."

"It's too late," Alex said. "I already turned down the invitation."

"You could at least have asked me!" Lizzie said.

That was true, and any other time, under any other circumstances, Alex would have consulted her daughter. But not this time, and that did seem strange. "I'm sorry. I thought…"

"Mom! I'd give anything to see *Les Mis*."

"Maybe it's not too late," Jude said. "Call him back right now."

"Yes, Mom! Do it."

Alex didn't speak. She just drummed her fingernails on the tabletop.

After a moment Jude said, "Tell you what, Allie-belle. Call him back and tell him I'll go. If you'll watch Wesley, sis, I'll attend the play with Daniel and Lizzie."

"You? When's the last time you saw a Broadway production?" Alex regretted the snarky tone as soon as she'd spoken.

"So? What difference does that make? I don't think Lizzie should miss this." She winked at Lizzie. "I promise not to wear my denim skirt."

Alex knew she was defeated, and she almost didn't care anymore. Where just a few moments ago panic had seized her limbs, now a spark of excitement flamed to life. It was only a play. Just one night. And it was Daniel. "All right, I'll call him back," she said. "And I'll go."

"Thanks, Mom! We'll have a great time."

"I'm sure we will."

What was she doing? Walking to the study again. Dialing the last known caller back. Listening for Daniel's voice. Telling him she'd moved her schedule around. And hearing his enthusiastic response.

She realized that she had butterflies in her stomach like she had as a teenager whenever she was with Daniel. And she'd most definitely lost her appetite like she had during that first meal with him at Birch Shore.

Eighteen years earlier

"So you're from Fox Creek?" Daniel said. "That's really close to my town of Greenfield."

Alex took a nervous swallow of iced tea so she wouldn't talk with her mouth full. So far, during this meal together, Daniel had gotten up and refilled her tea glass twice. He must think I'm a bottomless pit, *she thought. "I know. My dad used to go to your father's hardware store."*

"What's your primary job at the resort this summer?" he asked, showing no sign of the

anxiety she was experiencing. Daniel seemed as if he'd be at home in any environment.

"I'll be working in the gift shop," she said. "I start learning the inventory and pricing system tomorrow." Another sip of tea. "What about you?"

"Glorified bellhop," he said. "I greet the guests, find out their room numbers in the hotel and arrange to have their bags brought up. Then I see if they have any special needs or requirements." He smiled. "I'm basically making tips this summer, but after working in the buffet last year, I wanted this assignment. If you're nice to people, they can be quite generous."

Probably doesn't hurt that you're so gorgeous, *she thought. "Are you saving for college?"*

"Yep. Taking political science courses at Ohio State. I'll be a junior this year. What about you?"

Her parents had agreed to pay for whatever her scholarship and this job didn't cover. Still, she knew a private school might seem an extravagance to this boy. "I...ah, I'll be going to Wittenberg as a freshman."

He nodded. "Good school. What are you taking?"

"Art history courses." Why did her chosen major suddenly seem like a course in looking at pretty pictures? "I want to have a career in museum acquisitions."

"Cool. Sounds interesting."

Daniel just had a way of taking everything in his stride. He didn't even raise an eyebrow at her college choice. And if he wasn't impressed with her career decision, he didn't react in a negative way. He was just...well, nice. He'd seemed nice when she first met him, and she had no reason to change that opinion now.

"Hey," he said. "You should join the revue. The summer employees put on a show six nights a week. We start rehearsals tomorrow, but we only have a week to get ready."

A show! Unless the revue had a full orchestra and needed a violinist, Alex couldn't see a role for herself. "I don't know," she said. "I can't sing. I can't dance."

He grinned. "Anybody can dance, Alex. I can teach you in one lesson. And you can always work backstage. It's a great way to earn some extra money in the evenings.

Better than hanging out with the other kids and playing cards or going into town for a movie."

She didn't know what to say. She'd looked forward to her free time here when she could read and listen to music. But this boy... There was something special about him.

"Come on," he said. "I'll take you to the auditorium myself, introduce you to Glen Spenser. He's the director. He'll love you."

Alex sighed. This was going to be the best summer ever.

CHAPTER SIX

DANIEL PUT THE kitchen wall phone back on the hook and went to the refrigerator. He realized he was smiling as he cut a slice of cherry pie for his father and scooped vanilla ice cream on top. He hadn't thought Alex would say yes, and in fact, she hadn't. The return phone call had been a wonderful surprise. He wondered what changed her mind. Lizzie probably, but he hoped it might be him.

He handed his father the dessert.

"Looks good, son, but you don't have to wait on me," Gus said.

"After force-feeding you my special recipe meat loaf," Daniel said, "it's the least I can do."

His father chuckled and dug into the pie.

Daniel sat in one of the easy chairs that had flanked the practical plaid sofa as long as he could remember. "Pop, I have to ask you something. I've got a busy weekend coming up, and I need to know if you'll be okay here by yourself."

Gus wiped his mouth with a napkin. "Danny, I know I'm going to die, but I'm not dying yet. I'm perfectly capable of taking care of myself. Besides, you've got every neighbor on this block and my sister on call for emergencies. So you go and do what you have to do."

"Okay, then. I will."

"Just to satisfy my curiosity, what plans have you made?"

"I've got town hall meetings on Thursday and Saturday nights. Going to concentrate on the millage proposal for the new recreation area at Crabapple Lake. I really want the voters to approve the raise. Residents of the entire district will benefit from the improvements."

"You've got my vote," Gus said, causing Daniel to wonder if his dad would still be here when voting came around in November. "You going out Friday night, too?"

"Yes, but this time it's not business as usual for me. I'm taking Alexis and her daughter to the theater in Cleveland."

"Good for you, Danny. You should get out and have some fun." They discussed the musical and possible plans for afterward, and then Gus said, "So what about Alexis's daughter? Is she as pretty as her mother?"

"She's a cutie," Daniel said as an image of Lizzie came to mind. "But now that I think about it, she doesn't look like her mother. You know Alex has that fair skin and blond hair. And she has blue eyes. Lizzie is darker. Her hair is brown and her eyes, well, I don't know. I think they're green, but an unusual shade."

"She must look like her daddy, then," Gus said.

"I suppose." Daniel scratched the back of his neck. Odd that Lizzie didn't display many characteristics of her mom. She was pretty in her own right, sure, but usually daughters looked more like their mothers than their fathers, right?

Daniel picked up the empty pie plate and headed to the kitchen. He'd just gone through the door when he stopped, took a deep breath and held it. When exactly did Alex marry Teddy Pope? He knew it was at the very beginning of fall—just after Daniel had experienced the most memorable few months of his life with a girl he thought he could love forever. And why would they have a child right away? Because Teddy was older? Well, sure, that was a reason to hurry up with a family. Still, Daniel couldn't keep his thoughts from going back to that one special night under the pier.

Eighteen years earlier

THE BREEZE OFF *Lake Erie was cool, but the temperature of the sand, warmed from a day of bright sun, seeped through the blanket and erased any chill. Daniel reached into a cooler and removed another beer. He didn't drink much, but tonight he had two reasons to commemorate the occasion. This was their last night at Birch Shore, his last night with Alex, for a while at least.*

He popped the cap. "Here, Alex, one isn't going to hurt you."

She took a long swallow while he quickly finished his fourth. He'd probably polish off the six-pack. Heck, he needed something to help him deal with leaving Alex. She would be several hours away at Wittenberg.

He would stick around Birch Shore for three days to clean up and store summer furniture, and then his dad was picking him up to take him directly to Ohio State. Daniel didn't have a car. All the great tips he'd made had gone right into his college savings. If he wanted to see Alex, he'd have to make friends with someone who owned a vehicle and didn't mind lending it out.

Alex nuzzled her long, sweet-smelling hair under his chin. With his arm around her, he gently traced a line from her shoulder to her elbow. He'd fallen hard for her.

She drank the entire beer and giggled when she burped. "It was good," she said.

He kissed the top of her head. They'd found moments and private places to be together during the summer. Some of their kisses had turned passionate, but Daniel knew she didn't have much experience and respected that. Tonight he'd have to watch himself. Five beers were like a stiff shot to a guy's libido.

His intentions were noble. He and Alex would spend their last night, precious hours under the dock, hugging, kissing and holding hands. They would discuss the future and make plans to see each other again. He would make it clear to her that he wanted what they'd found together this summer to be permanent. He would ask her not to date at

Wittenberg. He was a one-woman guy, and he hoped she'd treat him the same way.

She turned her face up to his and offered her lips. As he kissed her, he realized something had changed. The kiss was like no other. Alex poured her heart and soul into it, and it lasted for the sweetest, longest forever Daniel could remember. She seemed to melt into him, her body fitting perfectly to his. And his hands started to wander. She felt so good, so warm.

She didn't stop him, and it took all of his willpower to put the brakes on his desire. "I'm sorry, Alex," he said. "I didn't mean..."

"It's okay," she whispered. "I want this."

"We can't," he said. "I don't have a... What if you get pregnant?"

She was silent a moment, her hand splayed over his chest. "I won't get pregnant," she said. "I'm on the pill."

"What? Why are you on the pill?"

"It was for irregular periods, but I'm protected."

His heart beat furiously. "Are you sure, Alex? Is this what you want?"

"Yes, I'm sure..." Her voice was a gentle hiss, a perfect blend with the waves rolling *on shore. He placed his hands on either side of her face and kissed her as if his life depended on it.*

As clear as that cloudless summer night, Daniel recalled making love to Alex as he'd recalled it so many times since that night. What if…

"You're nuts," he said aloud in his father's kitchen. "No way. Alex would have told you if she'd gotten pregnant. She wasn't the kind of girl to keep something like that bottled up inside. She was honest and principled." Wasn't she?

He made up his mind to find out what he could about Dr. Theodore Pope. He hoped the good doctor had tan skin and brown hair. Besides, Alex told him she was on the pill, and that was practically foolproof, wasn't it? Daniel wasn't Lizzie's father. It simply couldn't be.

CHAPTER SEVEN

THE THEATER BUZZED with anticipation, and despite her misgivings, Alex was pleased to be a part of it. What Daniel hadn't mentioned was this was opening night. Wearing press credentials, critics from newspapers and online blogs were in the front-row seats. Wine was served in sparkling glasses. The musicians tuned their instruments to the rhythm of a sea of excitement. Daniel's tickets were for the sixth-row center.

With a quick glance over her shoulder at her mother, Lizzie carefully and quickly maneuvered her way into the row of seats first. Daniel waited politely while Alex went in next, and then he followed. When they were settled, Alex pretended to look at her playbill, though she wasn't focusing on any of the words.

Only an hour and a half ago, Lizzie had lain on Alex's bed as Alex dressed in her basic black sheath and rhinestone-studded heels. She added a black-and-white bolero jacket at the last moment. "I guess this will do," she'd said to her daughter.

"It's nice," Lizzie said. "But why don't you wear a scarf instead of that jacket?"

"What's wrong with the jacket?"

"Nothing, Mom. But it does kind of date you." When Alex started to protest, Lizzie added, "I mean, you're still so pretty, and you have a great body. Why hide it under something so boxy?"

"Because I'm not on a hunting expedition, Lizzie," Alex said, but she returned to her closet and fingered through the few scarves she'd brought with her from Chicago. She chose a silver-and-black gauzy one, tossed the jacket to the bed and loosely framed her shoulders with the scarf. The look seemed to transform her from matron to date. Unsettling? Yes, but she felt feminine, and, well…

"Daniel is here, ladies," Martin called from the foyer.

Alex grabbed her bag and followed Lizzie down the stairs. The tails of the thin scarf fluttered behind her like the wisp of a cool breeze. The look in Daniel's eyes made the last-minute change worth the trouble.

Now, sitting in row F in the ultramodern theater, next to a handsome man she once thought she loved, Alex felt younger, vibrant, more womanly than she had in years. Not that Teddy hadn't complimented her often. He had, but she'd never tossed aside an expensive jacket for a simple scarf to please him.

As if reading her thoughts, Daniel leaned in close and said, "You look lovely tonight, Alex."

Her face flushed, a pleasant but slightly embarrassing reaction. She wanted to return the compliment but didn't. Daniel was, to use an almost archaic term, *dashing* in a dark suit and black tie. The footlights reflected off the tops of his polished black loafers. But the other Daniel, the one who could build a set and inventory a hardware store, was still present under all that finery. His hair was skillfully mussed. His face was shadowed with a hint of beard. His cologne, woodsy and fresh, rattled her senses whenever he leaned close enough for his shoulder to touch hers.

Yes, she wanted to tell him that he looked nothing short of magnificent. If they had been friends, she could have. If they had been lovers, she could have. But in truth, they were neither. They were practically strangers who once knew the magic of a few idyllic summer months. And far from being on the verge of romance tonight, if she wasn't very careful, they could be headed for disaster. So she muttered a simple, "Thank you."

After what they all agreed was a remarkable performance, Daniel took them to a popular restaurant near the theater where the adults had champagne and Lizzie a ginger ale. They all indulged in decadent desserts served on delicate china plates, each sharing bites.

When Daniel turned into the drive of Dancing Falls at nearly midnight, Lizzie thanked him for the evening. He had barely stopped the car when she jumped out of the backseat flashing her smartphone. "I'm sorry to rush off," she said. "But I have calls to return to my friends in Chicago." She smiled at Daniel. "I told my girlfriends I was going to *Les Mis* tonight."

Scurrying toward the house, she called back, "No hurry, you two. Finish your conversation."

Alex couldn't help smiling. Lizzie had been

steering her and Daniel together all evening. They had been talking about a key child care facility for single working mothers that Daniel had initiated. Alex thought they had finished the discussion.

Daniel turned and placed his hand on the back of her seat. "So, back to politics, eh? What would you like your senator to do for you, Alexis?"

Such a leading question! Maybe it was that second glass of champagne, but Alex had to stifle a giggle.

"What is so amusing?" he asked.

"My daughter," she said. "Lizzie is about as subtle as a cyclone."

"Well, good. I need someone on Team Daniel."

She smiled. "What exactly does Team Daniel want?" She was enjoying the innocent flirting much more than she should. It *was* innocent, wasn't it?

"First of all, I'd like to know if your memories of that summer are as vivid and happy as mine are."

Probably more. Except for an outcome that changed her life, her memories were indeed happy ones. She'd made love with Daniel.

It had been perfect. But she couldn't admit to that. "We were kids, Daniel. Everything that happens when you're young seems to be monumental in importance, both the good and not-so-good."

"Come on, Alex," he said. "What happened between us was all good. At least that's how I remember it. Every night, waiting for the show to end so we could steal a little time together. We were so close…for as long as it lasted."

His voice took on a dreamy, sad quality. She wanted to wrap her hand around the arm that lay on her seat back. Of course she couldn't. "We can't go back, Daniel. You know that."

"I'm not talking about going back." He leaned in close to her and she caught another light but heady whiff of that cologne. "I'm suggesting we go forward from now, tonight." His hand slipped to her nape, and he gently rubbed the tender skin under her hair. "I really want to take advantage of this moment Lizzie gave us. I want to kiss you, Alex, see if some of the magic still exists."

She backed away from him and wondered why the simple motion seemed to take an extraordinary amount of effort. "Daniel, we can't. I can't."

He smiled. "Too soon?"

"Yes, that's it."

He removed his hand. "Okay. I get it. But I wonder if we should talk about your husband sometime? I'm a good listener."

"I don't know. The pain of losing Teddy is too fresh."

"I'm here if you change your mind, for the next two weeks, anyway," he said.

A small, painful clinch numbed her chest. "What do you mean?"

"I have to go back to Columbus, Alex. I'll be here for the opening of the play two weeks from tonight, but then it's back to business as usual for me. Hopefully, I'll have finished at Pop's store and listed the property with a Realtor."

She didn't speak. Just focused on her hands in her lap. This should have been good news. She couldn't think about any sort of relationship with Daniel, not when they were so intimately connected in ways he didn't even know. But two weeks. It was so soon.

"Alex?" He whispered her name. A low

timbre that vibrated deep inside her, just like he used to say her name. "Are you okay?"

She reached for the door handle. "I'm fine. I'm going in now. Thank you for a lovely evening."

He held her wrist. "Wait. What about a picnic on Sunday, just the two of us." He held both hands in the air. "No funny business, I promise, but I'll bet you haven't even been to the Cuyahoga Valley Park since you've been back. Let's spend the afternoon together, take the train ride, shoo ants off a couple of sandwiches." His grin was so enticing. How could it hurt? *So many ways.*

And yet she heard her voice accept his offer. "Sounds like fun," she said. "I guess I could. But Daniel…"

"I know. We're grown-ups now." He leaned in and kissed her cheek. "But you never know, Alex. There still could be some magic."

She touched her cheek as she walked to the front door. Could there be magic? Enough to allow for a profound confession and ultimate forgiveness? Or would it take a miracle?

CHAPTER EIGHT

MARTIN FOSTER LOVED his home when it was filled with the women he adored. This Saturday had been nearly perfect with his daughter and granddaughter chatting nonstop about the play they'd seen the night before, and the opening night of *The Music Man* coming up soon. His Maggie had been resting peacefully, showing no signs of the demons that often seemed to plague her. And even Jude had come to the big house and lay in the sun while Wesley did cannonballs into the pool.

Only Carrie, Martin's youngest, and truly the one he worried most about, was absent. But to make up for the loss, the girls had called her that afternoon, and they'd all caught up with Carrie's latest escapades in her attempt to find herself in some forest setting, this time in Washington State. How ironic that the one daughter who had breathing and asthma problems would be the one who wanted a career in forestry.

"So how are you feeling, honey?" Martin had asked before hanging up. "And tell me the truth. Do you need any meds?" He constantly reminded her to take the medications that kept her breathing difficulties from becoming too severe.

"I'm fine, Daddy," she'd said in that always hopeful, always cheerful way she had of imparting information. "Don't worry about me. You sent me enough antibiotics to last into the next century."

"They don't do you any good if you don't take them," he urged.

After being told he worried too much for about the hundredth time, he allowed Carrie to disconnect. He joined his grandson in the pool, where they fought galactic battles with water guns until dinner.

After supper, the girls cleaned up the dishes, Wesley fell asleep on the sofa and Martin watched the sun set over the gently rolling hills of his chosen spot in the world. Just after dark, sirens exploded on the serene calm of his evening.

Jude came running to the front porch. "What

the heck?" She darted down the steps. "Sounds like they're coming here." The family watched flashing lights race by their property line about a quarter mile away.

"Something's going on," Martin said.

"Yeah, and it looks like the epicenter is the old Jamison place, where Miss Fix-a-Fence lives!"

Martin stood. "Aurora's? All these emergency vehicles are headed to Aurora's?"

Jude darted a glance at Alex, who'd just joined them on the porch. Jude shrugged her shoulders and mouthed their neighbor's name as if to say *Since when have they been on a first-name basis?*

Alex mouthed back, "Beats me."

Ignoring his daughters' less-than-subtle exchange, Martin dashed into the house and returned with his keys. "I'm going over there."

He climbed into his Lincoln Navigator and spit gravel as he headed down the drive. He told himself he was only going because he was a doctor. If something had happened to his neighbor, he could be of some help.

When he entered Aurora's drive, the area near the house looked as if an amusement ride had been set up. Blue and white lights flashed from three police cars. The red lights of another vehicle at the back added to the crazy display. And Aurora was nowhere to be seen.

Getting out of the car, Martin dashed to the nearest officer, a young man whose father had recently been the recipient of a heart monitor. "Carl, what's going on? Where's Ms. Spindell?"

"Oh, hi, Doctor Foster. How are you?"

"Carl…?" he said impatiently.

"Yeah, the lady who lives here, that's her name? She's in back with the EMTs."

Martin ran around to the rear of the house, where he found Aurora seated on the back of an opened ambulance, her leg elevated on an overturned flowerpot. EMTs were checking her vital signs. She glanced up at Martin and tried to disguise a grimace with a smile. "What are you doing here, Marty?"

Marty? No one had called him that since his grandmother died forty years ago. In spite of the emergency situation, Martin realized he liked the way his nickname sounded coming from Aurora's unpainted lips. Her crazy hair bristled around her delicate features as if it had been charged from a light socket.

"I'm your closest neighbor, Aurora," Martin said. "It wasn't hard to determine that something was going on here. I thought I might be able to help."

Turning to the two EMTs, he added, "What's the situation? Why is her leg elevated?"

"She has either a sprain or mild fracture of her left ankle," one of the medics said.

"I'm fine," Aurora insisted.

"We're urging her to go to the hospital, but she claims she doesn't want to."

"I don't need to," Aurora said. "All they would do at the hospital is x-ray it, tell me what we already know and wrap an Ace bandage around it. I can do that here."

"Aurora, if you have a fracture…" Martin said.

"I don't. Look." She wiggled her foot as if that was all the proof needed. And if that wasn't enough, she restated, "No hospital."

Martin asked the EMTs to fill him in on Aurora's condition and discovered that her vital signs were fine and she probably was only suffering from a sprain.

"But that's not all," one of the medics said. "What Ms. Spindell didn't tell you is that her house was broken into tonight. She came inside while the intruders were still here and chased them out the back door."

Martin shot his new friend a look meant to convey both his admiration and horror. This explained the presence of half of Fox Creek's police force. "Aurora, that's crazy. You could have been seriously hurt, or worse."

"They were cowards," she said, nodding to an object a few yards away. "See that toilet plunger? That's the only weapon I had, and those two kids took off like spooked rabbits."

"When she was chasing the thieves, she fell through a step, and that's when she hurt her ankle," the EMT explained.

Martin leaned over and probed the hurt leg. "Does this hurt badly?" he asked.

"No. It's fine. A few days off my feet and I'll be good as new." A quick intake of breath indicated that she was lying.

"I am officially recommending a trip to the hospital," Martin said.

"I am officially refusing," she said. "I want to sleep in my own bed."

"Okay, then." Martin turned to the medics. "You guys can go. I'll look after her. If she needs any further care, I'll bring her to the hospital tomorrow."

"You're the doc, Doc," one of them said.

The medics helped Aurora to a lawn chair and climbed into their vehicle. Within a minute, they were gone, their taillights disappearing around a curve in Aurora's drive. Martin moved the flowerpot, added an outdoor cushion for comfort and settled her leg on top.

"Don't budge," he said, and went into her house. A minute later he came out with an ice pack, which he put on her ankle. Then he pulled up another chair and sat down. "I take it you were able to call 911," he said.

"Always carry my cell phone," she answered.

"And a toilet plunger."

She smiled. "A girl can never be too careful."

"Was anything taken?"

"I don't know. Probably some junk jewelry my son's father gave me. I don't lock it up, so I suppose it was easy pickings."

Martin pondered the odd reference she'd just made. Why did she refer to the man who gave her the jewelry as her son's father instead of her husband or ex-husband? "Were you out when the intruders broke in?"

"I was at the grocery. I didn't know anyone was in the house until I opened the front door and saw a flashlight beam coming down the stairs. That's when I grabbed the plunger from my downstairs bath."

"These kinds of crimes, breaking and entering, are rare in this neighborhood," Martin said. "But that doesn't mean that you should be careless. Had the door lock been tampered with?"

"No. I didn't lock it."

"Aurora…"

"I'll lock up from now on," she said. "Learned my lesson."

"What you need is a security system, one that notifies authorities if anything is amiss in the house. I can recommend a good company."

"I'll probably take that advice," she said. "Can't have robbers busting in when I start having guests."

"Or when you're here alone," Martin added. "I'm sure most of the population in this part of the state knows that a single lady lives out here. You're almost inviting trouble."

"I can usually handle trouble," she said. "Though I admit that I am a little shaken by what happened tonight." She shivered. "Thanks for coming by, Marty. I'll call you tomorrow for the name of the security company."

"I'll help you inside. It's getting chilly."

Martin slipped his arm around Aurora's shoulders and helped her navigate the rough patches of lawn. She was amazingly agile for her age and hopped up the steps and into her home almost effortlessly. A police officer met them inside and asked a few more questions about what she remembered.

"We'll come back tomorrow for a list of anything that's gone missing," he said. "And we'll make sure a car passes by a few times during the night."

Aurora nodded. "Thank you, Officer." In the dim living room light, her face was flushed. Perhaps the difficult trip from the backyard had taken a toll.

The police officers left, and Martin was careful to lock the door behind them. He checked the back door and first-floor windows, as well. "Do you have an Ace bandage?" he asked when he came back to the living room. "If not, I can get one from my house."

"There's one in the downstairs bath," she said. He went to get it and gently wrapped the elastic around her slightly swollen ankle.

"You'll need to stay off this for a few days," he reminded her.

"Thanks for everything, Marty, but don't worry about me. I've been taking care of myself for longer than I care to remember."

"Aurora, don't you have any family you can call? Maybe you shouldn't be alone tonight."

"Family?" She uttered the word as if the notion was ridiculous. "This may come as a surprise to a family man like you, Marty, but not everyone values their kin like you do. I can't count on anyone, and that's fine with me."

Hmm... There was a story here, and Martin didn't feel he should pry. But he was worried. Aurora couldn't tip the scales at more than a hundred and ten pounds. Despite her tough talk, there was an air of fragility about her, as if she might break in a stiff wind. What if those thugs came back? What if she tried to walk and fell, further injuring herself?

Martin had been away from Maggie only

a few nights during their thirty-eight years of marriage. Still, he said, "If it's okay with you, Aurora, I think I'll help you into your bedroom and then grab an extra pillow. I'll bunk down here on the couch for tonight."

"That's not necessary."

"I hope it isn't, but it's what I'm going to do. If I can use your phone, I'll call my daughter and tell her my plans."

Aurora leaned against the back of the sofa and released a satisfied sigh. "You're really a pretty good egg, Marty," she said.

He chuckled. "As eggs go."

MARTIN RETURNED TO his house the next morning after accepting Aurora's offer of coffee. Lizzie was in the kitchen when he came through the back door.

"Hi, Grandpa. How was your sleepover with Aurora last night?"

He smiled at the grin on her face. "Don't read anything into that, Lizzie. I just wanted to make sure that Ms. Spindell would be safe through the night."

"And was she?"

"Yes, and thankfully, her sprained ankle is

better this morning, too. How is your grand-mother?"

"The nurse is with her. Everything is okay, I guess. Nothing new."

Martin headed straight for the coffeemaker to pour his second cup of the day. *Nothing new.* Always the same answer. Maggie was "holding her own." There had been no change in her condition. The life of his once vibrant wife was now described as *nothing new.* And as usual, there was nothing he or the entire field of medicine could do about it.

"Where's your mother?" he asked.

"She's upstairs getting ready."

Martin stirred one sugar into his coffee. "Ready for what?"

"She's going out today. A picnic with our handsome senator. Can you believe it?"

Actually, he was shocked. Not disappointed, though. His Alexis was still a young woman, a pretty one at that. She needed to go out and accept the fact that the end of Teddy's life did not mean the end of hers.

"Really?" he said. "She's going out with Daniel?"

"It's the best, isn't it?" Lizzie said. "He's so nice, and I think he likes her."

"Hmm…" Martin took a sip of coffee. "Did you know that those two have a history?"

Lizzie pulled out a chair and sat. "You mean beyond the summer they both worked at the resort? Did they used to date?"

"I don't know if they dated, exactly," Martin said, "but while Alexis worked at the resort, she told Grandma and me that she'd formed a friendship with Daniel. I knew he was Gus Chandler's son from the hardware store. They were a good, well-respected family in Greenfield. I always wondered if your mom had sort of a crush on him."

"I didn't know that part." Lizzie took a bagel from a basket on the table and tore off a small piece. "You know what they say, Grandpa. History can repeat itself."

But was it always the best thing if it did? he wondered. What had happened to end that crush all those years ago? When Alexis announced her pregnancy, Martin had a fleeting thought that perhaps the father was Daniel. He quickly banished the possibility. Alexis would have told him if the father was a local boy, knowing the families would have worked together for the benefit of both the parents and baby.

He clearly recalled the resolve on Alexis's face when she said, "It's no one you know, Daddy. Just someone who stayed at the resort. It was a mistake…" She'd dissolved into tears, and a look from Maggie quickly silenced any more questions. Days later Martin decided the father couldn't have been Daniel. Alexis had been fond of him. She wouldn't have kept this information from him. And then Teddy, dear, sweet, honorable Teddy, admitted his adoration of Alexis, and a solution presented itself.

Martin often pondered about Lizzie's real father, but everything had worked out for both his daughter and granddaughter. He resigned himself to accepting that, for her own reasons, perhaps pride, perhaps shame, Alexis had made the decision that secured a comfortable, safe future for her.

Nevertheless, it was kind of nice that romance was in the air at Dancing Falls. He'd known that Alexis had been terribly fond of Teddy. She had a good life with him, but he often regretted that she might not have enjoyed the kind of passion he'd experienced with Maggie. All of his girls had suffered too much heartache in their short lives, and he needed to remind them that we only go around once. They owed it to themselves to make the most of every opportunity.

CHAPTER NINE

At 10:30 ALEX came downstairs to a pair of grinning Cheshire cats that strongly resembled her father and daughter.

"You look lovely, darling," Martin said.

"The outfit is okay, Mom, but I have a pair of shorts that would fit you and they'd show off a little more leg."

Alex swept a glance down her perfectly appropriate clothes. "This is fine. Bermudas are making a comeback, and the blouse is feminine, don't you think?" She frowned. "And both of you can just stop imagining all sorts of…well, whatever it is you're imagining."

"I'm not imagining anything," Martin said. "Are you, Elizabeth?"

"No, I'm not imagining anything."

"Conspirators, both of you," Alex said.

Jude swept into the living room wearing a pair of denim cutoffs and a short-sleeved plaid shirt. "I just got off the phone with Carrie," she said. "Lizzie told me about the big date, and Carrie wants you to call her when you get home."

"It's not a date!" Alex protested. "At least not to me. I'll be eating food with insects buzzing around and scrambling to find an outdoor restroom. That's not a date."

"Maybe not to you," Jude said, "but…" She narrowed her eyes. "That's what you're wearing?"

Running out of patience, Alex said, "And what exactly do you find so offensive about this outfit?"

"The blouse is a little too froufrou, isn't it? I mean, the neckline is okay, and the itty-bitty cornflowers are cute, but ruffles went out of style a long time ago."

Alex gave her a scathing look. "This from the Foster family fashion guru who hasn't had on a print or a ruffle since kindergarten, and doesn't read a magazine that doesn't have a four-legged creature on the cover."

Jude frowned, looking adorably hurt. "Point taken."

The doorbell rang. "Never mind. Let me go on this so-called date and get home as fast as I can before you all have me married!"

She opened the door to a man who had lost nearly twenty years in the past three days. In loose-fitting beige shorts and a light blue crew-neck shirt, he looked less like a polished politician and more like the boy she'd had a hopeless crush on one summer. She could hardly catch her breath. And no way could she think about eating.

"I've got our lunch in the car," he said. "You look great, Alexis."

She shot a look at her family over her shoulder, and Lizzie laughed. "Have fun, you two."

Alex walked out ahead of Daniel, her head swimming. Many years had passed since anyone had told her to have fun on a date.

MARTIN STOOD IN the doorway until Alex and Daniel had pulled down the drive. He scratched the back of his neck.

"What's wrong, Dad?" Jude said, coming up behind him.

"Nothing, honey. Really. I was thinking that Alexis deserves to have a nice time today."

"I couldn't agree more." She took his arm and urged him away from the door. "Let's do the Sunday crossword together, what do you say?"

"Sounds good." But he couldn't keep the persistent thought from niggling at his brain; the same one that pestered him eighteen years ago. He'd looked closely at Lizzie, stared at Daniel. It couldn't be, he told himself. And yet the timing was so right. But Alex had told him that she'd known Lizzie's father for only a few days and just got carried away. And Alex wouldn't lie.

Still... He shook his head. One thing was for sure. If Daniel Chandler was Lizzie's father... If he'd known the truth and hadn't stepped up to do the right thing all those years ago... He stood to lose a lot more than Martin's vote in the next election.

ALEX HAD ALMOST forgotten how beautiful this part of Ohio was. The Cuyahoga National Forest was green, lush and sprinkled with ponds and slowly rippling streams, home to extensive wildlife. She and Daniel explored the park, dangled their feet off the rocks to cool off, and at one o'clock they were ready for the lunch he had picked up at the Wooden Fork in Greenfield.

"I hope the sandwiches are good," he said. "My mom used to buy her deli meats at this place."

"Right now anything would be wonderful," Alex said. "I'm starving."

"Let's find a table."

She looked up as a cloud darkened the sky. "Uh-oh. Look at those thunderheads. I think our picnic is going to be washed out."

"You could be right." He tucked the lunch sack under his arm securely. "Maybe we should make a beeline for the car and eat inside."

They'd made it only about a quarter of the way to the parking lot when the skies opened up with a fury.

Daniel took her hand. "We won't make the car without getting drenched, but I know a sheltered place just around that curve."

She quickened her pace to keep up with him and was soon entering the opening of a covered bridge. The roof provided decent shelter, though a few determined drops fell to the bridge floor. Alex shook water from her hands. "I never knew this was here."

Daniel looked around. "Apparently, no one else thought of it today." Sweeping his arm, he added, "The Bridge over Sprat Creek welcomes you to a unique dining experience." After a moment he said, "Oops, I forgot to bring a blanket, but once we empty the insulated bag, we can squeeze together on top of it."

She nodded her approval, but inside her nerves were tripping to a strange tune.

"How long has this bridge been here?" she asked when they'd somehow managed to keep their backsides dry on one bag.

"I remember doing a report on bridges when I was in middle school," he said. "I think this one was built in the 1880s." Looking up at the rafters, he said, "When it first opened, it accommodated horse and buggy traffic, then Model Ts. It was deemed unsafe for modern cars in the fifties and has stood here quietly ever since."

"Besides all that, it's a great place for lunch," she said.

When they'd finished, Daniel pointed out that the storm had faded to a gentle drizzle. "We'll get wet, but we can start back to the car if you'd like. You're probably chilly."

She thought a moment. A breeze rustled the leaves overhead, and fat raindrops plunked on the tin roof, which covered the bridge. There was a peace here she hadn't experienced in a long while. Maybe it was the storm, maybe the bridge, maybe the man, but she said, "Let's wait it out. I'm fine and I'd kind of like to stay."

He leaned against the side of the bridge interior, raised his knees and wrapped his arms around them. "Good. I don't want the day to end yet anyway." Smiling at her, he said, "I'm having fun, Alex. Feels a little like it used to when we were younger."

She chuckled. "I don't know about that. We were kids and hopeful about our futures."

"You aren't hopeful now?" he asked.

"Not so much. Now I'm thinking about Lizzie's future. You'll understand when you're a par..." She stopped, bit her lip. "Lizzie's excited about her studies and being a teacher someday. She's such a bright girl..." Alex looked down, avoiding Daniel's interested gaze. Too much information, she thought.

"She's that, all right," Daniel agreed. "She's taken to her part in *The Music Man* like she was born to do it."

"She puts her heart and soul in everything she attempts," Alex said.

"But what about you? You're young. You have a long life ahead of you. I know you've suffered a loss, but there is still so much you could do."

She clasped her hands tightly in her lap. "I don't know."

"Do you want to talk about him, Alex? Why don't you tell me about Teddy."

She didn't want to talk about Teddy, but an adamant refusal might look more suspicious than allowing the conversation to happen. At least she could control what she said. "There's probably nothing so extraordinary about Teddy. Despite being a gifted doctor, he was a simple man, a good and kind one, a great father."

He shifted so he could see her better. "How did you meet him? It must have happened very soon after our summer at Birch Shore."

She didn't have to guard her words for this question. "Actually, I'd known Teddy since I was a teenager. He and my mother and father were friends. He often came over for dinner. We'd play games, watch movies. I think Teddy was lonely since he'd never found anyone."

"So your family became his family?"

"I guess. But there was never anything in-appropriate between Teddy and me. I could talk to him, depend on him. There were things I told Teddy that I never even told my parents. He just seemed to get me so well." She glanced into Daniel's eyes and was sur-prised to see such understanding there. Al-most as if he had known Teddy himself.

"And when did this admiration turn to something stronger?" he asked.

"Just before I went off to college. In that month after I worked at the resort. I missed all the fun we had, and I missed you, too. I knew we'd be miles apart and hardly ever see each other."

Daniel opened his mouth to speak, but ap-parently thought better of it.

"Anyway, I felt lost," she continued. "I came home and saw Teddy in a new light. He admitted that his life was not fulfilled." *Be careful, Alex.* "He wanted children, a wife, someone to share the ups and downs with." She continued staring into Daniel's eyes. "I adored him, I really did."

"And the age difference?"

Alex should have been prepared for this question. Over the years she'd been called everything from "child bride" to "trophy wife." She'd heard supposed friends accuse Teddy of robbing the cradle. But the truth was, she did care deeply for Teddy, and she resented all the unkind comments.

She looked Daniel straight in his eyes. "Aren't you pushing forty, Daniel?"

"In three years, yes, I'll be forty."

"Teddy was in his forties when I married him. I'd known him almost my whole life. His age was never a factor in our marriage. To me he was just Teddy, one of the kindest, gentlest men I've ever met." She ended by clearing her throat and saying, "I'm sure you've heard the expression that age is just a number."

"But you were a teenager. I'm a little surprised your parents approved."

"But they did. My parents often said that I was born with an old soul. Maybe they were right. At any rate, Teddy and I grew together through almost two decades."

"I heard that you never went to Wittenberg," Daniel said.

"No. I moved to Chicago with Teddy, had a baby and enrolled at the University of Chicago. After getting my degree, I worked at the Art Institute of Chicago." She smiled. "I loved my job."

He remained silent for a few moments, stared at his clasped hands and finally said, "What do you remember about us, Alex? About that summer?"

She thought about her answer before evading the truth. "I remember the fun, the work, the other kids, Mrs. MacIntosh, our dorm leader. And I remember a talented, dashing, captivating boy who could make me laugh with just a look and a goofy smile."

He nodded. "Okay. But do you also remember that I was crazy about you? You must have known."

I was the one who was crazy in love, she thought. *You never told me you had similar feelings.* She had to tread carefully with her response. "I recall moments where I believed we had something special," she said. "But in the end, I think we were caught up in the moon and the beach and the adventure of it all. I was away from home for the first time in my life. I was experiencing a freedom I'd never known. You were part of that freedom."

"Do you remember that night under the pier?"

She held her breath. Would he mention what they'd done?

"We made love, Alex. Maybe it wasn't the best it could have been. Maybe you deserved better than an old blanket spread on the sand and a couple of beers. But to me it was the ultimate way to bring the summer to a close. It was more than special to me, and I thought about you every day after we left the resort."

A huge knot seemed to form in her chest, and she wasn't sure if it was the anguish of regret or remorse. Or a deep sadness. Maybe Daniel hadn't recognized her right away that day in the theater, but he did remember her, and her heart was caught somewhere between the joy of mattering to him and the pain of having to continue lying to him.

"That night meant something to me, too," she admitted. *But I can never tell you how it changed my life.*

"I called you a bunch of times after we separated, and then you stopped taking my calls. Why?"

What could she tell him that he would believe? Whenever someone in her family said that Daniel was on the phone for her, the pieces of her heart crumbled more. "I married Teddy less than a month after the summer ended," she said. "Isn't it obvious why I could no longer continue any sort of relationship with you?"

"Yes, of course, but I still don't understand. We made promises to each other about the future that night, and I don't think you were the kind of girl who made promises she didn't intend to keep."

For the first time she realized that she had actually hurt him. She'd never seriously considered that he had deep feelings for her. He was extraordinarily nice to everyone, as charming to the summer employees as he was to the guests. She'd always assumed she was the proper small-town girl who was swept off her feet by the charismatic summer heartthrob, the one all the girls wanted, and she was lucky enough to end up with. But to think that she might have hurt him was an incredible revelation. Maybe if she'd taken his calls…

Alex had suffered for days when she considered whether or not she would tell Daniel about the pregnancy. In the end, she didn't tell him for several reasons. He had a bright future ahead of him and the scholarships and part-time jobs to see him through his university education. His finances would have been much different if he'd had a baby to support.

Also, she really believed that she was just a summer fling for him, and when she discovered she was going to have his baby, he was probably already thinking about next summer's conquest. And last, she had lied to him about being on the pill, and to tell him a baby was on the way was to admit she'd purposely deceived him. She was afraid he'd think she'd trapped him.

And then Teddy, gallant, thoughtful Teddy, gave her the path to make her troubles go away. He promised her a secure and happy life, and he had provided that. He said he'd raise her child as his own, and no one would ever know that he wasn't the father. He'd kept that promise, too. Sometimes he treated her so well, so carefully, that she believed he thought she might break. If Teddy hadn't died, she would be married to him today. She wouldn't be on a picnic in the rain with the man she'd never forgotten.

Alex looked into Daniel's eyes now.

He reached for her hand. "Are you crying, Alex?"

His question shocked her. She hadn't been

aware that her eyes were filling with tears over so many mistakes, so many regrets, so many promises not kept.

"I'm sorry," she said. "I guess I just didn't believe that the promises meant that much to you."

"I've never been one to say what I don't mean. I don't make empty promises to the people of this district, and I didn't make any empty promises to you." He rubbed the back of her hand with his thumb. "I cared for you, Alex. What we shared that summer was real. As real as this…"

He reached up and cradled her chin in his hand and then bent lower until their foreheads touched. Alex told herself to stop him before this went any further, but just like so many nights in the moonlight, words failed her on this gray afternoon on a covered bridge.

His lips touched hers, lightly at first. When she didn't pull away, he increased the pressure of his mouth, and the kiss became demanding, needy. They might have been kids again, experiencing the splendor of that first kiss, frightened, excited and wanting more. She leaned into him as his arm came around her, and with simmering emotions rising to the surface, she kissed him back with all the passion she'd kept buried for eighteen years—passion that she'd never quite been able to feel for Teddy.

She didn't know how long the kiss lasted. Maybe a minute, maybe just a few sparkling seconds, but in that short time, the feelings of that long-ago summer came rushing back, enveloping her in a flowing warmth that made her wish for an eternity of Daniel's kisses.

But scruples, especially for a woman like Alex, had a way of restoring logic. Breathless and dizzy, she managed to say, "We'd better go."

"Okay." He stood, offered his hand and she got up. Her legs felt weak and insubstantial. He wrapped his hands around her arms. "You felt it, too, just now, Alex. I know you did. Whatever we once had, it's still there."

"I don't know," she said. "I'm still grieving, adjusting. I shouldn't have…"

"It's all right. No explanations necessary." He picked up the lunch bag and slung it over his shoulder. "But for the rest of the time I have here, I'm going to keep asking to see you. I think we owe it to each other."

They emerged from the bridge into spears

of sunlight breaking through the clouds. Daniel took her hand as they walked in the fresh, moist air to the car. They didn't talk, each occupied with their thoughts. And Alex remembered what he'd told her. *The time I have here*... Just under two weeks. The realization made her sad, but really, wasn't Daniel's return to the capital what she should hope for?

CHAPTER TEN

ON TUESDAY ALEX drove Lizzie to the theater. Her mind was occupied so that she barely kept up with Lizzie's chatter. Daniel hadn't called the day before, but that wasn't so strange, especially when he had so much going on with his father, his town hall meetings, the theater. And she'd done nothing to encourage him to contact her.

Alex found out from Lizzie that Daniel had come to the Red Barn late Monday afternoon. She cleverly, or so she thought, questioned her daughter and discovered that Daniel hadn't mentioned her or their date. Again, not so strange. Why would he talk to her daughter about something that didn't concern her?

Still, Alex was feeling out of sorts as she drove into the parking lot. A bit moody, a bit sullen, maybe even disappointed.

Until she saw Daniel's SUV and his tall, imposing form stepping from the driver's side. In tune with the warm day, he wore denim shorts and a Cleveland Indians T-shirt. Funny, she'd never known that he was a sports fan.

"Look, Mom, there's Daniel," Lizzie said. "I'm glad he was able to come this morning. We're running out of time to get the gazebo built for the country dance scene."

"If you need an extra hand, I can stop by later," Alex said. "I can wield a mean paintbrush, but I'm not much good with a hammer."

"We'd love your help, Mom. I wasn't much good, either, until Daniel gave me a carpentry lesson. I swear, he knows how to do everything."

Daniel stopped at the door and turned at the sound of their approaching car. He smiled and waved.

Lizzie jumped out of the passenger side and headed quickly to the entrance. After speaking to Daniel, she went inside. Daniel came over to Alex, who had remained in her vehicle.

"Hey, Alex, how're you doing?" he asked.

She expelled the breath she'd been holding. He wasn't angry or avoiding her. "Great.

You?" For one fleeting, anxious moment she felt as if she were back at Birch Shore.

He leaned on her open window. "I'd be even better if I knew you were going out to dinner with me tomorrow night."

She swallowed. "You never asked me."

The smile widened. "No? Must have slipped my mind. Alex, will you go out to dinner with me tomorrow night? How about the Bristol Falls Inn? It'd be perfect. A little candlelight. A little music."

The possible consequences of a wrong decision raced through her mind. Anticipation at just the thought of spending more time with Daniel raced through her blood. Alarm bells rang. She knew what she should say.

"That sounds lovely," she said instead.

"Super. Pick you up at seven."

He tapped on the hood of her car as a goodbye and then waited while she backed up, turned around and zoomed out of the parking lot. Only when she was rounding the curve that would hide the Red Barn from view did she see him go inside.

"What are you doing, Alexis?" she said aloud. "You know this is trouble. You know seeing Daniel can only mean more risk, more complications."

But then the other side had its say, convincing her that she only had to watch her words, think before she spoke. She could be with Daniel without revealing the one bit of information that could seriously affect all their lives. Her conscience tugged at her. Should she keep silent? Should she tell him the truth? Could she tell him? When would the time ever be right? She knew she should tell the truth, but she'd held back for so long, she could do it for a while longer. And didn't she deserve some happiness? Shouldn't she explore these feelings she had for Daniel? How could she do that if she didn't see him? And so, as she drove back to Dancing Falls, she contemplated the choices in her closet, wondered how she would wear her hair. She might as well be a pretty little liar.

DANIEL AND LIZZIE took a break from painting the gazebo and went outside for a breath of air. They sat together on the redbrick planter box in front of the theater. Daniel had a pair of energy bars in his pocket and offered one to Lizzie.

"Thanks." She unwrapped the treat and took a small bite.

"Are you getting nervous about opening night?" he asked her.

"Yes, but in a good way. I don't have that many lines, so I'm not worried about forgetting them. But I could still use some help with the dance numbers." She gave him a rueful smile. "I've never been especially co-ordinated."

"I hear ya," he said. "I cringe whenever I have to go to an official function where dancing is involved, although when I was your age I wasn't too bad. But my feet have obviously given up on me lately."

"My mom says you were a good performer."

"That's kind of her. I enjoyed it, but now I'm a performer of a different sort. Being a politician is like being under a microscope. I never know when someone's cell phone camera is catching me with a frown on my face or when a reporter is looking for a juicy story."

Lizzie crumpled the empty wrapper in her hand. "But you're one of the good guys, aren't you? You're genuinely concerned about the people of Ohio."

"I try to be, and for the most part, I'd say I am a good guy. But you never know when someone could uncover a detail from the past, which might drop a bomb on all my plans."

She giggled and made the sound of an explosion. "Now you've made me wonder what's in your past that could be so damaging."

He laughed. "I'm a man of mystery and I intend to stay that way." He knew he shouldn't pry, but he felt a compelling need to learn more about Teddy Pope. "Speaking of mysteries, Lizzie, how about your father? He was a doctor, wasn't he?"

"Yeah. His patients really liked him."

"So he was one of the good guys, too?"

"He was."

"I'll bet you really miss him."

She only nodded.

"Do you look like your father?" he asked.

"Not so much. No one knows where I got this dark hair, though my grandma Maggie's hair is light brown. My dad had blond hair until it fell out. He was kind of bald when he died."

"Sometimes traits can skip a generation, or so I'm told," he said. "I look more like my mother than I do my father, and Mom told me once that I look even more like her mother. Weird, I guess, being told you look like a woman."

"Not really," she said. "A man can have eyes like his mother's or the shape of her mouth. Your eyes are really pretty, kind of like mine—the color's hard to describe."

Yes, he'd thought that, too. He'd always put the word *hazel* on ID forms when asked for eye color. That was as close as he could come to a description. He wondered what Lizzie put on her forms.

"So how long were your parents married?" he asked.

"Eighteen years." She smiled. "Mom must have gotten pregnant while they were on their honeymoon. I was born before they'd been married a year."

He wanted to ask for specific dates but didn't want Lizzie to think he was probing too deeply into her family's history. But more and more he was starting to wonder...

He put the thought out of his mind. Alex was the most genuine, honest woman he'd ever met. She wouldn't, *couldn't* hide something like this from him. And she had to have known how he felt about her. He would have supported whatever she decided to do. No, Lizzie was definitely Teddy's daughter. And it was the only scenario he could live with.

He stood. "Guess we'd better get back to work. Glen is starting to look anxious about pulling the sets together."

"Only nine more days to the dress rehearsal." She stood, as well, and gave him a grin. "My mom said she'd come help us this afternoon."

"That's nice of her. Unfortunately, I have to leave in a few minutes and go to the hardware store."

The grin faded. "Are you planning to see her again?"

He feigned surprise. "My, aren't we nosy. But, since you asked, yes. We're going out to dinner tomorrow night."

"That's good. She needs to have some fun. Even before Daddy died I was starting to worry about her."

"How so?"

"Mom always had so much energy, and Daddy was much older. He was slowing down, and Mom had to cut back on some of her activities to be home with him more often." She shrugged. "She loved him and all, so it was okay, but now she has a chance to start over."

"Are you thinking she might start over with me?" It was a blunt question, and Daniel realized that he shouldn't have asked.

"Couldn't say. Depends how you treat her, I guess."

Daniel held the door for Lizzie, but before she went in, he added, "I like your mother, Lizzie. I don't want you to worry about her when she's with me."

"I don't. But I wonder what will happen when I go away to college and she's back in Chicago. Who will worry about her then?"

He didn't answer, but hope flared that maybe it would be him.

DANIEL WAS IN a good mood as he drove to the hardware store and he knew why. If Alex had turned down his invitation, he would have conceded that she wasn't interested in him. But she had not only accepted, she had also seemed glad that he'd asked.

He parked behind the store and went in the back entrance and through the warehouse to the front. He expected to see his father behind the counter, but instead he found Jerry Miller, the young man Gus had hired to help out on occasion. There was only one customer wandering the aisles.

"Hey, Danny, how's it going?" Jerry called.

"Good. Where's Pop?"

"He didn't call you?"

The first tingle of alarm skidded down Daniel's spine. "No, why? Is something wrong?"

"Not wrong. Right. Your dad thinks he's going to accept an offer for the inventory. Some guy from Steubenville who is opening up his own shop was here all morning checking the list you made. He said everything looked in order and he made an offer pretty close to what Gus wanted."

Grateful he wasn't facing bad news about his father, Daniel sighed with relief. "That's terrific," he said. "So why didn't Pop tell me himself?"

"I don't know," Jerry said. "He was fine one minute, and the next he handed me the key to the cash register and said he was going home. Maybe he needed to think things through."

Daniel scratched the back of his neck. He didn't want to jump to conclusions, but Gus Chandler never left work early unless there was a family emergency or he was really sick. "How long ago did he leave?"

"About an hour."

"You okay here?"

"Sure. I'll drop the keys and cash at your place later. Tell Gus I've got everything under control."

Daniel thanked Jerry and headed back to his car. In ten minutes he turned onto Elm Street, where he'd grown up, and pulled into the single drive behind his father's car. He went in the back door. "Pop!"

No answer.

"Pop, where are you?" He opened the door to the basement since his dad often puttered around there and called down. No answer.

Still calling out for him, Daniel walked through the dining room and into the parlor. He could no longer ignore the feeling of dread that threatened to banish all logical thought.

"Pop, answer me…"

Daniel stopped just inside the living room, and his heart leaped into his throat. His father lay on his back on the sofa, a familiar photo frame clutched to his chest. His other arm hung over the cushions, the fingers almost touching the floor.

Panic spurred Daniel across the room. Blood pounded in his head. He told himself to breathe. "No, not like this. Not alone," he said.

He crouched beside the sofa and lifted the frame from his dad's hand. The smiling face of his mother didn't bring him any comfort like it usually did. He set the portrait on the floor and laid his head on his dad's chest. If there was a heartbeat, he couldn't hear it. Tears clogged Daniel's eyes and burned in his throat.

And then there was a sputter and a cough. A few seconds later Gus lifted his arm from his chest and swatted the air around his face as if he was battling a pesky fly. Daniel jerked away, landing on his backside. "Pop?"

"What are you doing, Danny?" Gus said. "Why were you leaning over me like that?"

Daniel clutched his own chest. "Good grief, Pop, you scared me half to death. I thought you were…" He couldn't say the word.

Gus sat up. "Dead, Danny? You thought I was dead?"

"Well, you had that picture of Mom over your heart, and I assumed…"

"I often nap with your mother's picture," Gus said.

"And I called you a bunch of times. You didn't answer."

"I was sleeping on my good ear," Gus said. "Been supposed to get a hearing aid for the other one for almost a year now." He smiled. *Smiled?* "Under the circumstances, I didn't see the point."

"This isn't funny, Pop," Daniel said.

His dad's face grew serious. "No one knows that better than I do, son, but you've got to lighten up a little. You're not the one dying."

"But when I walked in here, saw you on the couch… I thought you'd been alone, and I don't want that to happen."

"I promise you, Danny, when my time comes, I won't let you miss it. I'll go out with you by my side, and we'll have one last laugh for old times' sake."

Daniel felt a grin spread across his face. "I wouldn't want it any other way. Now, why don't you tell me about the deal you made to sell the inventory? And I guess it's time for us to call the Realtor and get the building listed."

"Yep. Say goodbye to that inheritance,

Danny. No hardware store for you. Glad you've got that politicking gig to fall back on."

Daniel listened to the details of the sale while his brain kept going back to how strange his day had been. Starting with the best news this morning when Alex agreed to go out with him again, and ending with the biggest scare of his life. This day had been a perfect example of life's highs and lows. And despite everything, he couldn't wait until tomorrow.

CHAPTER ELEVEN

THE BRISTOL FALLS INN was as lovely as Alex remembered it from her childhood when her parents brought the whole family there to celebrate birthdays and anniversaries. The inn was a special place filled with happy memories, but nothing could compare with the memory she was making tonight, because after the salad course and one glass of wine, she was quite certain she was falling in love.

How can this be happening? she asked herself. Teddy had been gone only a few months. She'd loved Teddy. Admired and respected him. But this was different. Exciting, passionate, thrilling. She quite literally couldn't tear her gaze from Daniel's face in the candle's dim glow.

They talked about that summer, not the intimate details, but the fun, crazy times they'd had. They talked about *The Music Man* and the frenetic pace of getting ready for opening night.

They talked about politics and Daniel's plans for the district, all the ideas he had for making life better in his district and the state in general.

His voice hypnotized her; his eyes held her transfixed; her mind recognized the goodness in him, and her heart opened to let him in again. In a little over a week he would return to Columbus, but she knew that until he had to go, she was his, for however many times he wanted to see her. And then, if they had a future, she would tell him the truth about Lizzie. And if they didn't have a future, if he didn't feel for her what she felt for him, she still would tell him.

Alex felt empowered by her decisions. Battling with her conscience was killing her, quite literally starving her of her confidence, her belief in herself. She might have gone on keeping her secret, right or wrong, if she hadn't seen Daniel again, but being with him like this changed everything. Daniel's compassion for his constituents, his balanced way of looking at the world, had taught her this. And he deserved to know he was the father of a very remarkable young lady.

Later, when Daniel took her home, his kiss was gentle, his arms strong and comforting. Alex was able to give in to his embraces without examining all the consequences of getting close to him again, without experiencing all the guilt that came with the pure enjoyment of being in his arms. She had made up her mind. Now she just had to wait for the right time to tell him and hope that he would try to understand.

"I'll be here through opening night," he said as he walked her to the door. "I'm leaving on Saturday morning after the cast party." Slipping his arm around her shoulders, he added, "Of course, Columbus is just three hours away, Alex, maybe less if I break the speed limit on Friday afternoons."

She laughed. "I don't want to be responsible for our newest senator ending up in jail for reckless driving."

At the door, he pulled her close. She laid her head against his chest, relishing the warmth of his hands on her back.

"I have three more town meetings before I go," he said. "But when I'm not talking to crowds of people, I want to be with just one person only. Let's make the most of these last days, okay?"

She looked into his eyes and smiled. "I'm in."

He kissed her thoroughly, sealing the pact they'd made. "Call you tomorrow."

She went into the house and found Lizzie, Jude and Wesley watching a movie in the family room. "Where's Dad?" Alex asked.

Jude pointed toward the window. "He's at Aurora's place." She smirked. "Just left before you got home. If I didn't know Dad so well, I'd think they had a thing going on."

"Dad?" Alex shook her head. "No way."

"I know, but he must find something awfully fascinating at her house."

"How was your date, Mom?" Lizzie asked.

"Great. The dinner was wonderful." She sat next to her daughter on the couch and for one fleeting moment wished she weren't the older, responsible sister, the mother, the aunt. She longed to be just a girl again and admit that the food, as terrific as it was, was the least wonderful thing about the date.

But then she looked into Lizzie's eyes and realized that the decision she'd made earlier was going to change her daughter's life. And all at once the burdensome weight of responsibility settled on her shoulders again.

As HE TURNED into Aurora's drive, Martin thought about her voice on the phone. Normally so self-assured, she'd sounded frightened, nervous. "Marty, this is Aurora. I'm sorry to bother you but I've had a little mishap."

"I'll be right over," he'd said.

He tried the front door, knocked and called Aurora's name.

"Around back," she answered. "The door's unlocked."

He scurried around the side of the house, watching his step so he wouldn't stumble over contractor supplies. His worry increased when Aurora didn't meet him at the door. He turned the latch and entered. "Aurora?"

"Over here," she called from the direction of the pantry.

He rushed over and found her lying under a shelf unit and surrounded by canned goods, her body visible from only the waist up. "Good heavens. What happened?"

"Darned leg," she said. "I was climbing up the shelf to store items on the top when my ankle gave out. I slipped and pulled the whole dang thing down on top of me."

He cleared a path to be able to remove the shelf. His voice was breathless when he asked, "Are you hurt?"

"I sure am," she replied. "My pride and my dignity have been torn to shreds."

He smiled. "I'd say your common sense suffered a blow, as well. Why in the world would you climb up a shelf? Why didn't you use a stepladder?"

"I do this all the time," she explained. "Never had a shelf and about a hundred cans fall on top of me before."

He grunted, lifted the shelf. "Can't say that I don't wonder why not."

Picking her up by her shoulders, he assisted her to a kitchen chair and immediately began flexing her limbs and checking for injuries.

"I'm fine. Quit fussing. I just couldn't get my arms free to move the shelf. Might have lain here all night until the construction crew arrived if I hadn't called you." She patted her trusty cell phone.

"At the risk of wasting my breath again, I should ask, do you want to go to the hospital?"

"No. I'm okay. You can go. And thanks."

He stood with his hands on his hips, looking down at her. She was quite a contrast from Maggie, who was nearly as tall as he was and pleasantly filled out from years of her own great cooking. Maggie was a large, comfortable woman, but there was something to be said for Aurora's petite angles.

"Aren't you even going to offer me a cup of coffee?" he asked. "I'll make it."

She laughed. "Sure, but I'd suggest green tea for this hour of the night. Coffee will keep you up."

"Ugh, tea!" he said, plugging in her coffee-maker. "Where's the coffee?"

She looked at the pile of cans on the floor. "Somewhere in that mess."

He found the appropriate can and made a half pot. Despite her warning, she had a cup with him. "I appreciate your help tonight, Marty, and the other night, too. I promise you won't have to play my knight in shining armor in the future. I'll think before I do something stupid."

He took a sip, set the mug down on her table. "I don't mean to harp on this, Aurora, but I really think you should have someone stay with you until the inn is up and running. A friend, maybe."

Her face clouded. She looked down at her coffee. "I don't like putting people out." As if more explanation was needed, she added, "Everyone I know is busy with their own lives. You must understand how that is."

He did. His life was two-thirds perfect right

now since Alexis had come home. Jude was a constant concern, but she was less than a mile away. And Carrie—he never stopped worrying about his youngest daughter. She had such high, impractical hopes, but her poor body couldn't keep up with the goals her ambition demanded. Why a bright young woman like his sweet Carrie would ignore her asthma to live in nature was a mystery to him. He tried at least once a month to get her to come home.

"I do understand," he said. "If you promise to be careful, I promise to come over when you bury yourself in groceries. But don't dig that grave during the daytime when I'm at work."

She chuckled. "You're a good friend, Marty. I'm sorry I was so hard on you that first day when I brought your dog back."

"Correction. My *daughter's* dog. I like the mutt, but I don't claim any ownership." He glanced toward the back door. "I see you have the security system installed."

"Took your advice. Makes me sleep easier."

"Good. Now I'll give you some more advice. Have one of these construction guys nail that shelf to the wall."

"I will."

He got up to leave. "I meant what I said,

Aurora. Call if you need anything. If I'm home I'll come help you."

She nodded. "If things get too hectic over at your place, you've earned yourself a free night in the Howard Taft Bedroom. One thing I can offer here is peace and quiet."

"Do I have to drink tea?"

She laughed. "No."

"My wife is a tea drinker, though not so much anymore."

Aurora's expression changed. She blinked, looked away.

"Is something wrong?" he asked.

"Of course not."

"You did know I was married."

"Sure." She shook her head slightly. "Doesn't matter to me one way or the other, though I guess I'm a little surprised you never talk about your wife."

"She's ill. I take care of her."

"Admirably, I'm sure," Aurora said. "But you certainly don't have to take care of me, so you should run on home."

He thought about explaining more of his situation to her, but decided against it. "Good night, then." He opened the back door. "Lock up after I leave."

"Will do."

As he drove home, he thought about what she'd called him, her knight in shining armor. He'd often considered that the reference might apply to him. He enjoyed helping people. He wanted his daughters to rely on him, his patients to know they could trust him with their lives. But his poor Maggie, locked and lost in the blankness of her mind. He hadn't been able to help Maggie, and his heart broke a little more every day when he had to face that failure. All the doctors and medicine in the world couldn't stop her decline.

But it wasn't in his nature to stop lending a hand. And when he thought about the strong but soft hand belonging to Aurora Spindell, the one that had wrapped around his arm when he walked her to a chair, he smiled, though he told himself not to enjoy helping Aurora *too* much. He was, as he'd just admitted, a married man.

ON THE FOLLOWING Thursday night, the dress rehearsal for *The Music Man* went very well. Alex was there with Daniel. They shared the auditorium seats with approximately fifty honored guests, critics from local publications, the mayor, the chief of police and relatives of the cast. By this time, Alex had become so comfortable with Daniel that it seemed the years that had separated them were only a distant memory. They had gone to dinner twice, a movie once and another picnic, this time at Dancing Falls, near where the twenty-foot waterfall cascaded down the boulders at the back of her family's property. Alex loved the scenic spot. As waterfalls went, it was unimpressive. But as a date, the picnic had been spectacular.

They sat watching the musical, their shoulders touching, their whispered comments only positive.

"Isn't Lizzie just perfect for that part?" Alex said. As soon as she spoke, she felt remorse because he could be sharing in Lizzie's success on a far more personal level—as her father. Soon, Alex thought. She and Daniel were growing closer every day. She was almost ready to trust him with the most intimate details of her life, including this one.

"She's wonderful," he said. "And she seems to be in her element up there on stage."

"This has been a terrific experience for her. She's been so happy and involved. This play has done more than any of the antidepressants the doctor gave her after Teddy died. I feel so much better about sending her off to college in the fall."

When the cast came on stage for a last bow, Glen rushed down the stairs to grab Daniel. He brought him on stage and introduced him as his right-hand man and the state's newest and brightest star in Columbus. In typical fashion, Daniel minimized his importance in the production and reminded the audience that he would be back on duty in the capital on Monday. And then he disappeared behind the curtain with the actors.

Alex watched the crowd file out of the theater and waited patiently for Daniel to return. They would take Lizzie for ice cream to celebrate and then drop her off at Dancing Falls so the two of them could have some alone time. Alex checked her watch. She'd waited for almost fifteen minutes and wondered what was taking so long backstage. She decided to give them fifteen minutes more and then she'd investigate.

DANIEL CONGRATULATED ALL the actors, but he hugged Lizzie.

"I couldn't have done this without you,"

she said. "You ran lines with me and helped me with my dance moves. Thank you, thank you, Daniel. This has been so much fun, the best summer ever!"

He laughed. "Wow, we could use more of that enthusiasm for summer stock theater around here. Maybe you'll come back next year for whatever production Glen has in mind for the Red Barn."

"Or maybe I'll come back sooner," she said, her face breaking into a grin.

"What do you mean, Lizzie?"

She took his hand. "Come with me, Daniel. I have to talk to someone, and you're it."

He followed her to a quiet corner of the prop room, where she turned over two flowerpots for them to sit on. "I'm glad Mom isn't here," she said. "I'm glad it's just you and me."

His inner warning bell sounded a faint alarm. Was this going to be news he shouldn't be hearing? What did he know about communicating with a teenager?

"Lizzie, your mom is here. She's in the theater waiting for us."

"I know. But what I want to say is just between you and me."

He decided the most expedient way to deal with this was to hear her out. "Okay, what's on your mind?"

She took a deep breath. "I want to go to drama school, Daniel. I know now that this is what I was born to do. I want to act. I *need* to act. I had to tell someone, and since you and I share a love of the theater, I knew you'd understand."

Oh, he understood, all right. He understood that Alex was likely to be devastated when she heard of Lizzie's change of heart. Many of their conversations had been about her daughter's future. He cleared his throat. This conversation was a bit like walking on quicksand. "Have you considered that maybe this decision is based on the excitement of the moment, Lizzie? Maybe you should wait until the play's run is over and then rethink the whole thing."

She clasped her hands in her lap. "I could think about this from now until I'm a dithering old woman and I wouldn't change my mind. I'll still go to college, but I'm going to learn to be an actor."

"I'm assuming you haven't told your mother this plan," he said.

"Not yet, but I'm going to."

"She seems pretty set on you going to Bryn Mawr."

"I know, but that's just it. *She's* set on it. My father's mother graduated from that university, and from the time I was maybe three years old, that's all I heard about. Bryn Mawr. 'Lizzie's going to Bryn Mawr.'"

"It's a fine school," Daniel said.

"It is, I know that, but I want to go somewhere else."

"Have you investigated other schools?"

She smiled. "You bet. I went online and looked up the Department of Theater at Ohio State University. It's wonderful, Daniel. They do a full range of drama training, and the students get to write their own plays, direct and act in them."

Daniel knew about the theater department. He'd thought about going there himself when he finished his summers at Birch Shore. At the time, he'd had aspirations similar to Lizzie's. The excitement of the resort stage, the lights, the applause—it had all combined to make him seriously consider acting as a career choice. He wasn't sorry he'd opted for political science, but always in the back of his mind was the question, "What if…?"

"It sounds like a fine program," he admitted. "Still, you need to discuss this with your mother."

"Of course, and I will. But I bet she'll be much more receptive to the idea if I have your backing."

He choked on his next breath. "My backing? What difference will that make? I don't have any say in your future."

"But you and Mom, you're dating and getting on so well. She'll listen to you."

He took a moment to think. "You know, Lizzie, I feel a bit like I'm being railroaded here, as if you're using my relationship with your mother to help you get your way. I'm not comfortable being in this position."

"But you said I have talent, right? Be honest with me."

Of course he was. "Yes, you have talent." He kept his voice as even as he could. The last thing he wanted was to exaggerate his opinion of Lizzie's acting ability. But the girl was darn good. He knew it, and so did the audience tonight.

"And you believe that everyone should follow their dreams?"

For the most part, he did. When he'd first met Lizzie, she'd been quiet and withdrawn, still grieving over the loss of her father. The theater had brought her out of the dark place she had been, allowed her to grow and develop her creative skills. No one, not even Alex, could deny that this summer at the Red Barn had been just the tonic Lizzie needed. And maybe acting was truly the stuff of her dreams.

Unfortunately, he didn't know how strongly Alex had her mind made up on Lizzie going to Bryn Mawr.

"Daniel?"

He realized he'd been lost in thought. "Oh, sorry."

"You do believe in dreams?"

He managed a slight smile. "Sure. Dreams are important for everyone. But your mother has dreams, too, dreams for you."

"Those are her dreams. Mine are at Ohio State. And it's a lot closer than Bryn Mawr." Lizzie grinned. "You live in Columbus, just minutes from OSU. It would mean so much to me to have you as a mentor, someone I could talk to. And I'll be much closer to Mom, as well, than I would be in Pennsylvania."

He couldn't argue those points. Maybe having Lizzie nearby would be enough reason for Alex to at least consider the other school.

"Say you're on my side, Daniel," she pleaded.

He sighed. "I'm not *not* on your side, Lizzie. I want you to be happy. I want your mother to be happy, too. And I'm not your father…"

He recalled his earlier pondering about whether or not he actually might be Lizzie's dad, but he'd accepted that he wasn't. He and Alex had grown so close. She would have told him. They'd had deep conversations about Lizzie.

"I don't have a father, Daniel," Lizzie said. "You are as close as a father to me as anyone could be. I trust you. I admire you." She leaned forward, rested her palms on his hands. "I need you to believe in me. I know acting is what I want to do. I don't have any doubts. Please say you'll talk to Mom for me."

"I can't tell your mother, Lizzie. It's not my place. You have to tell her. You've got to be as honest with her as you've been with me. See how she reacts. She might surprise you."

Lizzie gave him a petulant look, but she followed it with a nod. "Okay, I'll tell her tomorrow night after the opening and the cast party. As soon as we get home. She'll be in a good mood."

Yes, she probably would be, Daniel thought. And the next morning he would be on his way to Columbus, already missing Alex, but grateful he wasn't taking sides between these two strong women. Being a politician had its challenges, but maybe dealing with policy and budgets was slightly easier than being a parent.

"Here you are," Alex said from backstage. "I've been looking all over for the two of you."

Daniel stood, walked over to her. "I think we're ready for ice cream."

"What were you guys talking about?"

"Oh, nothing," Lizzie said. "I was just getting some tips from Daniel on how to make my portrayal of Zaneeta even better tomorrow night."

Alex smiled at Daniel. "He's a pro," she

said. "I'm sure he would only give you good advice."

Lizzie smiled, a little too brightly.

CHAPTER TWELVE

THE THEATER WAS filled the following night for the official opening of *The Music Man*. Once again Alex was so proud of Lizzie and grateful that her daughter had chosen to join the production. At the final curtain call, she said to Daniel, "Thanks for coming with me and enduring this two nights in a row."

He smiled. "I wouldn't be anywhere else."

"I know I mentioned this last night, but isn't she fabulous?"

"You're a proud mother and you have a right to be. I agree with you. The best part is she loves performing so much."

Alex put her hand on Daniel's arm. "That's the mystery to me. Lizzie acted in a couple of school productions, but I never knew she had such talent for the other things, the singing and dancing." Her face flushed. She well knew that Lizzie could have gotten her talents from her biological father.

The crowd began filing out of the theater. Alex and Daniel remained seated, knowing they had to wait for Lizzie. Alex appreciated the time alone with him. In just a few hours, he would be headed back to Columbus, and she wouldn't see him for at least a week.

"How does your father feel about you returning to your job?" she asked.

"He's okay with it, better than I am, actually. His sister is coming for a few days beginning on Sunday. I'll call every day to check up on him."

"And how's he doing?"

"He's getting weaker, but his pain meds are keeping him mobile. He's still planning on taking that trip west, and if the doctor's prediction is correct, he should be able to do that."

"Is he satisfied with the deal he made for his inventory?"

Daniel had told her about the offer that came in and how grateful he was that finances wouldn't be a problem for Gus. Once the building sold, there would be even more capital.

"He says it's a fair proposition and the

guy's deposit check didn't bounce, so all is going forward."

She leaned her head on his shoulder. "I think it's wonderful that you could take some time to be with your dad through this ordeal. You're a good son, Daniel."

He smiled down at her. "Thanks, but right now I'm just as interested in being a good boyfriend." He took her hand. "I am your boyfriend, aren't I, Alex? I feel like I am. I definitely want to be."

She sighed. "We've been together almost every day for a week, and even before that. If you're not my boyfriend, then I've become awfully fond of a stalker."

He chuckled. "Can you imagine? You and I calling each other boyfriend and girlfriend just like we were teenagers again. I have to admit, Alex, the first couple of times I ran into you I didn't think we'd make it to this point, although I wanted it to happen."

She turned her hand over in his and threaded their fingers. "I kind of wish we weren't celebrating with the cast tonight. I'd like to find a park bench somewhere and just sit and look at you."

"We'll do that after the party. I don't plan

on getting any sleep tonight, and it's a short drive to Columbus."

Glen came out on stage and waved to them. "Hey, you two lovebirds, let's get moving. They're waiting for us at the Tinker's Tavern on the green. Appetizers, drinks and of course—" he waved his arm with a flourish "—champagne!"

Daniel stood and put his hand out to help Alex. "Is the cast going together?" he asked Glen.

"Yeah, everyone has a ride, including Lizzie, so we'll meet you there."

When the two of them got in Daniel's SUV, he leaned over and gave Alex a long and passionate kiss.

"Wow," she breathed. "You're not leaving for nine hours yet. I hope you have more of those saved up."

"I do, and for the record, I'm crazy about you, Alexis Pope."

She stared out the windshield. Daniel's words brought back all the guilt and anguish she'd kept buried for so long. How could Daniel, how could any man, love her after what she'd done, what she was still doing? Confessing the truth to him would be the hardest thing she'd ever had to do. When her eyes burned with tears, she blinked hard to clear them.

"Alex, what's wrong?" he asked. "Did I say something to upset you? If you don't feel the same about me, it's okay. But I should warn you. I'm not giving up."

She shook her head. "I don't know what's wrong with me, but it's nothing you've done." That was a lie. She was falling in love with Daniel a little more each day. And the realization devastated her even though she let it happen. She cleared her throat. Daniel was waiting. She had to say something. "I was just wondering how you'll feel when I go back to Chicago."

"The same. Chicago is still less than a day's drive from Columbus, and I have a feeling you might be driving to my city with some regularity."

"Oh, really?" She turned to see his profile. "And what makes you think that?"

He opened his mouth as if he would speak, but then closed it again and shrugged. "Just a thought, that's all," he said after a moment.

She wondered what he meant by the comment as they drove to the Tinker's Tavern. Did he believe she would come to Columbus to see him? She would, anytime she could, but would he want her to after hearing the truth? Alex no longer believed that she would return to Chicago taking the secret with her. That had been her safe plan, and it was falling apart a bit more every day. She couldn't keep telling herself that this summer would be like the one so many years ago. A magical, wonderful dream she could take with her, and no one would get hurt.

THE CELEBRATION LASTED until after midnight. Daniel drove Alex and Lizzie home. When they stopped in the drive at Dancing Falls, Alex assumed Lizzie would go in, and she would have alone time with Daniel. After all, Lizzie knew Daniel was leaving in the morning, and she had been enthusiastic about matching her mom with Daniel since she met him.

Lizzie stood outside the car. "Mom, I need to talk to you. Can you come in with me?"

Surprised, but not worried, Alex looked at Daniel. "Do you mind?"

"Not at all." His features had taken on the sharp angles of concern.

Alex wondered if perhaps he minded more

than he let on. "I'll call you when we're done. Maybe we can still find that park bench."

"Sure. I'll be waiting."

She got out and walked to the front door. The living room was quiet, with just a low lamp glowing in a corner. Martin, Jude and Wesley had gone to the performance but not the party. Alex assumed her father was in his room with Maggie, and Jude and Wesley had gone to their place above the tack room. Alex lit a brighter lamp. "Is this good?" she asked. "Can I get you something, a glass of milk, maybe?"

Lizzie furrowed her brow. "Mom, I'm not a kid anymore. You don't have to bring me milk and cookies."

"Okay. I'll try to remember that." She sat on the sofa and patted the seat next to her. "What did you want to talk about, honey?"

Lizzie sat but did not lean back. Her demeanor was guarded, her back straight. She didn't waste any time. "Mom, I've changed my mind. I don't want to go to Bryn Mawr."

Alex told herself to stay calm. This was just a young girl getting carried away by her opening night success.

For ten minutes the conversation was mostly

one-sided as Lizzie went over all the details about her choice to go to Ohio State. Most of what she said was mixed with the continuous buzz of alarm that had begun playing in Alex's mind ever since Lizzie's announcement.

...great Department of Theater

...cutting-edge program

...closer to Chicago

...acting is what I was born to do

When she finally drew a breath, Lizzie regarded her mother thoughtfully. "So, is everything okay, Mom?"

Alex licked her dry lips and swallowed. Her first instinct was to play the role of mom and declare the idea was nonsense, and she would hear no more about it. But she'd never assumed such a dictatorial attitude with Lizzie before, and she couldn't now. Though, in fairness, Lizzie had never come up with such an illogical choice before, either.

"Is everything okay?" Alex repeated. "No, honey, everything is not okay. I don't agree with or approve of your decision."

"Mom, I just told you all the best reasons why I want to do this."

"Yes, you did. And not one of them is good enough to cancel the plans we made for you to go to Bryn Mawr. Do you realize what an honor it is to be accepted by this institution?"

"Well, sure, but..."

"This is your future, Lizzie. We had it all mapped out for you."

"You and Daddy mapped it out, Mom."

"You were sitting right there at the dining room table when we were looking at catalogs. Why didn't you say something if you didn't want to go to Bryn Mawr?"

"Well, at first I thought I did. I mean, Daddy was so excited that I would be following in Grandma's footsteps. It meant so much to him. And teaching literature seemed like a solid, safe thing to do."

"It is. Teaching is a rewarding profession. What could be better than introducing books to a new generation? Once you have your master's you can join a small college community and enjoy all that life has to offer. Sabbaticals, opportunities for study overseas, lasting friendships..."

"All that may be true, but it doesn't excite me. Not anymore."

"You mean not since you snagged a small role in a summer stock theater?" Alex realized she was minimizing what Lizzie had devoted the past weeks to, but she had to make her daughter see the foolishness of this irrational and impulsive decision.

"That's not fair, Mom! You were totally behind me getting a part in the play. You drove me there!"

"Yes, I did, so you would have an opportunity to clear your head this summer, so you could forget your grief for a few blessed weeks. And you did! The play worked wonders for you. But it will be over in a few nights and you'll be off to college."

"I don't want to go to Bryn Mawr, Mom. Or be a teacher. I've always enjoyed acting, so don't make it sound as if I heard applause for the first time and became a completely different person."

Alex stood, paced in a small area. After a moment she said, "I can't let you do this, Lizzie. What sort of a future will you have with a degree in acting? I can just picture you waiting tables in Los Angeles, hoping your agent calls with an audition—that's if you're even fortunate enough to get an agent."

"Why do you have to paint the absolute worst picture?" Lizzie said. "Who knows if I'll end up in California? Maybe I'll go to New

York or some other city. The point is I want to act. I know that now, and it's not too late for me to change my mind and withdraw from Bryn Mawr."

A solution occurred to Alex, the last card she could play. "Have you checked into acting classes at Bryn Mawr?" she asked. "Why can't you have a double major, theater and literature? You can make up your mind what you want to do at a later date."

"No. I want to go to Ohio State."

"Why?"

"Because of the program there. And Daniel is close by."

Daniel? Did he know about this? Alex recalled his comment about her driving to Columbus, his wary expression when he dropped them off at the house a while ago. If he did know, the decent thing would've been to have given her a heads-up.

"Have you discussed this with Daniel?" Alex asked.

"Yes, and he agrees with me."

"What?" The sting of betrayal gnawed at Alex's stomach. How could Daniel have gone along with this wild plan? He had no right to interfere! At least, no right that he knew about.

"What did he say?" she asked. "That he thinks it's the best choice for you?"

"Not in so many words," Lizzie admitted. "But he said that everyone should have dreams and be able to follow them. And he went to Ohio State, and he knows a lot about the theater department. And look what an OSU education has done for him."

She paused as if waiting for her mother to say something positive. Alex kept quiet, so Lizzie pressed on. "And he's my mentor, Mom. He's helped me all summer, and I can call on him for advice anytime since he'll be in Columbus, too. He's already promised that I can call him whenever I want. It's perfect, don't you see that? I mean, I like Daniel, you like Daniel. What could be better?"

What would be better is if this entire conversation could be rewound and deleted from Alex's memory. She sat back on the sofa, took a breath. "Think about what you're saying, Lizzie. All at once you're ready to give up everything you've planned based on a few weeks of summer stock theater and a man you've known for such a short time. You've always loved books—novels, poetry. Literature is the ideal major for you. I'm sorry, but this doesn't make any sense!"

Lizzie leaned forward, stared into her mother's eyes. "Mom, think about this. I'll be within a few hours' drive from you in Chicago. Daniel and I can take off for occasional weekends together and come and see you."

Daniel and Lizzie confined in a car together for hours? As what? Mentor and protégée? Father and daughter? Alex didn't know anymore. If Daniel was having this much influence over Lizzie as a good friend, maybe she should rethink her resolve to tell him the truth.

She tried the most immediate and practical rebuttal she could come up with. "What makes you think I have any plans to see Daniel once I go back to Chicago?"

"I just thought… I mean, you like him, and he obviously likes you. You're great together. Why wouldn't you see him?"

Great together. In the back of Alex's mind, she believed that she and Daniel might have a future. Once she told him about Lizzie, once he'd processed that information, maybe they could make a go of a relationship. Or maybe not. He might never forgive her, never want to see her again. She couldn't let Lizzie base her entire future on the possibility that Daniel would become a permanent fixture in their lives.

"You're jumping to conclusions, Lizzie," she said. "I don't know that I'll ever see Daniel again once I leave Ohio." And now that she knew he'd encouraged *her daughter* in this ill-thought-out plan with his speech about dreams, Alex didn't know if she wanted a future with Daniel. He hadn't mentioned anything to her about Lizzie's plans, and yet he clearly knew that this conversation was going to take place. He'd allowed her to walk into an ambush. What about these past weeks, the time they'd spent together? Did that mean nothing?

Right now Alex didn't know if she wanted to scream at Daniel that he'd overstepped his boundaries as a family friend, although not as a father, she reminded herself, or jump in the car with Lizzie and return to Chicago. Of one thing she was certain. She felt betrayed by Daniel in more ways than one. He'd backed Lizzie's plan without discussing it with the girl's own mother, and he'd let Alex face Lizzie without preparation. She'd begun to think of Daniel as an ally, and he'd betrayed her tonight.

"Lizzie," she began calmly. "It's late. I'm tired. You're tired. But you need to know that I am not in support of this idea. I think you would be making a mistake. How many young girls have set their sights on something as flimsy as an acting career? And how many have failed? I can't let you throw away everything your father and I hoped for you, not to mention what you wanted for yourself, until you got this taste for acting. This is just a whim. Hopefully, once we're home, you will forget about it and start thinking about your real future."

Lizzie's eyes filled with tears. "I won't forget about it, Mom. I won't! If you won't let me go to Ohio State, I don't know what I'll do. I can't afford to pay all my expenses myself. I know you control my college finances…"

This was true, but Alex hadn't played that card yet and hoped she wouldn't have to. "Go up to bed, honey," she said. "We'll talk more in the morning."

"And will the outcome be any different?" Lizzie asked.

"Probably not."

Without another word, Lizzie stood and strode to the stairs. The echo of her footsteps pounded in Alex's heart. She hated arguing with Lizzie. They so rarely disagreed. But she had to be the wiser, smarter one now. She had to be the mother.

Alex didn't know how long she sat in the living room, but sometime later, her cell phone rang. She checked the caller ID. Daniel Chandler. Without connecting, she turned off the ringer and went up to bed.

CHAPTER THIRTEEN

"GOOD GRIEF, DANNY, you look worse than I do!" Gus set down his coffee mug and stared at his son.

His eyes gritty from lack of sleep, Daniel went to the counter to fill a cup for himself. "I'm not surprised. I didn't sleep well." *Or at all.*

"You're getting an early start," Gus said. "It's barely eight o'clock."

"I have one stop to make before I take off for Columbus," he said. "But I'm glad you're up. I want to go over some stuff with you first."

"If it's about my well-being, you can save your breath, son. I think you've got me prepared for any eventuality."

"That's my job, Pop. Aunt Margaret is coming tomorrow and she'll be here as long as you need her. I hope you'll let her stay until the deal is done with the hardware store and the building is listed. I don't want you trying to cope with any additional stress by yourself."

"We don't know how long that will be, Danny. You know I don't want to disrupt everybody's life. It's bad enough that you've spent your entire time off helping me out. You could have had a real nice vacation, but instead…"

Daniel leaned against the counter. "Stop it, Pop. I've been where I want to be, and I'm coming back as many weekends as I can." He opened a drawer and took out a tablet. Sitting at the table with his father, he flipped through a few pages.

"You're going to wear that book out," Gus said.

"Just making sure all the phone numbers are correct. We've got your doctors, Aunt Margaret, Bill Justin down the street, Phyllis Conklin from your church…"

"And the butcher, the baker and the candlestick maker," Gus added. "I'll be okay, Danny. Go save the world, or at least this part of Ohio."

Daniel took a last long swig of coffee. "Still got a few things to pack up in my car and then I'll head out. I can't believe my assistant has me scheduled for dinner with the Ohio Corn Growers Consortium tonight. I won't have time to unpack." He got up, strode around the table. Without embarrassment he bent down and gave his father a long hug. "I'll miss you, Pop. Be sure and call if you need anything."

"I'll call if I do, Danny. Now go on before we both turn into weepy old women."

Five minutes later Daniel drove down the main street of Greenfield. But he didn't take the highway south toward Columbus. Instead, he headed toward Fox Creek.

LYING IN HER BED, Alex heard a car pull into the drive of Dancing Falls. Her body felt like lead, and she didn't even try to get up. She knew her father was an early riser and would answer the bell. But when the front door opened, and her dad's booming voice identified the visitor, she padded to the bedroom door and listened through the crack.

"The girls aren't even up yet, Daniel," Martin said. "Can I get you a cup of coffee while we wait for them?"

"No, thank you, sir. If you wouldn't mind, I'd like you to tell Alexis that I'm here. I wouldn't ask, except I'm leaving for Columbus, and the matter is urgent."

"I guess I can do that," Martin agreed. "Why don't you wait on the back patio and give her a minute to pull herself together."

Alex listened to Daniel's footsteps through the main-floor hallway as he walked toward the back of the house. She threw on a pair of yoga pants and a T-shirt and tied her hair at her nape. At the last moment she squeezed a dime-size amount of toothpaste on her finger, rubbed it over her teeth and rinsed.

She met her father halfway down the stairs. "I heard. I'll take care of it, Dad."

"Is something wrong, Alexis? Do you want me to go with you?"

"No, but thanks. I think Daniel just wants to say goodbye." And ask why she didn't pick up his call last night. After a restless sleep she was ready to tell him the answer and a whole lot more! Her anger hadn't abated in the overnight hours. If anything, she was even more determined to let him know he'd disappointed her.

Her heart hitched in her chest when she stepped out on the patio. There, seated at the table, was her Daniel, the man she'd once loved, the man she was falling for all over again, until last night. He looked as if he hadn't slept, either. His hair was mussed, his eyes blinking in the bright sun. He was dressed for driving in shorts, a T-shirt and sneakers. A ball cap lay on the table.

At her approach, he turned, stood. "Alex, we need to talk."

She smoothed her hands down the sides of her pants and took a chair. Only then did Daniel sit back down. Always the gentleman.

"That's funny, Daniel," she said. "I think we should have talked last night before Lizzie told me she's decided to throw her future away."

"It was Lizzie's place to tell you, not mine."

She huffed out a long breath. "Daniel, we've become so close—at least I thought we had."

"I feel the same."

"Then didn't you feel any compassion for what I was going to face? Any compunction to give me a heads-up? You know how I feel about Lizzie's future."

"It wasn't my place to interfere with a mother and daughter," he said. "I'm Lizzie's friend, but that's all. Otherwise, I'm an outsider."

His innocent words brought a fresh stab of guilt to her heart.

"What would you have had me do?" he asked.

"Tell me what I was facing! Include me in what you and Lizzie talked about. You encouraged her without consulting me!"

He looked genuinely confused. "What are you saying? I didn't encourage her. I told her to talk to you."

"Then you didn't tell her that everyone should follow their dreams, as if we only get one shot at life, so we should do what makes us happy?"

"Yes, I suppose I said that, but I was speaking in general terms. I certainly didn't say that she should drop out of Bryn Mawr and go to Ohio State."

Alex shook her head and lowered her voice. "I think she's been planning this for weeks, ever since she met you and got that part in the play. Last night was just the culmination of all those hours at the theater. And all those hours with you."

He leaned slightly forward. "Alex, is it really fair to blame my influence for this? It was you who brought Lizzie to the theater in the beginning. You thought the diversion would help her get over her father's death. And it has. So a lot of good has come out of her experience at the Red Barn."

"Maybe so, at first," she said. "But a bit of good does not make up for altering an entire future. Lizzie is smart. Her IQ is in the top five percent of her age group. She's a girl with a bright career ahead of her." When her voice began to tremble, Alex paused and swallowed. "I can't let her throw all that away." She stared hard at Daniel. "And I can't let you tell her that dreams can become reality."

He waited a moment before responding. "But can't they, Alex? Can't dreams become our reality? Since you've come home, I think I've become a believer."

"Don't be so sentimental, Daniel." At his shocked expression she sat back, ashamed of the way she'd spoken to him. It wasn't as if her own dreams hadn't been filled with Daniel lately. "I'm sorry, but Lizzie will be throwing her future away if she follows these impossible, impractical dreams." She crossed her legs and stared out over the expansive back lawn. "An actress! What chance does she have, really? How many young girls head out on this path only to end up disappointed, living hand to mouth, waiting for their phone to ring?"

"I might be able to help her," Daniel said.

Alex cringed, turned her gaze back to him. "Haven't you helped enough?"

He looked as if she'd struck him. "Hear me out, please. I'll be close to her. I'll visit her at the university, monitor her progress. I think I'm qualified to judge if she has talent. Right now I'd say she's got plenty, but I won't flatter her if she doesn't show promise."

Alex placed her clenched hands on the table. "That won't be necessary. Don't you get it, Daniel? She's not going to Ohio State. She's going to Bryn Mawr. And it's time for you and everyone else to stay out of her life!"

"So you've made up your mind?" His eyes had taken on a combative spark. "That's it?"

"She made up her mind last night," came a voice from the back door. Lizzie stood in flannel pajama bottoms and a tank top, her eyes bleary, her hair in disarray. "It seems I'm not to have any say in my own life."

Alex stood. "Lizzie, there is no need to be so dramatic."

"That's right, I forgot. There's no room for drama in this family, is there?"

Alex's heart was breaking. She and Lizzie had never spoken so angrily to each other. In twenty-four hours Alex had lost most of what mattered to her. But she wasn't going to sacrifice her daughter's future just to end an unpleasant scene.

"Go back inside, please," she said. "We'll talk later. Right now this conversation is between Daniel and me."

Anger flared in Lizzie's eyes. "That figures. I'm standing right here listening to the two of you talk about the next few years of *my* life, and I'm told to go back in the house. How is that right, Mom?"

"Lizzie…"

"Fine. I'm going!"

When she'd gone inside, Daniel did the strangest thing. He smiled, reached out and took Alex's hand. "Being a parent can really suck, can't it?" he said.

His compassion was her undoing. The lack of sleep, the emotional turmoil—it came spilling out in a huge sob and a flow of tears. And his arms came around her. He held her close but she felt cold and lonely.

"I've got to go," he said. "But I'm not giving up on us, Alex. I'll be back on Friday, and I hope you will be waiting for me."

He kissed the top of her head. "If I screwed this up in any way, I'm sorry, honey. Really, truly sorry. You're the parent, not me."

She shuddered in his arms.

"I won't interfere again. I promise."

He picked up his cap and walked around the side of the house. Alex waited until she was sure his car had left the property, and then she went inside. She actually wanted Daniel's help, needed it, and though he had every right to give it, she had no right to ask.

CHAPTER FOURTEEN

DESPITE THE WARM summer temperatures, the next few days were the most bitter Alex could remember. She missed Daniel. She was sorry they'd quarreled and that she'd assigned so much of the blame to him. He was just being sympathetic to Lizzie's problem. But she still resented his influence in Lizzie's life. He was changing everything about the comfortable relationship she'd built with her daughter and she didn't know when that would stop. Or if it should. But most of all, she didn't know what she would do when he came back on Friday.

Lizzie continued with her role in *The Music Man*, putting aside her disagreement with her mother to do the best job she could. Alex attended two more performances, and at each one, she had to agree with the audience and critics that her daughter had talent. But that did not mean she should give up the plans Teddy and she had made with Lizzie's blessing.

Alex hoped that Lizzie would wake up one morning to the realization that her goals to attend Ohio State were impractical and would ultimately be unfulfilling. By Friday afternoon that hadn't happened, and there were only two more performances of *The Music Man* before the run ended on Saturday. And only two weeks until Alex and Lizzie planned to return to Chicago and shop for the necessities for college, a chore they once looked forward to with enthusiasm.

Just before noon Alex was making sandwiches when her father came into the kitchen. "What are you doing home so early, Dad?" she asked.

"I moved around some appointments and got everyone taken care of this morning. Thought I'd just spend the afternoon in the pool. You and Lizzie want to join me?"

Was it Alex's imagination or did her father's invitation sound less than sincere? "I don't know, Dad. I'll see. You should ask Lizzie yourself. These days she does what she wants without any coaxing from me."

Martin poured lemonade into a pitcher to take to the pool. "Things still aren't better on the mother/daughter front?"

"We're speaking, so I suppose that's some progress. But I haven't relented on this crazy idea to go to acting school."

"And she hasn't changed her mind, either?" Martin asked.

"No, and I feel awful about it, but I'm going to have to play the mother card on this one. I feel like I've always done what's right for Lizzie, and this is no exception. Her decision was based on pure impulse, and that's no way to decide the rest of your life."

Martin added ice to the pitcher. "Hmm… I suppose you've talked to your sister Jude about this."

"Of course, but so has Lizzie. As you might expect, Jude professes to be unbiased, but she's really on Lizzie's side. But you know Jude. She runs her life by being spontaneous, and we all can recall some of the consequences of her behavior!"

Martin chuckled. "I've bailed her out of any number of jams. Remember when she posted those No Hunting signs all over northern Ohio? She had them printed so they looked like authentic Government Issue, and it had the hunters around here up in arms."

"I remember. She was only twelve or thirteen and got someone to drive her to all the hunting areas."

"I never worried about you doing those fool-hardy things, Alexis. But to give Jude credit, usually her heart's in the right place," Martin said, "though she often acts before she thinks. I'm not surprised she sides with Lizzie on this one."

"What about you, Dad? You haven't weighed in on this situation. Do you think I'm doing the right thing as far as Lizzie is concerned?"

"Oh, honey, I don't want to get in the middle of this one. I love you both and want what's best for you. I trust your instincts. You've always been a good mother. Can I just leave it at that?"

Alex smiled. "Coward." She nodded at the pitcher in his hand. "Plan on drinking a lot of lemonade, I see."

"Not just me. I'm having company."

Alex raised her brows. "Really? Who?"

"Aurora Spindell from next door. I told her I'd show her some water exercises for her sore ankle." He looked at his watch. "She should be here in a few minutes."

Alex knew her father was an honorable man, but she was concerned about his interest in Aurora. "What's going on, Dad? You're seeing a lot of our new neighbor."

"Haven't seen her in a week, Alexis. And, like you say, we're neighbors. Helping each other is the right thing to do. She's alone over there with no one to give her a hand."

Alex shrugged. "Okay. Have fun." She had enough to worry about without exaggerating her father's interest in Aurora. After all, he slept every night in a narrow bed in his wife's sickroom. He never complained about his responsibilities. In fact, he seemed to thrive on them. If he wanted to befriend a neighbor lady, what was the harm?

"You'd better get out there, Dad. Your patient has arrived."

He stared out the window. Aurora sat on the edge of the pool next to Lizzie, and from the looks of things, they were having a spirited discussion. Alex could well imagine the topic. Lizzie was collecting supportive opinions like soldiers collected ammunition.

A FEW MINUTES LATER, Lizzie had gone inside, and Martin patted Aurora's hand as she clung to the side of the pool.

"Ouch! I don't think I'm ready for this, Marty."

"Yes, you are, Aurora. The swelling has gone down. You're just left with some residual pain. These exercises will help."

She gave him a doubtful look. "If you say so."

"I do say so. I'm a doctor, remember."

She continued flexing her ankle with the front of her foot poised on a pool step. Martin enjoyed the view of her springy red hair bound in an elastic band and her ultraconservative flowered bathing suit with its ruffled skirt and blousy top. He wondered why she tried to hide her slim figure. And then he glanced up at the second-story window where his wife stayed and thought perhaps he understood. Someday he and Aurora would have an honest and open conversation about Maggie and eliminate Aurora's concerns.

"Now stand on your toes and count to ten."

She lasted less than two seconds.

Martin laughed. "You know, for a tough gal, you are a sissy when it comes to pain." He offered her his hand so she could exit the pool. "Try sitting on the side and doing some simple flex and retract positions. Keep your toes pointed."

"Can I have another glass of lemonade first?"

"No. Do you think a physical therapist would let you stop for refreshments in the middle of a session? Five more minutes. You can do it."

She reluctantly complied and worked the sore ankle in the water. "The pool feels great, actually," she said. "We should make a profit-share deal whereby my guests can use your pool." She grinned at him. "That's assuming I will see profits, a detail I'm not at all sure of right now."

"You're pouring a lot of capital into that house," Martin said. "You're not running out of money, are you?"

"Not yet. But I don't have enough for a pool. What I am running out of is patience, with code enforcement officers and electrical and plumbing inspectors. It seems to take days for one little project to be accomplished and then along comes a bureaucrat to tell me what's been done wrong."

He brought her a glass of lemonade. "Here. You've earned a break." Taking a seat next to her on the cool tile, he said, "You are making progress, though. I can see the changes from the road as I drive by. The new yellow paint is particularly attractive."

"Thank you. That is the only project the inspectors didn't find fault with." She took a sip from her glass. "So how are you, Marty?"

He was taken aback at the question. He spent hours every day asking people the same thing, but few asked him. "What do you mean?"

"Just that you are a busy man. You have an important job. You take care of your wife and your family. And from what I've heard, you're active in several community activities."

Since Aurora brought up the subject of Maggie, he decided to pursue it. "What have you heard about my wife, Aurora?"

"Probably close to the sad truth," she said. "The people in this town like and respect you. I don't think they would exaggerate your role in your wife's care, or the seriousness of her condition."

"Maggie's diagnosis was the greatest disappointment in my life. Her continued decline was my greatest failure. Modern medicine can only do so much, and it took a lot of soul-searching until I accepted that fact."

"She's lucky to have you," Aurora said.

"They all are. I could tell from talking to your granddaughter that your girls love you very much."

He laughed. "So that's what you and Lizzie were talking about out here, how much they all love me?"

"In a roundabout way," Aurora said. "They do love you, but Lizzie was telling me that she's having a problem with her mother."

"I know all about it, and I hope you didn't get involved."

"I've learned not to interfere in another family's problems. But if Lizzie wants to tell me the details another time, I'll listen."

"And will you have an opinion?"

She grinned. "One thing you'll learn about me, Marty, is that I *always* have an opinion. Once I tried to influence a family member of my own about his future. I'm still paying the price for that mistake."

Again, Martin thought about Aurora's words. There was definitely a story here, maybe an explanation about why she was alone now.

Her concise affirmation that his girls loved him made him sit a bit taller. He knew his daughters appreciated what he did for their mother, but the simple praise from a practical stranger almost meant more. *A practical stranger.* He'd known Aurora only a few weeks. Their initial meeting had been less than auspicious, and yet he felt connected to her in a way that defied logic. Aurora didn't treat him like a doctor. She didn't expect anything of him. She didn't ask too many questions. And yet her concern seemed genuine.

If his situation was different... But it wasn't. If he was starting over... But he wasn't, and had no idea when, or even if, he would be. So for now he would take what pleasure he could from this plainspoken, gutsy neighbor, who embodied the will and determination of a lumberjack.

One simple realization stunned him. Aurora was fun. And fun, the laughing, teasing kind that could inspire closeness, was what a mature man craved, and was lacking in his life.

"Get your whip out, Marty. I've got about ten more minutes to devote to this torture before I go home. Make it good."

He smiled.

ALEX'S CELL PHONE rang at 7:30. The caller ID identified the call she'd been waiting for, agonizing over. Was he on his way to Greenfield or had he stayed in Columbus? After their argument, she wouldn't blame him for turning his attention to his constituents and considering her a lost cause.

She connected. "Hello, Daniel." He'd called her twice during the week, both times to say that he hoped the situation between her and Lizzie had improved. It hadn't. Sometimes Lizzie seemed close to accepting that her future lay at Bryn Mawr. Still, Alex worked to break down the wall of silence the girl had built between them.

"I'm a half hour away," he said.

Her heart contracted. He hadn't given up on them.

"And I'm starving," he added. "Are we speaking?"

"Yes, we're speaking. I'm sorry…"

"No apologies necessary, Alex. Once we start down that road, one or the other of us could be apologizing every day for something. I believe in the principle of *get over it*."

She laughed. "I'm willing to go along with that. Now, about feeding you…"

"Can I stop and pick you up? We can order a pizza and take it over to my father's." He paused. "You understand I need to see him."

"That sounds lovely. I'd like to see Gus, too."

"Great. I'll be there in—" he paused, as if checking his watch "—approximately twenty-six minutes."

"Oh, that long? Can't you hurry it up?" She felt her face flush. She was shamelessly flirting again, and it felt so good.

He chuckled and hung up. Alex went to her room and changed her shorts for a pair of jeans. She tossed aside the old T-shirt she'd been wearing and chose a pink Oxford cloth blouse. Last, she applied a minimum of makeup and swept her hair into a topknot, which she secured with a tortoiseshell clip.

Before going down to wait for Daniel, she stopped at the door to the guest room where Lizzie slept. Lizzie was out, but Alex wrote her a note explaining where she was and left it on the dresser. Then she called Jude to see if her sister would pick Lizzie up if she called. Naturally, she had to explain about Daniel to Jude.

"Looks like your argument with Daniel is over," Jude said. "You two might make it after all."

There was no point in denying her feelings

for Daniel anymore, Alex thought. She'd protested for so long, saying that her relationship with him was purely platonic, that they were friends and that was all, that she wasn't dating him in the traditional sense. She didn't know if anyone in her family believed her. She didn't believe herself. Once she'd admitted that she was attracted to Daniel, she'd careened headlong into a spiral of emotions that both terrified and excited her. She'd missed him this week. She'd agonized over the harsh words she'd spoken and the genuinely sweet gestures he'd made before leaving. She'd worried that he wouldn't want to see her again.

As Alex went downstairs, she wondered if this was love. Her feelings for Daniel were certainly different from the ones she'd experienced for Teddy. And yet she'd loved Teddy. But she hadn't felt this… What could she call it? Passion? Desire? Crazy winged creatures playing racquetball in her stomach? If this was love, she thought, it was absolutely, horribly wonderful.

And so tonight, or at the latest tomorrow, but definitely this weekend, she would tell him about his daughter.

She watched out the front window for his car to pull up. Without waiting for him to come to the door, she dashed out and got in the passenger seat. His arm was slung over the steering wheel. The dome light showed the sparkle in his eyes, the genuineness of his smile.

She sighed. "It's nice to see you…"

He cut her off by pulling her close and kissing her. He smelled so good, as if he'd driven with the windows open. She ran her fingers through his hair, mussing it even more than the wind had done. The kiss lasted until she finally noticed the gearshift sticking into her thigh. She backed away, rubbing the afflicted area.

"Oops," he said. "I'll do better later."

She smiled. "You're doing fine right now."

They stopped at Lorenzo's for pizza and headed into Greenfield. Alex had never been to the Chandlers' house before. In the increasing dusk, she found the modest bungalow warm and inviting with lamps shining from the windows. The landscaping was trim and neat. A few flowering bushes surrounded the small front porch, imparting their scent to the night air. Streetlights illuminated each corner on Elm Street, showing off the residents' pride in ownership.

"What a nice place to grow up," she said, walking to the porch.

"It's okay," he said. "Two bedrooms was enough, but have you ever tried to get by with only one bathroom?"

She hadn't.

Gus met them at the door. He hugged his son. "How was the drive?"

"No problem," Daniel said.

"It's nice to see you, Alexis," Gus said. "Come in. Make yourself comfortable." He sniffed the air. "What's that I smell?"

"Pizza, Pop," Daniel said. "Do you want a slice?"

Gus chuckled, rubbed his hand over his thinning abdomen. "And ruin this pretty waistline? I don't think so."

"So how are you feeling?" Daniel asked.

"I'm okay, son. Good days and bad. Today was a good day. Your aunt Margaret left this afternoon. I wanted to tidy the place up for you, but Margaret didn't leave me anything to do. So I fixed my own supper."

Gus looked from Alex to Daniel. "But it's

now past my bedtime, so I'll leave you two kids to your pizza."

"Don't you want to tell me about the sale of the inventory?" Daniel asked.

"Now? It can wait. Everything is going according to plan, so you concentrate on pizza and this pretty girl beside you."

"We'll talk tomorrow," Daniel said. When Gus had left the room, Daniel took a bottle of wine from a cabinet in the corner. "It's Pinot Noir. Is that okay?"

"Perfect," Alex said.

He went into the kitchen and returned with the bottle opened and two glasses. He poured for each of them. Holding his glass up, he said, "To the weekend."

Alex clinked her glass against his. "And to forgetting the last time we were together and starting over, right?"

"No. I don't want to forget anything. Everything that happens is part of this relationship, Alex. You, me, Lizzie—I don't want to scare you, but I feel like we're meant to be together through the ups and downs. Maybe I'm speaking too soon. Maybe you don't want to hear this, but I feel a connection to you and Lizzie that grows stronger every day."

She took a long swallow of wine, a tactic to give herself time to think. He felt a connection. Of course he did. He'd been the first man, the only other man besides Teddy, that she'd ever made love with, and that one time, that expression of her deepest longing, had produced a baby. His baby.

He took the glass from her hand and set it on the coffee table. "I want to hear all about your week with Lizzie and how that's working out, but first, I have to know if you've thought about me this week, if you've felt even something of the connection I'm talking about."

Only every time I look into my daughter's face, into those gold-green eyes that defy description and are a perfect match when I look into yours.

"I missed you," she answered honestly. "I wanted to call you, but I knew you were busy."

"I was, but I would have made time." With his knuckles, he traced a line down her cheek, her neck. She bent her head to the side, giving him access to continue. And then his lips followed, nibbling at the soft skin under her ear, the smooth slope of her neck until they found her mouth. The kiss was hungry and passionate, and if she'd wondered at all about that special connection they professed to feel for each other, all doubts vanished.

In this little bungalow, with this man, she was home.

THE WINE BOTTLE EMPTIED, the pizza box thrown away, Alex and Daniel sat on the sofa. The TV played softly, a documentary they both thought they would like to see, but had abandoned a few minutes ago when Daniel turned down the volume.

"I thought you wanted to watch this," she said. "It's about America's national park system, and you're trying to put through a bill to make improvements to the Cuyahoga Park, aren't you?"

"I am, but we have to talk, Alex."

A flash of alarm skittered down her spine. His voice sounded so ominous. She turned, letting his arm fall away from her shoulders. "What is it? What's wrong?"

"I don't know if it's wrong," he said. "But

it's important, and it might change some things." He took a deep breath. "Something happened this week…"

CHAPTER FIFTEEN

SHE TRIED TO smile and failed miserably. "Daniel, you have me worried."

He took her hand. "I'm sorry. I don't mean to worry you, but what I'm about to tell you is life-changing. And since I've found you again, since I've grown close to you and your daughter, I'm not at all sure I want my life to change, especially if it will change us."

She exhaled a long breath. "Just tell me."

"Okay. In a way, what happened is fairly unusual. I mean, I'm only in my first term as a state senator. I had expected to serve at least two terms before seeking another office."

"A higher office, you mean?"

"Yes, that's right. State government is satisfying in many ways, but I can't deny that I have ambition beyond Ohio's boundaries."

"And has an opportunity presented itself?" She asked the question, but she had no idea what she wanted the answer to be. Like Daniel, she was just becoming comfortable, hopeful with the way things were.

"It has." He cleared his throat, held her hand a bit more tightly. "An exploratory committee met with me this week. Their job is to suggest a replacement for Senator Dillingham, who will be retiring at the end of his term."

"Senator Dillingham from Dayton?"

He nodded. "He's been one of Ohio's representatives in the US Senate for years."

"Yes, and he's quite well respected, though he is a member of the 'other' political party."

She remained silent for a moment and then said, "So, what you're trying to tell me is that this committee thinks you would make a good US senator? They want you to run?"

"That was the purpose of the meeting, yes." A slight smile curved his lips. "I have to tell you, Alex, I was flattered. I'm not one to respond to other people fawning over me or patting my back for any reason. Usually people who flatter you want something, but there were some important people in this steering committee."

"And you value their opinions?"

"Yes. They think I can win the seat." He

stood, paced in a small circle. "It's so early in my career to be considering a move like this. I know I've barely gotten my feet wet in state government, and now I'm setting my sights on Washington. Maybe I'm reaching way beyond my grasp. Maybe I should stay where I am for a while. I don't know."

"What does your heart tell you, Daniel? Do you want to stay where you are?"

He sat down next to her again. "No, I want to try for that senate position. I know it will be a lot of work. Hours of speech writing, campaigning, learning the other candidates' positions. Too many public functions to even think about. If I decide to do this, my life will hardly be my own for a while."

"And when would the election take place?" she asked.

"Next November. If I win, I'd take office in January." He rubbed the back of his neck. "You have to understand, Alex. If my father… if his future were…different, I wouldn't consider this run right now. But by the time campaigning kicks into high gear, Pop will be gone." His voice hitched.

She rubbed the back of his hand. "Maybe this is just what you need."

"I'm thinking maybe I do. Or I will. I'm really going to miss him."

"I know. It sounds to me like your mind is made up. And you stand a wonderful chance of winning. You've done so much for the people of this district. Once word spreads of our charismatic young senator looking toward the nation's capital, supporters will flock to you."

She believed what she said. Daniel seemed to have the whole package politically. He was smart, honest, courageous and handsome as sin, but the consequences of his decision weighed heavily on her mind. What would happen to their relationship once she returned to Chicago? If Daniel ran for higher office, he would be required to campaign in every Ohio district, not just this one. She would hardly see him.

Daniel chuckled. "I think I need you as my campaign manager. But I'm also thinking about us, Alex. I don't want what we've started to end because of my ambition. You know I'm crazy about you. You've made me think of a future of a different sort. I don't want to regret losing you the rest of my life."

"But wouldn't you regret not taking this

chance, Daniel? And wouldn't that regret be as profound as any other?"

He nodded in a contemplative manner. "I'm caught, honey, between here, with you, and there, where I see my star shining. I know I can do so much good…"

"You should accept the nomination, Daniel. Start gearing up for the election as soon as possible. Get out there. Let people know your name and what you stand for."

"But…"

"If you're about to mention us, remember, I won't be here anyway. I'm going back to Chicago. I have a life there. We'll see each other when we can. Don't let this opportunity slip away because of the feelings you have for me tonight."

"You talk as if those feelings aren't real, as if they'll vanish. And I don't think that."

"We don't know what will happen." *I still haven't told you the truth about Lizzie. I still don't know if you'll be able to forgive me or if you will want me as you say you do now.* She laid her hand on his arm. "As my mother used to say, 'If it's meant to be, it will be.'"

"There is one other reason for me to seriously accept the offer now."

"Oh?"

"I'm sure you're aware of the political climate in this country these days. It's a tough gig. Seems like mudslinging is all around us. Candidates have staff members whose job it is to dig up dirt on the other guys. Candidates for national office have to be pretty squeaky-clean."

"I'm aware," she said, smiling. "I live in Chicago, remember? It seems like every morning there's another front-page scandal."

"True. The point is I'll have to be vetted. Every little detail from my past will be examined under a microscope. I don't think I've done much to be ashamed of. Haven't dated any married celebrities or embezzled any money, or even stolen a candy bar that I can remember. I don't have any children wandering around Ohio wondering where Daddy is…"

Suddenly, Alex couldn't breathe. To keep him from seeing her face, she stood and walked to an open window. She had to pull herself together. She had to think. How could she tell him about Lizzie now? This news could destroy his plans. But if he counted on a future with her, how could she not? And what if she kept silent and a political opponent found out about Daniel Chandler's secret child? What would that do to his chances of winning in November?

But how would anyone find out? She'd covered her tracks so carefully for so many years. If she abandoned her plan to tell Daniel the truth and continued to keep the secret, no one would ever know. Except her.

Thank goodness he hadn't picked up on her anxiety. "So you're in?" he said, coming up behind her.

His hands wrapped around her upper arms, giving her support. She leaned against his chest. "I want whatever you want, Daniel."

He kissed the top of her head. "We'll make it work, Alex. You've given me the courage to believe that it's possible for a man to have the future he wants, the woman he needs."

"I'm glad," she said, cupping her hand over her mouth as if stifling a yawn. She had to get home, shut herself in her room and think this through. She had to protect her daughter. She wanted to protect Daniel's future. But the secret seemed to have taken on a life of its own. The consequences of her decision eighteen years ago were now like a spiderweb, growing daily, becoming more tangled. She wondered, if she could go back to that time in her life, would she do things differently?

"You're tired," he said. "Let me take you home. We have all day tomorrow to be together."

"Thank you," she said. "I am tired." She turned in his arms when she was certain her expression would not reveal her inner turmoil. "And I'm so proud of you," she added.

They discussed plans for the next day as Daniel drove her home. As soon as she was in her father's house, Alex ran up the stairs and went straight to her mother's room. She knew her father hadn't gone to bed yet. He was watching a movie in the family room. She went in, left the door open a crack and sat next to her mother's bed.

MAGGIE FOSTER'S EYES were closed. Her breathing was regular. Alex spoke softly into the monitor, which connected to a receiver in the family room downstairs. "Dad, it's Alex. I'm with Mom right now, so I'm turning off the system, okay?"

"Sure, sweetheart. I'll be up in about a half hour."

She switched off the machine, picked up her mother's hand and said, "It's time to tell you everything, Mom. I feel like I'm at a crossroads and I don't know which way to go. Maybe I should have told you then…"

Eighteen years earlier

"MOM, DADDY, *I have something to tell you.*"

Alex tried to draw breath into her lungs so her voice wouldn't sound so weak, so terrified.

"Sure, sweetheart," Maggie said, patting the sofa beside her. "Come sit down."

Alex sat. "Are we alone? Are Jude and Carrie in the house?"

"Not right now. Jude is outside with an eyedropper and that batch of new kittens we found in the garage. Carrie is at a girlfriend's." Maggie looked worried. "What's wrong? You look so serious."

"I've probably never been so serious," Alex said.

"Nothing we can't fix," Martin said. "Just tell us."

She'd rehearsed her words so many times. She knew what she wanted to say, what she wouldn't reveal. Yet now she didn't know how to start. "I've made a terrible mistake."

Her father smiled. Smiled! He probably thought that his firstborn daughter's idea of a mistake was writing in a schoolbook or littering in a park.

"Toward the end of my time at Birch Shore, I met a guy. He was the son of one of the guests. They were from California. They stayed at the resort for a week, so I got to know him pretty well."

"Okay," Maggie said.

"I really liked him," Alex continued. "His last night we were alone in his room..." Her voice had dropped so that her parents had to lean in to hear her. She wanted to cut out her tongue rather than disappoint them.

Martin cleared his throat. "Alexis, are you saying that you and this...boy..." The words seemed as difficult for him as they were for Alex. "Had sex?"

She nodded. "It was only one time." She looked at her mother. "But as you always told us, Mom, it only takes once."

Maggie held her daughter's hand. "Oh, honey. Are you pregnant?"

Another nod brought an onslaught of tears.

Martin stared down at his hands. Maggie began to cry. She gathered Alex into her arms.

"What is this young man's name?" Martin asked. "We'll call his parents right away."

"No," Alex said. "I don't want him to know. I want to deal with this myself."

Martin released a long sigh. "Besides the fact that he left you in a terrible situation, Alexis, he does have a right to know."

Alex sat back and straightened her spine. She was certain of what she wanted to say now. "I don't want him in my baby's life," she said.

"You want to have the child?" Maggie asked.

"Yes, absolutely. But this boy, he doesn't love me. What we did was wrong. It shouldn't have happened. I don't want a relationship with him based on the baby. I'd rather raise the child by myself."

The veins in Martin's temples throbbed. "But he's responsible! He has to bear some of the burden."

"We were both equally guilty," Alex said. "But Daddy, I have a plan."

"It's all right, honey," Maggie said. "We'll

raise the child, the three of us. It will be okay."

"No, Mom, it's not okay. I need to make this right." She paused, remembering Teddy's kind words. "I spoke to Teddy about this."

"Teddy! You told Teddy before coming to us?" Her father was clearly hurt, angry.

"He listens, Daddy. He understands me." She fortified herself with another long breath. "And now he has offered to marry me."

Martin stood. "Oh, he has, has he? How generous of him!"

Maggie held up her hand. "Martin, sit down. Hear her out."

"I said that all wrong, Daddy," Alex said. "Teddy wants *to marry me, and I want to marry him. He'll raise the baby with me. He will take care of us."*

Martin returned to his chair but didn't speak.

"Honey, have you thought this through?" Maggie said. "You know we love and respect Teddy, but he is quite a bit older than you."

"That's my point exactly," Martin said. "I can't allow this. It doesn't make sense."

"I have deep feelings for him, Daddy. I

really, truly do. I want to marry Teddy. I'm going to marry him."

"Are you sure, honey?" Maggie asked. "Because there are other options. Have you thought about growing older with a man who is almost thirty years ahead of you? You don't have to sacrifice a full life with someone your own age because of this one mistake. For a marriage to work, there has to be sharing, honest communication, and pardon me for being so blunt, but passion."

"I can have all that with Teddy," Alex said. "My mind is made up."

LETTING GO OF those memories, Alex took a deep breath to calm her nerves. She knew she'd feel better once she admitted the truth to someone, even if that person couldn't advise her. But right now the facts were almost as painful to reveal as those from eighteen years ago.

"I told you before, Mom, I've run into Lizzie's father since I've been home," she began. "Seeing him has made me remember how I felt about him back then. I would never have done what I did if I hadn't cared for him. And you know, too, that I loved Teddy. He was so good to me and Lizzie. Every day I spent with Teddy was secure and comfortable. And content."

Alex wiped tears from under her eyes as she recalled the desperate few days between finding out she was pregnant and marrying Teddy. He'd been so sweet and forthcoming. He said he loved her and wanted to spend the rest of his life making her happy. And he'd kept that promise.

So, only one short month after leaving Birch Shore, Alex married Teddy in the living room of Dancing Falls. It was a simple ceremony with only family present, and Alex's parents supported the decision. After all, Teddy and Martin had been friends since medical school, and Maggie had come to love him almost as a brother.

"If anything, Mom," Alex said, "Teddy treated me too well, better than I deserved. He gave me security and joy. Maybe not the passion you once told me about, but I didn't think I missed it." Alex cleared her throat. "I've often wondered if our arrangement was fair to Teddy. Oh, he never complained. Never once, but I can admit to you now that I never believed I deserved such a selfless, loving man in my life." Her next words came out on a sob. "I will miss him always, Mom, and I will always be grateful.

"But now, Mama, I am in such a mess. I think I'm in love with Lizzie's father. He, too, is a good man, a respected man, and seeing him again has made me come alive. I've been able to put my grief behind me for a few blessed weeks. But he doesn't know he has a daughter, and I am so afraid of the consequences if I tell him.

"Will I lose Lizzie when she discovers her life has been a convenient lie her mother concocted so she could face the future? Lizzie is a strong, independent young woman. You would be so proud of her, but her independence could be the undoing of our relationship. If I don't lose Lizzie for good, I know that at least I will lose her respect."

Alex gripped her mother's hand as if it was a lifeline. "And Daniel, Mama, what of him? That's his name, by the way, Daniel Chandler. He's the son of the man who owns the hardware store in Greenfield. Maybe you remember me speaking of him that summer at Birch Shore. Now he's a senator with a bright future. He's done many good things for our state, and he's likely to continue his good works in the nation's capital. For this reason alone, I'm glad I made the decision I did all those years ago. I'm glad Daniel had the chance to get a top-notch education and to become the man he wanted to be.

"He deserves to know about Lizzie. I realize that. But what will happen to his plans if word leaks out that he has a daughter? Will the news be presented as some sort of sleazy backstory? Will Lizzie be labeled the illegitimate child of our state senator? And what of her? Lizzie could be hounded by the press for comments. Will she become a media headliner for all the wrong reasons? How would such scrutiny affect her life at college? Her future? I've spent my life trying to protect Lizzie, and the truth could destroy her now."

Alex raised her mother's hand to her face and cupped Maggie's palm against her cheek. "Oh, Mom, what should I do? How will this ever come out right and fair to everyone? Should I continue the lie and give up Daniel? Because I would have to. I couldn't be a part of his life if I carried the lie with me. And now that I've seen him again, I don't know if I can go on living the lie myself.

"I wish you could speak, Mom. I need you so badly. I need a sign that you're still in there somewhere." Her voice hitched. She forced the next words out. "Should I tell Daniel that he's Lizzie's father?"

A rustling at the door made Alex drop her mother's hand. She spun around to face her sister, who stood with one hand on the jamb.

"What did you just say?" Jude asked. "Daniel is Lizzie's father?"

ALEX GASPED. "JUDE! What are you doing here?" She knew it was a stupid question the moment the words left her mouth.

"I live here, remember?" Jude said. "Or very nearly."

Still, it was uncommon for her to come to the main house this late at night. It was close to eleven o'clock. She wouldn't leave her son at the apartment by himself. "Where's Wesley?" Alex asked.

"He's on a sleepover. I wasn't tired, and I sometimes use my quiet time to come and see Mom." She entered the room and pulled another chair close to the bed. "So, sister, you want to explain yourself?"

"I don't know what you heard. I was just

talking randomly like I often do with Mom."
Lame, Alex. Very lame.

"You picked a random name from out of thin air to identify Lizzie's father? And you just happened to pick Daniel Chandler?" She wiggled her fingers and said, "Give it up, Alex."

"You shouldn't have been listening at the door."

"Yeah, and if you didn't want anyone to know your business, you shouldn't have said what you did out loud. Now that we've established both of those parameters, let's have the truth."

Alex grabbed her sister's arm. "You can't tell anyone, Jude. Promise me. Besides me, and now you, Mom is the only other person on earth who knows the truth, and I just told her."

Jude tried to pull her arm free. "Relax, okay? And let go of me."

Alex did. Jude settled back in her chair and raised one booted foot to the opposite knee. She left a smudge of barn dirt on her jeans. "Wow. What goes around comes around, eh? You and Daniel had this thing at Birch Shore all those years ago. And you're having a thing with him now. And you two have a lot more in common than any of us thought."

"Don't make light of this," Alex scolded. "The whole situation is breaking my heart. I never meant to lie to Daniel, and keeping this secret so long has been the hardest thing I've ever done."

Jude leaned over the bed and spoke to Maggie. "Evening, Mom. If you can hear, you must be lapping up my sister's confession. Imagine." She turned her attention back to Alex. "So why *did* you keep it a secret? Daniel is a stand-up guy. He would have married you. Unless you never loved him… Unless you really loved Teddy…"

"Of course I loved Daniel, or at least I believed I did. I never would have had sex with him that night if I weren't in love."

"So it only happened one time?"

"Yes!"

Jude smiled. "Oh, that must have been a shock for Miss Pure-of-Heart, the one who never screwed up."

"Until I screwed up royally."

"So who knew the truth about you being pregnant? Mom and Dad? Teddy?"

"Yes. They knew that I was pregnant, but

I never told anyone who the father was. Dad pressured me to give the father the chance to do the right thing."

"Can't argue with Dad's reasoning. So… why didn't you?"

Alex sighed and began recounting the list of reasons that had made so much sense to her at the time. Daniel's future was dependent upon his scholarships to Ohio State. His parents couldn't afford to support him and a family. Daniel would have forfeited his dreams. She didn't know if he truly loved her. Jude nodded as she told the whole story.

"And the last reason? I didn't tell Daniel because I lied to him that night. I told him I was on the pill."

Jude's jaw dropped. "You lied?" Something awfully like a chuckle burst from her lips. "My Allie-belle lied about being on the pill?"

Alex shrugged. She knew she'd earned her squeaky-clean reputation honestly. When she'd finally told a lie, at age seventeen, it was a big one. "I guess I was caught up in the moment," she said.

"So, my devious sister, you are human after all."

"Don't kid about this, Jude. You're not so pure yourself."

"Never said I was. But I never had the sterling reputation to keep up."

"I'm devastated. This is the worst mess I've ever been in my whole life."

"Come on, we have to kid a little. If we didn't, I think we'd both sit here and cry our eyes out. Although now that I really think about this…"

Alex jumped at the sign of hope. "What? What are you thinking?"

"That our beautiful Lizzie was the result of your lie and your, ah, let's call it poor judgment, and she's about the coolest kid around. You and Teddy raised her well."

"And Lizzie will hate me if she learns what I did, what I've been doing her entire life. And all this is happening when we're already arguing over her college choice."

Apparently having nothing to say to refute that, Jude merely nodded. After a moment she said, "She can't hate you forever, Allie-belle. Over the years you've gotten an awful lot of points for being a good mother. All that doesn't just go away. You two are as close as any parent and child I've ever seen.

I hope Wesley and I have half the foundation you've built with your kid."

Alex sighed. "Thanks. So let's say eventually Lizzie would forgive me. She's only half the problem. What about Daniel? I really care about him, Jude. I never expected in my wildest dreams to come back to Ohio and fall in love, but I think I may have."

"That is a wrinkle," Jude agreed. "He's not likely to take this news well."

"And you don't know the full story." She told Jude about Daniel's opportunity to run for national office, pledging her sister to complete secrecy.

"No one will hear it from me," Jude promised. "And you're right. If this leaks, Daniel could be hit hard by the media. An illegitimate child in his background?"

"This is the twenty-first century, Jude," Alex said. "Surely once the circumstances are revealed, once I take the entire blame…"

"You haven't lived around here in a long time. I don't think you get how conservative this area is. I'm involved in politics to a degree with my charities," Jude added. "I know how spin doctors work. Daniel's opponent will probably use this story to his advantage.

And that's not even saying what the media might do to Lizzie."

Alex nodded, felt the first burn of tears. "I've thought of that." Her gaze latched on to Jude's brilliant blue eyes. "What should I do, Jude? What would you do?"

"Oh, sweetie, I'm a bad one to ask. I make more mistakes in one week than you've made your whole life, although this time your screwup is a chart topper."

"I know."

"And I don't have your knack for diplomacy. I say what I say and let the demons pick at my bones afterward."

"You would tell Daniel?"

"I would. But I'm not saying you should. If you don't, then the outcome is obvious, isn't it?"

Alex stared at her hands in her lap. "I give up Daniel and go on as I have, letting Lizzie believe that Teddy was her father."

"And if that hasn't been easy the last seventeen years, it probably won't get any easier for the next seventeen. And you'll have to give up a future with the man you've come to love—again."

"But if I tell him, I may lose him anyway."

"You might. Or he might offer compassion for what you've been through. He might have a solution. He's a smart guy. I don't think we can assume that Daniel will just walk away."

Alex considered what Jude said for a couple of minutes. During that time, Jude fussed over their mother, pulled her blanket up, smoothed the delicate ruffles on her nightgown. "This is just great, Mama," she said. "You have the rotten luck to raise three daughters who can't clean up their own messes, and now you're not even able to knock some sense into any of us."

"What's this?" Martin's voice came from the doorway. "I won't allow anyone to say my daughters aren't perfect, not even one of them." He chuckled. "Besides, I had something to do with raising you girls, too, and I think I did a darned good job."

Alex stood. "Movie over, Dad?"

"Yes, and I'm going to bed." He lifted Maggie's hand and checked her pulse. "How's our girl?"

"She gets a gold star for being a good listener," Jude said.

"Thanks for sitting with her, girls."

Alex and Jude kissed their father good-night and went into the hall. "Have you made up your mind?" Jude asked quietly.

"I'm going to tell him," Alex said. "I don't see any other way. I can't go on living like this. It was different when Teddy was alive. The lie was easier to believe, even for me."

Jude gave her a hug. "I've got your back, Allie-belle. Always will." She went downstairs and soon Alex heard the low rumble of her Jeep as she headed back to her rooms above the barn.

Alex knew she wouldn't sleep. Her thoughts would be focused on tomorrow. She would tell Daniel the truth before he returned to Columbus.

CHAPTER SIXTEEN

"How are you feeling, Pop?" Bleary-eyed from going over last night's conversation with Alex, Daniel headed straight for the coffeemaker, thankful that his dad was an early riser and had brewed a pot.

"I'm okay, son," Gus said. "I thought you'd sleep in this morning."

"Guess the sun had another idea. Anyway, I want to spend more time with Alex today."

"I like her, Danny. She's a good woman. Reminds me of your mother in a lot of ways. She has that same quiet composure about her, as if the world could go off its rails and she'd still maintain a steady course."

Stirring sugar into his coffee, Daniel thought about what his father had just said. Alex wasn't completely unflappable. She was having a tough time with Lizzie's change of plans. And he wasn't all that sure she supported his decision to run for higher office. She'd said she was, but Daniel had sensed a reluctance last night. That was why he couldn't wait to get to Dancing Falls this morning. It would mean everything if the woman he loved wanted the same future he did.

The woman he loved. A smile spread across Daniel's face. Where had that come from? Did he love Alex? He must because the past week without her had been long and empty. Last night he'd told her he was crazy about her. What he meant was crazy in love. Otherwise, why was he still smiling this morning after a restless night?

"What are you grinning about?" Gus asked him.

"Nothing, Pop. Just in a good mood, I guess."

"That's another way Alex is like your mother. Helen could make me grin like that for no reason, too." Gus shifted in his chair, obviously trying to find a more comfortable position. "If you ask me, Danny, you're a goner already."

Trying to keep the mood light, Daniel said, "You could be right, Pop. But what a way to go."

Both men sat at the table enjoying their coffee. Gus read the newspaper while Daniel stared out the kitchen window at the trees he and his dad had planted many years ago. Full and green and offering cool shade in the summers, those trees had grown up with him. Funny how they felt almost like family.

Just like the teenager who passed by the window on her way to the back door. "What's Lizzie doing here?" he said.

She knocked on the door and Daniel opened it. "Good morning," he said. "What brings you out this way? Thought you'd be sleeping late since it's the weekend."

"Can't," she said. "I may never sleep again."

He smiled. "I like drama as much as the next guy, Lizzie, but I kind of doubt that statement. Anyway, what's going on?"

She looked at Gus. "Hi, Mr. Chandler. I don't think I've ever met you."

Gus stood, slowly. "Hello, young lady."

Turning her attention back to Daniel, she said, "Can I talk to you? I don't know where to turn." She looked at Gus again.

He ambled away from the table. "I've got some annuals to trim in the backyard. If you two don't mind, I think I'll get to work before the sun gets too hot."

Daniel opened the door for him. "Call if you need anything, Pop." Once Gus had walked into the yard, Daniel pulled out a chair for Lizzie. He realized he could be crossing sacred ground here, but the kid looked as if she really needed a sympathetic ear. Her eyes were red, her hair pulled into a messy bun. "Sit," he said. "Talk to me."

"Can I have coffee?"

"You drink coffee?"

She nodded. "Sometimes."

He got her a cup and fixed it according to her instructions, lots of sugar and cream. "Does your mother know you're here?" he asked.

"No."

"Then am I going to get in trouble?"

She shrugged. "I'm probably going to get in trouble, not you. But something has got to make Mom open her eyes and see that I am serious about acting school."

"You don't think she knows that now?"

"She's so hung up on one stupid reason why I can't do it. She's sure that I'm going to end up busing tables, or homeless on the streets of LA."

"She's worried for you, Lizzie. All your life your mom had this image of you as a university professor living a sane, comfortable life. She always pictured you as a scholar, and you seemed to go along with that idea. Even you have to admit that acting is a big change, not to mention an even bigger risk."

"No, I don't agree. Look at the successful actors who are also supersmart. They graduated from top universities and still pursued their love of acting. I could study the arts, literature. Just because I want to enroll in the Department of Theater, doesn't mean I'll close my mind to everything else."

She had obviously done some research, and he couldn't refute her findings. She could take electives to broaden her scope, all the while concentrating on drama. But he absolutely, positively couldn't tell her this made perfect sense. It wasn't his place. He was in love with her mother. He'd already crossed the line as far as Alex was concerned.

Hoping a brilliant, heartfelt response would come to him, he cradled his coffee mug in two hands and waited. No luck, so he fell back on the one piece of advice he knew was irrefutable. "I see where you're coming from, Lizzie," he said. "But this is a discussion you should be having with your mother, not me."

She clasped her hands tightly together. "And just how am I supposed to do that? She won't discuss! She dictates…"

"I don't suppose there is a teenager anywhere who hasn't said that same thing about her parents."

Lizzie's eyes filled with tears. "Don't you understand, Daniel? Somebody has to be on my side. My grandfather won't go against Mom. Neither will Auntie Jude. It's like everyone is afraid of hurting her." A few tears fell onto her cheeks. "Well, let me tell you, my mother is not perfect. She makes mistakes. Not often but it has happened. And she's making one now by trying to live my life!"

Lizzie sank her forehead into her hands. "Please help me, Daniel. You understand better than anyone."

She raised her face and stared at him, and that was when he saw it. The glisten in her indescribable hazel eyes, a phenomenon he'd seen in only one other person. The tight lines around her stubborn lips, the deep furrow in her brow, the small widow's peak that gave her face character. Her face. Her beautiful face was exactly like another beautiful face he would always remember, the one in the frame that his father spoke to whenever he was lonely or uncertain.

The knowledge hit him hard enough to make him stumble if he'd been standing. His heart clenched. He couldn't breathe. This sad young girl looked enough like his mother to be… Yes, to be her granddaughter.

The realization sliced into him like a knife. Alex had lied to him for eighteen years. She'd become pregnant that night and taken an easy way out. She'd married a man who was already successful in life, one who didn't have to struggle to make his way. One who could give her everything she wanted, who would worship her. She hadn't chosen the man who simply loved her. Not the one who was the father of her child.

"You'll talk to her, won't you, Daniel?" Lizzie said. "You'll make her understand what this means to me."

It took every ounce of self-control he could muster not to stand up, walk around the table and enfold this girl in his arms. But he remained seated, the hurt shooting through his veins like white lightning. Slowly, deliberately, he nodded his head. "Yes, Lizzie, I'll talk to her."

CHAPTER SEVENTEEN

ALEX CAME INTO the kitchen around nine o'clock Sunday morning. She had stopped in Lizzie's room, as she often did, just to assure herself that her daughter was sleeping peacefully. This morning Lizzie had not been in her bed.

Not yet alarmed, Alex spoke to her father, who was reading the Sunday paper. "Have you seen Lizzie?"

"No. She's not in her room?"

Alex shook her head. "And I know she was up late last night. She went out with some kids from the show. I heard her TV going for a couple of hours after that. I figured she'd sleep until noon today."

Jude entered the house through the back door. "Hello, family. Can I interest anyone in scrambled eggs and bacon, as long as Dad has eggs and bacon in the fridge?"

"Sounds good to me," Martin said. "Where's Wesley?"

"He's on the front porch waiting for his ride to the water park. Aside from having to care for a few dozen animals, I am blessedly free from responsibility until the park closes this afternoon."

Jude was taking supplies from the refrigerator when Alex asked, "Have you seen Lizzie this morning?"

Her sister looked over her shoulder. "Nope. She's probably still sleeping, don't you think?"

"I checked. I don't believe she's in the house." Just then a car pulled around to the back of the house. "That's my car," Alex said. "And Lizzie is driving it. I wonder where she's been."

"One way to find out," Martin said.

Alex met her daughter at the door. "Where were you off to so early on a Sunday?"

Lizzie glanced around the kitchen as if she couldn't believe she had such a welcoming committee. She didn't immediately answer her mother, but when she saw Jude, she said, "I went over to the barn. Couldn't sleep, so I thought I'd help Auntie Jude feed."

"Funny, I didn't pass you on the road," Jude said.

"I took the long way. I was hoping to pick some wildflowers, but I didn't see any pretty ones."

"Too bad," Jude said. "But you're in time for bacon and eggs."

"I'm not hungry." Lizzie stifled a yawn. "I might try to catch a few more z's now, if that's okay."

Alex smiled. "We'll catch up later."

Lizzie left the kitchen, and Alex went to the sink to help Jude with breakfast. Jude nudged her. "So what are you going to do?" she whispered.

"This is officially clean-slate day," Alex said. "I'm going to do the right thing…finally. And hope I don't destroy the lives of everyone I love."

"When will you see him?"

"If he doesn't call by ten, I'll call him and arrange a meeting place, somewhere neutral where there will be other people around." She grimaced. "I really have no idea how he'll react."

"That's smart."

"What are you two whispering about?" Martin said, rustling his newspaper into submission.

"Girl stuff, Dad," Alex said. "Nothing important."

He put down his paper and cupped a hand around his ear. "Is that another car I hear? This place is like Grand Central Station this morning."

Alex looked out the kitchen window. Her heart seemed to slam into her chest wall. She gripped Jude's arm. "Oh, no, it's him. It's Daniel."

Jude patted her hand. "It's going to be okay. You know what they say. There's no time like the present. You might as well get it over with. Trust me, you're going to feel so much better when this weight is off your shoulders."

Alex smoothed her T-shirt over her jeans and then shoved her hands in her pockets to keep them from shaking. She wasn't ready. She'd had no warning. But Jude was right. Her mind was made up, so she would just get it over with. Her brain struggled to come up with an opening line. How did one tell someone his entire life was about to change?

Daniel parked and got out of his car. He strode purposefully to the door. Alex opened it. "Good morning." She sounded ridiculously chipper. "I didn't expect you yet."

"No? Well, I'm here."

He didn't look anything like a man who wanted to impress a woman. In fact, he looked as if he'd thrown himself together in a rush. His cargo shorts were wrinkled. He had on worn sandals. Even his shirt was only partially buttoned, the ends untucked.

"We were just about to have some breakfast," Alex said. "You're welcome to join us."

"I need to talk to you, Alex. It can't wait until after breakfast."

"All right." She glanced at her sister, hoping for a look of support. Jude seemed as puzzled as Alex was. "Shall we go into the backyard?" Alex suggested.

Daniel stood aside as she went out the door, and without speaking, he followed her.

"What's so urgent?" she asked when they'd walked some distance from the house.

His jaw muscles worked. "In the interest of fair play, I'll ask this one question to give you a heads-up. Where is Lizzie? Can she hear us?"

"She went up to her room. No, I don't think she can hear anything." A terrible premonition, like hundreds of prickling needles, worked its way down Alex's spine. She resisted the urge to squirm. Whatever Daniel had to say involved Lizzie, and the need to protect her daughter was like a fire burning in her stomach.

"What's the matter, Daniel? Why did you ask about Lizzie?"

He looked down at the ground, took a deep breath and then pierced Alex with an intense glare. She felt its impact down to her toes.

His voice was coarse when he said, "A man shouldn't have to explain why he's asking about his own flesh and blood, should he, Alex?"

She opened her mouth but no words came out. He knew! She didn't mean for him to find out from anyone but her. Yet how could he have? Her hands started shaking and she clasped them to ground herself. "What…what are you talking about?"

"Lizzie is my daughter, isn't she?"

When she didn't answer he said, "Never mind. Nothing you could say would change how I feel right now."

"But why do you think…?"

"I just know, and when I figured it out, it

suddenly all made sense. The connection I feel toward her, the similarities in our personalities, our looks, like-minded goals. And that's not even taking into consideration the calendar. But most of all, Alex, it explains why you've always been so protective of her around me, as if you would have been happiest keeping us apart. And now I know why."

Alex bit her lip to trap a sob that seemed about to tear her throat apart. When she'd managed to gain some control over her panic, she said, "Daniel, I was going to tell you today. You may not believe that, but it's true. I couldn't go on living with the lie."

"So eighteen years is your limit? You can only live with a lie that long?"

She could hardly bear to look at him. His features were so unlike Daniel's. His stare was cold, brittle. His stance was stiff, his back rigid.

"I'm sorry," she said. "You can't know how hard this has been. When I didn't see you for all those years, the lie wasn't so difficult to maintain. I could almost believe it myself. But then there you were, in the theater that day, and it all came crashing down around me. My perfect life, the beautiful family I'd built on a lie."

"If you're expecting sympathy, Alex, you can forget it. I don't care how hard this has been for you." He exhaled a shaky breath. "I don't know what's worse. The fact that you didn't tell me, or that you didn't tell Lizzie. She believes that Teddy was her father. For seventeen years she bought into your story, your lie."

Alex reached out her hand and let it fall to her side. "Don't tell her, Daniel, please. I have to think about the words, how to explain what I've done. I wanted to tell you before I faced her. Promise me you won't take your anger at me out on Lizzie."

"Oh, I won't," he said. "Unlike you, I'll make Lizzie's feelings, her needs, my top priority."

"That's cruel, Daniel. I know you're angry, but you have to know that Lizzie has always been my biggest concern. Her needs are all I think about."

"Really? What about her desire to go to Ohio State and study drama? By shutting her out on this issue, are you more concerned with Lizzie's needs or your own?"

"I'm always thinking about what's best for her."

"And I suppose a wealthy, successful doctor was better for her than a struggling college student with no prospects."

"That's not the way it was. I never compared you to Teddy. You make it sound like I was some gold-digging opportunist who grabbed on to the first wealthy man who came around."

"Sometimes the truth hurts."

"Daniel, you can't believe this. I had known Teddy practically my whole life. I respected and admired him."

"And how did you feel about me?" he asked. "What must you have thought about me not to even tell me that you were pregnant?"

A sob tore from her throat. "I loved you, Daniel! From the moment I saw you at Birch Shore, I couldn't get you out of my mind. When you paid attention to me I couldn't believe how lucky I was. You picked me! You can't know what that meant to a quiet, studious girl to have someone so charming…so talented…so full of life, want to be with *me*!"

"You loved me?" His voice was flat, almost as if he was repeating a food order to a waiter. "So let me understand. Did you lie to the man you supposedly loved about being on the pill?"

She bit her lip, tasted blood. "I did. It was wrong, but that night I wanted you in every way. I shouldn't have lied."

"I'm not through. You lied about being on the pill, and then you lied each time I called you after we left Birch Shore. You lied when you said you were in love and going to get married?" He scoffed. "I assume that was a lie unless you truly loved both Teddy and me at the same time."

She could barely get enough air from her lungs to answer. "I never loved Teddy like I loved you."

She didn't know if he even heard her. He was so quiet, his eyes cast down. After a long, torturous minute, he said, "That's good to know, I guess. But Alex?"

She swallowed, waited.

"Why didn't you tell me? I would have stood by you. I would have helped you."

"Yes, Daniel, I believe you would have tried, for a time at least."

"What does that mean?"

"Daniel, if you had become a father at that time in your life, your future would have been much different from the way it's turned out. Because I loved you, I considered what was best for you."

"*You* decided what was best?"

"Listen! I deceived you into thinking I couldn't get pregnant. That alone was enough for you to hate me. You would probably have lost your scholarship if you'd had to find a job to support the baby. I didn't have those concerns. My family was willing to do what was necessary. And Teddy was willing to marry me knowing I was carrying someone else's child."

He shook his head slowly. "Oh, no, Alex, you're not going to get away with trying to show how sympathetic you were to my situation. You're not going to come out looking like the compassionate one, the one who saved the poor lad's life and set him on the path to fame. Because…" He drew in a long breath. "Because it wasn't just your call! It was mine, too." His index finger jabbed at his chest. "Mine! My baby, too. And you chose to leave me out."

His voice shook. "When I think about the

years ahead if you hadn't come back to Dancing Falls. When I realize you never would have told me…" He stopped, breathed heavily.

"But I did come back. And now you know. We have to start from this day and go forward." She was openly crying now. "We have to do what's right for Lizzie. We have to protect her. Yes, I made a mistake, several mistakes, but Lizzie shouldn't have to suffer for them."

"Nor should you, right, Alex?"

"You can't believe I'm not suffering."

"I honestly don't know. What I do know is that you're suggesting we don't tell her." His voice rose in disbelief.

"Not immediately. I thought that maybe you would agree…"

"No, Alex. I don't agree. I've missed out on too much. I won't miss out on one minute of the rest of her life!"

She used the one argument she knew might reach him. "But Daniel, think about your future. What if your political opponents get wind of this story? The bright young senator running for national office has a child he never knew about, a child out of wedlock.

You don't know how the media could twist those facts."

"I don't care. Do you think I'm worried about a political office over having a relationship, an *honest* relationship, with my daughter?"

She took a deep breath, giving herself time to think. "This is so new, and I know the pain you're feeling is real. But we have to be logical. We have to examine all sides of this issue." She choked on her next words. "We can't destroy Lizzie's life to satisfy our own."

"That's what you think I'm doing? You think I'm only concerned with my feelings, what I want? This girl, our *daughter*, has been grieving over the loss of the man she believed was her father. Don't you think she deserves to know that she has a real father, one who only wants to love her?"

She knew he believed what he was saying, but he had to be realistic. "Daniel," she said softly. "You can't be a stand-in for Teddy. You can't substitute one father for another. It's not like Teddy just took a sick day. He was her father for her entire life!"

Daniel stared at something unseen over Alex's shoulder. If possible, his body seemed to stiffen even more. "Did Teddy adopt Lizzie officially?"

"No. He didn't have to. I listed him as her father on the birth certificate."

A sound much like laughter came from his throat, but it was bitter and cold. "This just gets even better."

"It made sense. Teddy was willing to raise her as his own. We'd gotten married. The names were the same…"

"Only *Pope* wasn't supposed to be Lizzie's last name."

She threaded her fingers and held her clenched hands over her mouth, speaking through them. "So what are you going to do? You really hold all the cards, Daniel."

He looked up at the sky as if seeking some divine guidance and then stared directly into her eyes. "The last thing I want to do is hurt Lizzie," he said. "But I'm not going to let you continue to live your lie under the pretense that this news will shatter her. I think Lizzie is stronger than you give her credit for. She has her own mind. She knows what she wants out of life and how to get it. She'll be wounded, but she'll be okay after a while."

Alex couldn't argue anymore. She wanted

to keep Lizzie from knowing the truth, for some time at least, but the resolute look on Daniel's face told her that her wish was not to be granted. Her throat hurt from holding back tears. Her eyes felt scratchy from a lack of sleep. Her shoulders fell; her spine seemed to soften. She was done. The sin was hers. Now the decision was Daniel's, as perhaps it should be.

"What's going on out here?"

They both looked at the house as Lizzie stepped outside. The girl stared at her mother's face. "Mom, what's wrong? Are you crying?"

She started toward them, but Jude flew out the back door to stop her. "Lizzie, honey, come back inside. Leave your mom and Daniel alone for a few minutes. I'll fix you breakfast."

Lizzie didn't seem to know which way to turn, as if she was aware that what was happening in the yard was huge, life-altering. "Do you want me to go back inside, Mom?" she asked.

Alex looked at Daniel.

"You should stay, Lizzie," he said. "Your mother and I need to talk to you."

CHAPTER EIGHTEEN

DANIEL HAD NO idea how he was going to start this conversation. He just knew in his heart that the truth had to come out. For Alex, who said she had suffered for years hiding such a monumental secret, for Lizzie, who had a right to know her father. And for him, the person who might benefit the most from Lizzie knowing the truth. He had a daughter, and she was charming and witty and independent. He was just getting to know her and already he was proud.

"Why don't we all sit down?" he suggested, pointing to a conversation area on the lower deck. The setting afforded privacy, and yet the women would still feel the security of being near their house.

"What the heck is going on?" Lizzie asked as she led the way. "Mom, why are you crying?"

"I'm okay, honey," Alex said. "It's just an emotional moment for me."

The wariness vanished from Lizzie's eyes, replaced with something almost like jubilation. "Oh! I think I know what's happened. And I couldn't be happier."

Daniel swallowed. Oh, no. Lizzie thought he'd talked Alex into letting her go to Ohio State. Or worse, she assumed he'd proposed to her mother. She thought they were going to be a family.

Daniel waited until the women had taken seats next to each other on the floral love seat. He took a chair on the other side of a serving table. Lizzie folded her hands in her lap. She smiled, looking from one to the other. Alex looked as if it was the first day of hunting season, and she was the only deer in the forest. Yes, he was angry at her, but until this morning, he'd thought he loved her. It hurt him to have to hurt her.

"Do you want to start, Alex?" he asked. It was only fair to give her the first chance to make this right. Truthfully, he believed she was too upset to begin the conversation.

She straightened her spine, took in a long breath and said, "Thank you. I would."

Surprised, he sat quietly, waiting. He half expected that she would dissolve into tears before getting the first words out, but her strength and will impressed him. She was going to be able to do this.

She took Lizzie's hand. "Honey, you remember that Daniel and I knew each other many years ago, the summer I graduated high school, to be exact."

"Yeah, I know. Grandpa told me all about this guy you had such a crush on at Birch Shore." She grinned at Daniel. "Did you know she had a thing for you, Daniel?"

"I remember wishing with all my heart that she did. But yes, I believed that we made a connection that summer."

Alex smiled. "It was more than a crush for me," she said to Lizzie. "I thought about Daniel all the time. I made up dreams of our future, how we would always be together."

"And here you are, close to living out those dreams," Lizzie said.

"Not exactly, sweetheart. I don't want you to think that Daniel and I have made a decision to go forward with the relationship we've shared this summer."

"Well, why not? You two get along so well. You've had lots of dates. Mom, I haven't seen you so happy in a long time."

Alex squeezed her eyes shut, took a moment to recoup. Daniel felt a sharp pain in his chest. His anger was fading fast in light of her suffering. He wished he knew a way to make this right for everyone without breaking anyone's heart. But the only path to reconciliation, if there was ever to be one, was through the truth.

"Yes, I've been happy," Alex said. "So much about this summer has made me grateful. Your enthusiasm for the play, your grandfather's joy in having you in his home again and seeing Daniel—all this has made me happy. But it also brought up memories that I've tried to bury for a long time."

Her voice hitched and Daniel's heart thumped against his chest. "Do you want me to take over?" he asked.

She shook her head and continued. "The summer I spent at Birch Shore was a turning point in my life. I was always the quiet, industrious one in our family. I wanted to achieve good grades, great things. I did whatever I could to keep from disappointing anyone. And then I went away to work for the summer and experienced a freedom I'd never known before. I was on my own, meeting new people, living in a dorm. I was exhilarated, excited, adventurous in ways I'd never been."

"And you met Daniel," Lizzie filled in for her. "And he must have helped you realize there was another side to Alexis Foster."

"He did. He was funny and talented. He helped me adjust to being away from home. He showed me a different kind of life, one with sparkle and fun and opportunities." She pressed on Lizzie's hand with her thumb. "I fell so hard for him, honey. I'd never met anyone like him. The truth is, I loved him. I really did."

"Then what happened?" Lizzie asked. "Why did you marry Daddy? And what did you mean before when you said you might not have a relationship with Daniel after we leave here?" She looked at Daniel and back at her mother. "This is so confusing, Mom. You loved Daniel, but you married Daddy. Now you can't have a relationship with Daniel."

Lizzie paused, thought a moment and then gave Daniel a piercing glare. "You didn't feel the same about her, did you? You didn't love Mom."

"That's not the issue, honey," Alex quickly

broke in. "I did a terrible thing. I had a se-cret, and I kept it from Daniel. I kept it from everyone except Grandma and Grandpa and your fa… Teddy."

"What secret?"

She looked at Daniel. He nodded once, en-couraging her.

"Daniel and I… We…" She rubbed her hand over her mouth. "Our last night at Birch Shore, we…"

"What?" Lizzie stared openmouthed at Daniel. Her eyes widened. "You two did it! You made love?"

Daniel had answered difficult policy ques-tions. He'd faced media scrutiny without bat-ting an eye. And yet this question from his daughter nearly toppled him. He nodded. "I loved your mom as much as she loved me, Lizzie. You have to believe that."

Lizzie focused on Alex again. "So you made love with Daniel and a few weeks later you married Daddy?"

Alex didn't speak. She just leveled an hon-est stare at her daughter.

"So what was the big secret?"

Daniel held his breath.

"I was already pregnant when I married Teddy," Alex said.

Lizzie's voice rose with shock. "You didn't use protection?"

"I was wrong not to plan carefully. But I wasn't wrong about Teddy. He knew I was pregnant, and he married me anyway. He gave us a good life. He loved us. He cherished you, sweetheart."

"Daddy's not my real father!" As if she couldn't find a target for her anger, she glared at Daniel as though snakes had suddenly sprung from his head. "You got her pregnant and didn't marry her?"

Daniel started to speak, but Alex held up her hand. "I never told Daniel," she said. "Remember, I kept the secret from him. I've always kept it a secret until we came back here." She looked down, sat straighter. "I would still probably be keeping it a secret, except Daniel figured out the truth."

"How? How did he know and not me?"

"There were clues," Daniel said.

"And Grandma and Grandpa?"

"They knew I was pregnant," Alex said. "They were very fond of Teddy and knew he would take care of both of us. They supported my decision."

"Didn't they ask who the father was?"

"Yes, and I think Grandpa strongly suspects. But I never revealed Daniel's name."

Lizzie stared down at the ground. Moments before she'd pulled her hand from her mother's grasp, and now she twisted her fingers in a frenzy of confusion and shock. "I don't believe this," she said. "All this time I've loved Daddy."

"And he loved you, with all his heart," Alex said.

"But it was all false! Poor Daddy. You used him, Mom. He would have done anything for you. He did! And all that time he could have married someone who hadn't tricked him. He could have had his own children. He could have been a real father!"

The disgust in her eyes was nearly Daniel's undoing. Then she said, "But instead, he got stuck with you, and with me!"

Daniel rose. "Lizzie, don't do this. Teddy was an honorable man. No one is denying that. And he cared for you as if he were your real father. I'm sure he never thought of you as a substitute for the real thing. And I'm sure he loved your mother. She was up-front with him. He never thought she tricked him in any way."

Lizzie stood, as well. She only came up to Daniel's shoulders, but she pierced him with a hurt-filled gaze. "You never even knew him!" Then she turned on her mother. "And how could you keep this from me?"

"I wasn't proud of what I had done," Alex said. "And I was protecting you."

"You were protecting yourself!" Lizzie said. "Your Little-Miss-Perfect self!" She whirled around and started toward the house.

"Where are you going?" Alex asked.

"Mother…" The word seemed to drip with venom. "At this moment do you really think you have the right to know?"

Alex started after her, but Daniel wrapped his hand around her arm and stopped her. "Let her go," he said. "She's angry and hurt. My guess is, she's going to her room. We'll probably hear a door slam in a minute, or maybe hear a lamp being thrown against a wall."

Alex dissolved into tears. She crumpled into the nearest chair. "Oh, Daniel, how will we ever get through this?"

He sat beside her. "Time, Alex. It will take time, but everything will be all right."

ALEX HAD NEVER thought her life was perfect, even though the outward trappings made it seem so to everyone around her. To their friends in Chicago, to Teddy's colleagues at the hospital, the Popes were an ideal family. Loving and supporting of each other. Alex believed that Teddy was proud to have her by his side, and he was proud of the accomplished child they raised together.

But always, Alex felt the pall of deceit over everything. She would find herself staring at Lizzie, trying to pick out similarities between her and Daniel. She would see him in Lizzie's eyes. She would remember Daniel's easygoing charm when she watched her daughter interact with others. Teachers, students, everyone liked Lizzie, just like everyone seemed to like her father.

And so, for eighteen long years, Alex suffered because of what she knew to be true while living a life built on a lie. Logically, she knew Lizzie had never been denied anything…except the identity of her real father. And she was never told that her mother, the woman many people admired and envied, the one who cautioned her own daughter about pregnancy and abstinence, had made a mistake when she'd been young. She had lied about it from the beginning and arranged all of their lives so no one would know.

And today, on this patio with the beauty of Dancing Falls surrounding her, Alex realized that the time of reckoning had come. When her tears dried, she simply sat and stared over the green expanse of manicured lawn. Daniel remained beside her, not speaking, not trying to console her. Just letting her deal with the aftermath on her own terms.

"I suppose you have to go," she said after more than a half hour had passed.

"Yes, I do. I'm sorry to leave you like this, Alex. We have so much left unsaid. And we should decide where we go from here." As if he thought she might misinterpret, he added, "With regard to Lizzie, I mean. I think she'll need both of us now. She'll have more questions."

The hurt inside Alex was so profound that she actually took Daniel's words as a sign of hope. Would Lizzie ask her questions? That would mean her daughter would at least keep the lines of communication open. But would they ever be as close as they were before coming to Dancing Falls? And what about Daniel? Would he become involved in their daughter's life, or would this be the last time she ever saw him? Would she go back to Chicago feeling even worse than she had all those years ago because she was forced to give up Daniel twice?

How could they stay together, build a future, when Alex had denied Daniel his daughter, the person who should have bound them for the past eighteen years? She needed to respond to him. "Lizzie has your phone number," she said, gathering the courage to look straight at him. "She'll call if she wants to talk to you. I would never try to prevent her from doing that."

"I never thought you would." He picked up his ball cap and settled it low on his head. "We…ah, you and I should talk soon. I'll want to know how Lizzie is."

He did not say he would want to know how she was doing, and she didn't blame him. The look on his face was resolute, but thank goodness she did not see hatred there. He would never forgive her just as she would never forgive herself. Some sins in life were simply unforgivable.

He walked around the table, paused a moment and lightly touched her shoulder. "Take care of yourself, Alex. We did the right thing today. Lizzie will realize that in time."

She didn't speak, just waited for him to round the corner of the house and get to his car. He'd just disappeared when the back door of the house opened. Jude came out with Martin. Each pulled a chair close to Alex.

"Jude told me," Martin said. "At first I wanted to throttle Daniel, but I guess I can't even do that."

"I'm sorry, Daddy. I wanted to tell you so many times."

"I wish you had. I could have done something…"

"No, Daddy, don't. You shouldn't have any regrets. This was my doing. If there are regrets—" she laughed bitterly "—and there are, they are all mine. Lizzie…where?" Her breath was coming in such short gasps, she couldn't even speak in sentences.

"She's in her room, Allie-belle," Jude said. "But don't forget. She's a Foster. We bend, but we don't break."

Four arms encircled her in love, and that was her undoing. She began sobbing and couldn't stop.

CHAPTER NINETEEN

AFTER ANOTHER NEARLY sleepless night, Alex awoke Monday morning with a sense of foreboding. She hadn't spoken to Lizzie since the previous day, not because she hadn't tried, but because Lizzie had remained in her room, disconnected from the family. Even Jude and Wesley, who'd taken trays of food up, hadn't been able to reach her. And Alex hadn't heard from Daniel, either. He must have made it back to Columbus, but he hadn't called her to check in.

Wearing only her pajamas, and not really inspired to get dressed, she went to Lizzie's room and knocked quietly on the door. "Are you up yet, honey?"

No answer.

"Lizzie, we have to talk eventually. There is so much we have to say to each other. The silent treatment is not good for either one of us."

No response.

Alex opened the door. The bed was rumpled, and Lizzie wasn't in it. Alex felt her heartbeat ratchet up. She went into the room and started searching. Lizzie's duffel bag was missing from the closet. Her cell phone was nowhere in sight. The top of the dresser had been cleared of her grooming products.

Alex pictured her daughter in several gruesome scenarios. In her delicate state of mind, anything could have happened. What if she'd taken the car and been in an accident? What if she'd taken off on foot and hitched a ride? What if she'd wandered off Dancing Falls property and gotten lost?

She left the room and darted for the stairs, taking them two at a time. She met her father in the downstairs foyer.

"Whoa, hold on, Alexis. What's the matter?" Martin asked.

"The cars," Alex said. "Are they all accounted for?"

"I assume so," Martin said. "I can check. I was just about to leave for the office. Why are you asking about the cars?"

Alex told him that Lizzie was missing. "You know how upset she was," Alex said.

"Who knows what she might do, where she might go. We've got to find her, Daddy."

Martin led his daughter to a bench by the front door. "Sit down, honey. We'll mobilize all efforts to find her. I'm sure she's all right. Just taking some time for herself. Upsetting us is probably the last thing on her mind."

He was trying to be positive, but Alex knew he was concerned. He took his cell phone from his pocket. "I remember Jude pulling the same stunts herself whenever she was angry with your mother and me."

He stared at his phone as if trying to decide a course of action. There was panic in his normally calm eyes.

"Should we call the police?" she asked.

"Let's check around here first. She could be at the barn with Jude. She could just be taking a walk. You head over to Jude's, and I'll get in my car and scour the property. Meet you back here in a half hour. If we haven't found her, I'll call the authorities."

A half hour later Alex returned to the house with Jude and Wesley. Martin pulled around to the back of the house. The passenger seat in his SUV was empty.

When Wesley saw Alex, he tugged on her T-shirt. "Did Lizzie run away?" he asked.

"No. Of course not," Jude said. "She's much too smart to run away."

"No luck," Martin said. "Let's look around for a note. If we don't find one, then I guess we'll get the police involved." He viewed his cell phone, which apparently hadn't left his hand. "I'll call Jeannie in the office and have her cancel my morning patients."

Before he'd dialed, his phone buzzed. He looked at the number and connected. "Aurora, good morning. Is anything wrong? We have sort of a situation over here this morning…"

"AND I CAN guess what it is," Aurora said. "Might you be looking for your granddaughter, Marty?"

"We are! Do you know where she is?"

"I do, indeed. She's here at my place, upstairs in a guest room. Poor thing was so tired, she had some eggs and toast and passed out a few minutes ago. She said she'd been outside in my yard since the middle of the night."

"The middle of the night? Why, in heaven's name…?"

"She said she didn't want to wake me. Such a sweet kid, but I wouldn't have cared." Aurora paused before saying, "What's going on over there, Marty?"

Martin gave a thumbs-up to Alex, and she collapsed on a chair. "It's a long story, one I don't have time to tell right now. Does Lizzie know you're calling us?"

"I didn't tell her I wouldn't, but she asked me not to. I figure she knows I'd call. She's awfully upset, Marty."

"You did the right thing, Aurora. I'll be over in a few minutes to get her. Just keep her there, okay?"

"That won't be a problem. But Marty…?"

"What?"

"I don't think you should come over here right now. Let her get some rest. She needs it. And, well… I don't know how to say this exactly, but she doesn't want to come home. She asked if she could stay here with me for a while."

"She has a home, Aurora, and we've all been worried sick since we discovered her missing this morning. I know Alexis wants her home."

"That's another thing… I don't like to interfere in family problems. Goodness knows I've had enough of my own, and I don't appreciate anyone butting in, but Alexis seems to be the problem. I questioned her a bit, and Lizzie says her mom doesn't understand her, won't let her make decisions on her own. Now, I know what kids can be like, and I figure this will blow over, but that child seems a long way from forgiveness at this point."

So Lizzie hadn't told Aurora the crux of the problem. She wasn't ready to reveal that part. "But Aurora, we can't expect you to do the job of a parent."

"You're not expecting anything. I'm offering, and I owe you, Marty. Let the girl stay with me for a few days. Let's see how this washes out. I'll take care of her…"

"I know you will. It's not that. Alexis is heartbroken over their argument."

"And to my way of thinking, so is this girl. I don't know what happened to get Lizzie so upset. I suspect she didn't tell me the whole story, and maybe she never will. But if she wants to, I'll listen. Sometimes it just takes another sympathetic ear for problems to work themselves out."

Martin looked at his daughter. Alex gave

him an expectant look that made him wish he could give her better news. Instead, he asked Aurora to hold on a minute. "Lizzie is at Aurora's," he said. "Aurora has offered to let her stay there a day or two, let her calm down, rethink the situation."

"She should be home. Here. With us."

"I know, sweetheart, but I think this might be a good idea." He didn't want to go so far as to admit that Lizzie didn't want to come home, didn't want to face her mother. "Some distance might be just what we all need right now. Aurora will take good care of her."

Alex let out a long breath. "Okay, then, if you think it's the right thing to do. But Daddy, tell Aurora to call us. I need to know how Lizzie is."

"I will." He returned to the phone and gave his instructions. Aurora promised to comply. When he disconnected, he went over to Alex and put his arm around her. "She's safe, Alexis. That's the best news for now."

ALEX ALMOST COULDN'T get her fingers to cooperate. She held her cell phone in a shaky hand, took a long, deep breath and punched in Daniel's number. Through the two short rings, she went over what she would say. But she never got the chance.

"Hello. This is Daniel Chandler, Ohio State representative, 6th district. Your call is very important to me. Please..."

Alex tuned out at this point and waited for the message to end. At the beep, she said, "Daniel, this is Alex. I need to speak to you. It's about Lizzie. Not really an emergency, I guess, not at this point, but..."

Alexis, quit babbling! "Please call me when you can. Thanks."

Less than five minutes later, her phone rang.

"Thank you for calling back so quickly, Daniel."

"You said this concerns Lizzie. What's wrong? Is she all right?"

He sounded winded, his words clipped and short.

"Yes, she's fine, but she's not here at Dancing Falls. She's at our neighbor's house, you know, the place where the owner is setting up a bed-and-breakfast?"

"Ms. Spindell's house?"

"That's right."

"What's she doing there?"

Alex tried to keep her tone light, to mask the panic clawing inside her. Remembering Wesley's words, she said, "I suppose you could say she ran away from home…"

"What?"

"It's all right. Like everything else Lizzie does, she did this responsibly. Only put a half mile or so between us. Aurora's a nice lady. She's offered to keep Lizzie for a couple of days until she calms down."

Daniel didn't speak, but Alex heard papers being shuffled.

"I should come home," he said eventually. "I can rearrange some things."

"That's up to you, of course," Alex said. "But I don't know if Lizzie would see you. She certainly doesn't want to see me, not yet, anyway. But I wanted you to know this latest development in case she contacts you. If she does, and if she tells you anything I should know that wouldn't violate her privacy, I'd appreciate a call from you."

She heard a light tapping, like a pencil eraser on a desktop. "Okay, I'll wait here and see if she calls. I suppose giving her time to adjust is important as long as you think this arrangement at Ms. Spindell's is best. And Alex…"

"Yes?" Just hearing him say her name gave her hope. Even false hope was better than none.

"I expect the same consideration from you," he said. "Call me if there's anything I can do or anything I should know."

"I will. Thank you, Daniel." She waited a moment and then, there being nothing left to say, she ended with, "Goodbye."

"Just a minute," he said.

Her traitorous heart skipped a beat. "I'm still here."

"How are you?"

It was just three words, a simple question, and yet it was as if an emotional dam burst. She let out a sob and bit her lips together to keep them from quivering. "I'm so sorry," she said. "So sorry for everything."

"I know you are," he said.

"But Lizzie is what matters now, the only thing that matters."

"Alex…" His voice was soft, almost a caress. "I could tell you not to be so hard on yourself, but I know you will be anyway. Lizzie is not all that matters. You matter, too.

You matter to a lot of people, but especially to Lizzie. I'll be in touch, okay?"

"Yes."

He disconnected and she sank into the nearest chair. She'd crossed a hurdle with that call and survived. But her body felt drained. And she couldn't help noticing that he hadn't said she mattered to him.

CHAPTER TWENTY

MARTIN HAD ALWAYS been proud of his oldest daughter, but he was especially proud of the way she adjusted to Lizzie's absence. Despite her anxiety, Alex had given Lizzie her space. She'd satisfied her longing for her daughter with calls from Aurora and a report from Jude. None of this could have been easy.

Wesley and Jude had gone over to Aurora's on Wednesday. They'd seen Lizzie and talked to her. Jude reported that everything seemed okay; Lizzie was understandably hurt, but she looked healthy and busy. She'd treated them to cookies she'd made herself in Aurora's kitchen, and Aurora said she'd turned the kitchen into a bakery. "Frustration baking," Aurora had called it.

But now it was Friday and Martin wanted to see his granddaughter for himself. A visit from him would ease Alex's mind, and it was a father's place to do that. Alex had lost so much in the past few days, not the least of which was the man she'd reconnected with. When Alex had been with Teddy, she'd enjoyed a life of comfort and attention. Now she was alone and lonely, and Martin was worried about her.

He hadn't yet sorted out his feelings for Daniel Chandler. More than a few times in the past week Martin had muttered a smattering of choice words about Daniel Chandler under his breath. "I'd like to…" He'd let the threat die on his lips. He wasn't in the business of hurting people, and besides, Alex had told him the whole story about that night, and Martin wasn't so sure he wouldn't have acted the same way, at that age, anyway. But Daniel's behavior now, his avoidance of Alex, was difficult to rationalize.

"Sure he's angry," Martin said to the mirror while dressing for his visit to Aurora's place. "He's hurting, too. And Alex did deceive him. But she kept the secret so he could have a future. Doesn't that mean anything to the man?"

To Martin's way of thinking, Alex's sacrifice should be taken into account when it came to forgiveness. But so far Daniel's only kindness had been two phone calls to check on the situation here. Martin had timed both calls. The longest had lasted eighty-two seconds.

"Not good enough, Senator," he said, pulling his boat shoes over bare feet.

Alex met him at the front door. "How long will you be, Daddy?"

"I'll stay about an hour if the ladies will let me," he said. "Don't worry, sweetheart. I'm sure Lizzie is fine, or we would have heard, and we'll have a good talk."

"I'm wondering if you should tell her that I will be the next one to visit," Alex said.

He patted her shoulder. "Let's see how it goes, Alex."

Martin knew his talents did not include peacemaking, but he hoped he could help. As he drove to Aurora's, he thought about what he could say to Lizzie, mostly a rehash of what he'd thought about for days. He wanted to tell her that he understood her anger and confusion, and even disappointment in her mother, but he also needed her to come back home. Mostly, he would tell her he loved her.

When he got to the house, he drove around back and found both women turning dark earth with spades and shovels. Lizzie kept working, but Aurora stopped and went to his car. She had on cutoff shorts, a T-shirt and a large brimmed hat. She wiped sweat from her forehead. Maggie had been fond of planting flowers, but this scene was different. Aurora's hands seemed built for getting dirty.

"Hi, Marty. Nice to see you."

"You, too, Aurora." He turned his attention to Lizzie. She, too, had on cutoffs and what looked to be a baggy cast-off T-shirt and a visor. Her hair was gathered into some sort of bird's nest thing on top of her head. Amazing. His perfectly put-together grandchild was taking fashion advice from Aurora Spindell. The notion made him smile.

"How's she doing, Aurora?" he asked.

"She's a dynamo, Marty. I can't keep up with her. If she's not concocting some bit of baked heaven in the kitchen, she's papering the bathrooms or starting a garden."

Martin could only marvel at the thought. "Wow."

"Believe me, I'm not making her do any of this," Aurora said. "She wants to help me. I'd say she's getting some stuff out of her system, and it must be working. That first morning I found her sitting on my back step with her head on a backpack. I could barely get her to eat a bite of eggs. Now she's wolfing down pork chops and mashed potatoes like they're going out of style." Aurora chuckled. "And making cake for dessert."

Martin stepped out of his car. He and Aurora leaned against the hood. "Lizzie's problem is more than just an argument with her mother. Has she told you what's bothering her, what caused this separation from her family?"

"She finally did two nights ago. It's a sad thing what she's going through. For years she thought this Teddy fella was her daddy. Now she knows different. And it's tough for Daniel, too. He missed out on the most joyous years of childhood." She smiled. "But then, he missed most of the teen years, too, so that can be a blessing."

"You sound like you're speaking from experience," Martin said.

She merely shrugged. "All families have problems, Marty. One that doesn't must be like those plastic people who live in a dollhouse." She gave him a sympathetic smile. "Well, you know how it is. Your daughter must be suffering most of all since she's carrying the burden of guilt."

"I've never seen her like this," Martin admitted.

Aurora looked at Lizzie. "Go on, Marty. Get her to take a break and talk to you. It'll be okay."

LIZZIE POURED TWO glasses of lemonade and set them on a refurbished table in Aurora's backyard. She took one lawn chair, and Martin took the other. She'd given her grandfather a hug, but now she gave him an earnest stare.

"I'm not ready to forgive her yet, Grandpa."

"Okay, but the word *yet* indicates to me that you might soon be able to."

Lizzie rolled her lemonade glass between her hands. "She's my mom. I've always loved her, admired her." She looked down as if the liquid in her glass held all the answers. "We were a happy family. Turns out now we weren't a family at all."

"I don't agree, sweetheart. You and your mom and Teddy were about as close a family as I've ever seen."

"You know what I mean," she said softly.

"Yes, I do, but you don't know what I mean.

What is a family, anyway, Lizzie? People brought together and staying together because of a strong bond of love. You had that in spades with your mother and Teddy. The way that man bragged about your accomplishments, every one from your first step to your piano recitals. No daddy could have been more proud.

"And the way he fussed over you when you were a baby. You'd have thought he was handling fine china." Martin laughed. "'She won't break, Teddy,' I said to him. I've had three and they've all survived."

Lizzie scrubbed a dirt-smeared finger under her nose, but didn't speak.

"Let me ask you this, honey. If you had been adopted by both your mom and Teddy, do you think they would have loved you any less?"

"No, I guess not."

"That's because blood isn't any more important than love. In fact, it's much less important. I knew you weren't Teddy's daughter. Didn't tell you because your mother didn't want me to, and I abided by her wishes."

He smiled. "Let me tell you something, honey. If Teddy had ever hurt you, father or not, I'd have chased him from here to the state line, just like I would have done to any man who hurt any of my girls, but that was one worry I never had. As far as I was concerned, Teddy raised you, protected you and, most of all, cherished you." He sighed. "To me, that's a daddy."

Lizzie looked up at him. Her eyes glistened with tears. "But what do I do now, Grandpa? Daddy... I mean Teddy is gone. I can't talk to him. There's this new man I hardly know. What do I do about Daniel?"

"What do you want to do about him?" Martin asked.

"I don't know. I don't know how to behave around him. Before I knew this, we were friends. We shared so many interests. Should we go on as we have been? Should we be different somehow? What do I call him?"

"Honey, you know the old saying that a person should never bite off more than they can chew. It's good advice, and you should listen to it. You don't need to handle everything all at once. Give a relationship with Daniel time. Let it jell. See what path it takes. Decide for yourself how big a role you want him to play in your life. And if it makes you feel any better, I'll bet he's worried about the same things, just like you are."

"You think so?"

"I do. And you're practically a woman now. If you don't want anything to do with Daniel or any of us, you can decide that, too. But that decision wouldn't include me because I'm not ever going to let you go. And I don't think your mother will, either."

Lizzie almost smiled. "I wouldn't want you to, Grandpa."

He opened his arms and she cuddled into his embrace. With her head on his shoulder, he gently rocked her, rubbing his hand up and down her arm. "You'll do the right thing about all this, Lizzie Pope. You always have. And I think it would have made Teddy proud."

She sniffled. "What about Mom?" she asked. "We can't leave things like this. There's her relationship with Daniel and my college future, and going back to Chicago together..."

"That's all true, but this is between you and your mom. I can't work that out for you. But I do know this. Nothing will ever be worked out if you don't see her."

She nodded against his chest.

"So I'll tell her it's okay to come over here?"

"You can tell her, Grandpa."

"When I do, I expect she'll come barreling right over."

Lizzie chuckled.

He leaned back and looked into her eyes, clearer now, determined and perhaps a bit hopeful. From the distance he saw Aurora leaning on a rake, smiling. "How you getting on with Ms. Spindell?" he asked.

"Aurora? She's great, Grandpa."

As he waved at his neighbor, Martin kind of thought so, too.

LESS THAN TWO minutes after Martin arrived back at Dancing Falls, Alex had thanked him for opening communications between her and Lizzie, and gotten into her car. Driving to Aurora's, she decided she would set aside all the rehearsed words she'd planned and let Lizzie steer the conversation.

Her first reaction upon seeing Lizzie was relief and then admiration for Aurora's skills. Lizzie's face and arms were tanned. Her hair showed subtle highlights of sun-streaking. Lizzie had always been pretty, but after a few days under Aurora's care, she seemed robust and even earthy.

It was good to see her out of the theater and in the sun, Alex thought, getting out of her car.

Lizzie came up to her. They didn't hug, which was strange, but Alex didn't care. She was happy just being in her daughter's presence.

"How are you, honey?"

"I'm okay. And you, Mom?"

Alex shrugged. "To be honest, I feel like I've lost my other half." Alex had meant to convey how much she missed Lizzie, but when the realization hit her that she could be speaking of Daniel, as well, an all-too-familiar ache squeezed her chest.

"Let's sit over here in the shade," Lizzie suggested. "Aurora is in the house, so we'll be alone."

"Okay." They sat and remained silent for a few moments while each woman gathered her thoughts. "How would you like to proceed?" Alex asked. "I'll answer any questions. No topic is off-limits."

Lizzie gave her a straightforward stare. "Tell me about my father, about Daniel," she said. "Not the stuff I know already, but the stuff you know."

Alex's mind went back eighteen years to warm, moon-kissed evenings at Birch Shore, and she said the first thing that came to mind. "He was so easy to love, honey. I think you will learn that for yourself.

"Daniel is friendly, funny and…noble. He pleases people without working to be a people-pleaser. Kindness and fairness come naturally to him. When we were kids, he helped everyone with their parts in the revue we put on at Birch Shore. I think that's why he's a good politician now. He listens. He evaluates. He doesn't judge. And he tries to make the best decision."

"What decision would he have made about your pregnancy?"

This was an easy question. "He would have stood by me, because of the kind of man he was even then. He foolishly might even have suggested marrying me, but that would have been a mistake. We were so young. Neither one of us was ready for that kind of commitment."

"But you married Daddy… I mean, Teddy."

"I'd known Teddy a long time. I trusted

him. Daniel and I were a summer romance. Our emotions were like a fierce storm, powerful and strong, but maybe as fleeting. I did a terrible thing by deceiving Daniel. I don't know if he would have gotten over that. I don't know if we would have lasted."

"And now?"

"Now I don't know. I've hurt Daniel. I've hurt you. I've had to question everything I did all those years ago. I told myself my silence was meant to give Daniel his freedom to determine his own future. I knew I could take care of you. We would be okay. But Lizzie…"

"What?"

"I believe I did two things right through the years. One, I never hurt Teddy like I've ended up hurting you and Daniel. Teddy was happy with me and ecstatic with you. And two…" She smiled and took Lizzie's hand. "I think I raised a great kid, not by myself, I admit, but still, you turned out pretty darned terrific."

Lizzie squeezed Alex's hand. "I don't know how to react to him now," she said. "I mean, when Daniel was my mentor, I knew, but now he's my father. Everything has changed."

Alex nodded. "Some things have changed,

but what is a father if not a mentor, one who guides you through life?"

"Grandpa says I should give it time with Daniel."

"And Grandpa is never wrong," Alex said. "Just ask him."

Lizzie smiled. "I don't even know when I'll see Daniel again."

"As soon as you want to, I'm sure of that." Alex knew the same was not true for her. She would have to give Daniel and Lizzie space to be together, just the two of them, time to connect on this new level. And she would have to accept that she'd hurt Daniel beyond his ability to forgive.

"I'll see him," Lizzie said. "We have to start somewhere, I guess. And in a few days we're leaving to go back to Chicago anyway."

"About that…"

Lizzie gave her mother an expectant look.

"We have so much shopping to do to get you ready for college. And now we have to choose an entirely new color scheme."

"What do you mean?"

"I scoured catalogs looking for dorm room accessories in white and yellow. Now I may have to leave the buying up to you so you can pick red and white."

Lizzie's grin broke through the last of the melancholy. "Ohio State colors!"

Alex shrugged. "If there's one thing this mess has taught me, it's that I made a whopper of a mistake when I was your age. You can't do any worse than I did. Fill out an application for OSU if that's what you want to do."

Lizzie hid a coy smile behind her hand. "I already did. I was accepted last week."

Alex faked a stern look. "I'm not the only Foster woman who can keep a secret!"

"I was going to tell you and then things got crazy."

"Yes, they did."

"Mom, who should I tell about this whole Daniel thing?"

"That's up to you, Lizzie, but it might be wise to live with the newness of what you've discovered for a while. Make sure you're comfortable with Daniel. And with me again." Alex wasn't ready to introduce Lizzie to her concerns about the media and her worry about Daniel's campaign. There would be time enough for that.

"You're probably right. I'll keep this between us for now."

Alex stood. "Go get your things. Let's go home."

Lizzie ran toward the house. Alex followed slowly. Before they returned to Dancing Falls, she had to thank Aurora Spindell for being a caring neighbor.

CHAPTER TWENTY-ONE

ONCE SHE AND Lizzie were home, Alex picked up the phone to connect with the other person in Lizzie's life who deserved to know what was going on. She got Daniel's recorded announcement and left a message for him to return the call. If nothing else, she would see if he'd call back as quickly as he did the last time she left a message.

The phone rang within a minute. "Hello, Alex. Do you have news?"

His voice sounded so strong, so good. "Yes. I wanted you to know that everything is improving here. I went over to Aurora's today and had a nice talk with Lizzie. She agreed to come home with me."

"I'm sure you're relieved."

"I am. There's one other thing you should know. I told Lizzie that it's okay with me if she filled out an application for Ohio State."

"You did?" He seemed surprised. She didn't blame him.

"Is she going to do that?"

"She already has, and she's been accepted," Alex said. "She's quite happy with that decision."

"I'm sure she is."

Alex wished she knew a way to keep Daniel on the phone. Just hearing his voice raised her spirits, gave her hope. But she couldn't kid herself. It was false hope, and she had nothing left to say that he would care about.

"I guess that's all," she said. "I didn't want you to worry."

"One more thing, Alex," he said.

"What's that?"

"Did you talk about me? I mean, will she want to see me?"

"I think so," Alex said. "Lizzie doesn't blame you for what I did, Daniel. I'm sure she sees you as a victim just as she is." As an afterthought, Alex added, "And she's right."

"I think I'll come home tonight, then," he said. "Maybe I can see Lizzie on Saturday, and I'll check on my father."

Nothing about wanting to see her. She wondered where she could go tomorrow so she wouldn't make the meeting between father and daughter any more awkward. As much as she wanted to see Daniel, she knew her presence would probably make everyone tense.

"I'll tell her you'll call in the morning," Alex said. "Or you can call her yourself."

"You tell her. That will be fine."

"Oh, Daniel...?"

She almost questioned him about his decision to run for higher office, but then she remembered that she had no right to ask about his personal or professional life.

"Yeah, what?"

"Ah, nothing. It can wait. Drive safely."

"I will. Thanks for calling, Alex."

"Sure." She disconnected and tried to tell herself that she should be relieved. Lizzie would be starting down a new path with her father. Alex truly believed the path would be relatively easy for these two—they were already so much alike. She was happy for Lizzie. She was happy for Daniel. Maybe in the end, that would be happiness enough.

"MOM, YOU'RE NOT even going to be here?"

"Not planning to, honey. Daniel's not coming over to see me."

"How do you know? I'll bet he wants to see you."

Alex rarely heard panic in her daughter's voice. All through the performances of *The Music Man*, Lizzie was composed and confident. Now, at the prospect of seeing Daniel, she was close to falling apart.

"I honestly don't see what the problem is, Lizzie. Daniel is the same man you idolized all summer. Your mentor, your friend. You've been comfortable with him for weeks."

"It's not the same, Mom. He's different now. I'm different. Everything is different. I don't know what to say to him."

Alex looked around the kitchen for her purse. Daniel called ten minutes ago and talked to Lizzie. He would be at Dancing Falls in another few minutes. Alex wanted to be gone. She found her bag. "Say what comes naturally to you, Lizzie. He's going to be as nervous as you are. Remember I told you that he's dealing with a relationship that is as new to him as it is to you."

Lizzie plopped down on a bar stool. "I know. I remember. But what if we can't think of anything to say to each other?"

"I don't recall a time in your life since you

were eighteen months old that silence was a problem."

Lizzie paused a moment and then tried a new tactic. "Don't you want to see Daniel, Mom? I mean, just a week ago I thought you guys might actually be in love."

So did Alex. And she wished she could go back to that time for just one more day, so she would have a chance to prepare Daniel for what was to come, a chance to tell him how she felt before their worlds came crashing down. This morning he hadn't even asked to speak to her. Clearly, there was no going back. Now all she had to figure out was how to go forward.

She tossed her purse over her shoulder. "Be yourself, Lizzie. That's the person Daniel already likes. I'm sure his opinion hasn't changed."

She went out the back door and got in her car. When she drove away from Dancing Falls to go who-knew-where, she saw Daniel's car entering the drive in her rearview mirror.

LIZZIE OPENED THE DOOR. Daniel took a quick look around the foyer, down the hall. He didn't see anyone else. "Hi," he said. "Thanks for seeing me. I believe we've got some things to talk about."

She walked toward the living room. "Yeah, I guess we do."

"Is your mom home?"

"No. She ran out… She left to do some errands." Lizzie sat in a chair, and Daniel sat on the other side of the marble coffee table. "We won't be interrupted in here," she said. "Grandpa's down at the barn with Auntie Jude and Wesley, and it's Rosie's day off."

Daniel smiled to himself. When he was Lizzie's age, he never had to contend with so many people in order to have a private conversation. This was merely one example of the different worlds they came from.

He exhaled. "Hmm, this is quite a situation we're in, right?"

"You can say that."

"Would you like to ask me any questions? I'll try to be as honest as I can."

She stared into his eyes for a moment. "Did you really love my mother like you said the other day?"

Whoa! Talk about starting with a bang. Daniel didn't know much about teenage girls, but he should have figured this question would have been on her mind. Thankfully the answer was an easy one for him. "Lizzie, I was crazy about your mother."

"Would you have married her?"

"I can't say. I would have wanted to do the right thing, but knowing what that was at the time might have been confusing. What I wanted and what your mom wanted could have been two different things. I do know this, however. I wish I'd known you from the beginning. I've missed out on so much." He smiled at her. "And I know another thing, too. Any father would be proud of what you've accomplished. I had nothing to do with that, but I can still be proud."

Thank goodness she seemed satisfied with that answer.

"Did you hear that she's letting me go to Ohio State?"

"Yes, I did hear something about that. It had to be a tough choice for her."

"I know. But I think she'll come to accept that this is what I want, and I'll make a success of my training." She waited before adding, "You'll still come to the university once in a while, won't you, Daniel?"

"Anytime you need me to or want me to." He sat forward in his chair. "Look, Lizzie, I don't know how to be a father. I know that you had a good dad in Teddy, but this will be a learning experience for me. I want to be there for you. I want you to be able to count on me. I don't expect that I'll take Teddy's place. It will be some time before you're even close to feeling about me the way you felt about him, if ever. But I'm going to try. And you have to tell me when I'm messing up, okay?"

She smiled. "You won't mess up, Daniel. You'll do fine."

His heart melted just a little, erasing a tiny bit of the anguish he'd felt these past few days.

"There is one thing we should talk about," Lizzie said.

"Shoot. Anything you want."

"Mom thinks we should keep our relationship just between us for a while. I think I get why she suggested that. You're a public person, and I can understand if you don't want the whole world to know you suddenly are the father of a seventeen-year-old."

"Lizzie, the truth is, I'd like to take out a headline in the local paper so everyone would know, but I understand where your mom's coming from. She's worried that the media will play this up in a way that puts you and me in a bad light.

"As I see it, the people you care about most already know. Your grandpa, your aunt, so I'm okay with respecting your mother's opinion on this as long as you are. In fact, I'd like for us to get to know each other before we take on the world." He thought a moment before saying, "But don't think for a minute that I'm going to be content keeping you a secret for very long."

"Sure. I'm fine with that."

"But Lizzie, there is one person you absolutely have to see again, so I'd like you to take a short drive with me. Would that be okay?"

A few minutes later they were in the car and headed toward Chandler's Hardware Store.

GUS WAS BEHIND the counter when Daniel and Lizzie arrived. Thankfully, he'd seemed in good spirits this morning, but then, he always did, even when the pain was bad. He'd taken the news about Lizzie exactly as Daniel thought he would. With understanding and compassion and forgiveness for everyone involved. "Life is too short to carry grudges, Danny," he'd said, and Daniel was still thinking about those words now.

"Besides, son," Gus had added, "you might need someone to help you through some tough times. I know you're a strong man, but I'll feel better knowing there is someone you can count on. And she seems like a real sweet girl."

So, with confidence, Daniel parked in front of the store and walked in with his daughter.

Gus smiled from the stool he was sitting on. "Hello again there, young lady," he said. "I'd like to come around this counter and give you a big hug, but it might be easier for both of us to just shake hands for now. The hugging can come later."

Daniel had told Lizzie about Gus's cancer. She knew he was frail, and moving was difficult.

Gus stared intently at Lizzie's face. "She's got your eyes, son, and she looks a lot like Helen."

Daniel smiled. He'd told Lizzie about her grandmother on the drive over.

"Hi, Mr. Chandler," Lizzie said, taking his hand.

"That won't do at all," Gus said. "Call me

Gus. Everybody else does and it'll suit me fine."

"Okay, Gus."

"I'm sorry I couldn't make it to one of your performances, Lizzie," Gus said. "Getting around isn't as easy as it used to be. But Daniel said you stole the show."

She grinned. "I don't know about that, but I had a great time."

Gus asked a few questions about *The Music Man*, which Lizzie answered with enthusiasm. When he asked where she was going to college, she told him Ohio State. Daniel figured that might be the first public announcement she'd made about her intentions.

"That's where Danny went," Gus said, staring fondly at his son. "And I suppose he turned out okay." He held one finger up toward Daniel. "You watch out for this young lady," he said. "She'll need someone to count on in the big world of higher education."

"She'll be able to count on me," Daniel said.

Gus shifted on the stool, and Daniel stood, ready to help him if need be. But Gus shooed him away. "So how are you doing with all this news?" he asked Lizzie. "I know it was a shock to me, and must have been doubly so for you. Are you okay?"

"I'm getting used to the idea," Lizzie said. "I'd already thought a lot of Daniel, so maybe the transition from friend to family won't be too hard."

Gus beamed at Daniel. "I always wanted Danny to have a child, even hoped it would be a pretty little girl like you. Always thought he'd be a good daddy." Still holding Lizzie's hand, Gus added, "But I never thought he'd hit the jackpot like this."

"Lizzie's special," Daniel said. "I'm already so proud of her. I hope I'll be a good father once I learn the rules."

"We both have a lot to learn about being father and daughter," Lizzie said.

From a few yards away, someone cleared his throat. "Ah, Gus, you want me to sweep off the loading dock?"

Daniel whirled around toward the back entrance. "Jerry! How long have you been standing there?"

"Not long. A few minutes." The young man shuffled his feet.

"Yes, you can sweep up," Gus said.

When the man had left, Gus turned to Daniel. "I know you wanted to keep this news within the family for now, son, but Jerry probably heard. I can tell him not to spread any gossip. I bet he'll listen to me."

Daniel looked at Lizzie. She shrugged and said, "Up to you. I'm okay with whatever happens."

"Me, too." He smiled. "Let it go, Pop. I've got nothing to hide."

CHAPTER TWENTY-TWO

ALEX FOUND OUT that Daniel had decided to run for one of Ohio's two senate seats by reading the paper Wednesday morning. The headline read "Local favorite Daniel Chandler making big announcement at town hall meet."

She handed the paper to her father at the breakfast table. "Did you see this?"

Martin scanned the article. "It says Daniel will be at Greenfield High School tomorrow night. Most politicians like to go back to their hometowns to share really big news. The reporter who wrote this article seems to think it's pretty definite. What about you, Alexis? How do you feel about Daniel announcing his intentions to run?"

Daniel would be in town soon. Alex hadn't seen him since that morning on the patio when the truth had come out and her life had fallen apart. That was almost two weeks ago.

She'd been able to keep up with his activities through Lizzie, who phoned and texted her father daily. Also, Lizzie had apparently not given up on her mother and new father getting back together.

"You should call him, Mom," Lizzie had said just last night. "You're both being so stubborn."

"Honey, it's not that simple," Alex had explained. "I caused so much hurt. Time has to pass before all those wounds can heal."

"You're going to wait until it's too late," Lizzie countered. "Daniel may find someone else or he may move to Washington and you won't ever see him."

Alex had thought about her daughter's dire predictions throughout another long, restless evening. And now to discover that he was coming to town tomorrow. Just the thought of seeing him again made her heart pound, her palms sweat. She missed him so much, but could she go to his speech? What if he resented her presence? What if he turned her away? Could she risk having her heart shattered again?

Martin set the paper next to his plate. "Are

you going to the town hall meeting?" he asked her as if reading her mind.

"I doubt it," she said. "Lizzie and I are leaving for Chicago the next morning. I probably should stay home and pack. I'm sure Lizzie will go if you want someone to go with."

"I'm on call at the hospital," Martin said. "So I'll have to miss the speech. Doesn't really matter. He'll get my vote unless he totally messes up between now and election time."

Her father leaned his elbows on the table and gave her an earnest stare. "You're aware, Alex, I was ready to kick Daniel Chandler to the curb when I first heard that he was the boy who got...well, you know."

"We've been all over this, Dad. He didn't force me to do anything back then. That's the truth."

"So you've told me, and often enough that I have to believe you. Plus, Lizzie seems to think a lot of him. And he's been a darned good senator for the folks around here. The improved water system, the additional lands devoted to parks, child care for the working mothers who need it... That's all Daniel's doing. And if I believe my granddaughter, he's making strides as a father."

"I doubt anyone can question Daniel's integrity," Alex said, recognizing that the wrong person with information about what happened eighteen years ago could seriously affect his sterling reputation. A political enemy could turn the story of what happened into something sordid. The facts could be twisted so Daniel appeared an uncaring, or even absent, father. But so far, as much as Alex could tell, the word about his unplanned fatherhood hadn't leaked.

"For what it's worth," Martin said. "I think you should go to the town hall. You've got no reason to hide from him, Alex."

Martin's accusation stung and Alex protested. "I'm not hiding! I'm giving him some space to sort things out."

"He's been sorting them for a week and a half now, Alex. And you're leaving in two days. Don't you see it's time you two had a good long talk about—" he paused, took a breath "—I don't know…about the daughter you share, the feelings you share, the future I believe you wish you could have had?"

Alex felt the familiar burn of tears in her eyes. "We don't have a future, Daddy. I ruined it. Daniel doesn't want to have anything to do with me."

All at once the food on her plate made her stomach turn. She couldn't eat. She wasn't sleeping. She'd made such a shambles of everything.

"But you do still have feelings for him, don't you?" Martin asked.

Alex answered with a slight nod. She didn't trust herself to speak.

"Here's an idea," Martin said. "I'll bet Aurora would like to go to that town hall. She's always talking politics and what needs to be done around here. What if I give her a call and you go to that meeting together? I have a hunch she can be a pretty reliable wingman... or woman."

Could she do that? Alex wanted so badly to hear what Daniel had to say, to have a glimpse of him one more time before she left for Chicago. It would help to have someone beside her, someone who wasn't judgmental. For some reason Alex knew she would feel comfortable with Aurora, and safe. She dabbed her eyes with her napkin and looked at her father. "I might be okay with that plan," she said. "But we'll have to sit in the back."

Martin smiled. "That's all right. You two can be fashionably late and get the worst seats in the house."

NORMALLY, DANIEL WAS at ease in front of crowds. He'd spoken at so many events and meetings that one simple town hall shouldn't bother him. Yet tonight he was anxious, fidgety. At first he chalked his unusual reaction up to the importance of this particular town hall. He was going to announce his candidacy for a national senate office and ask for the support of his constituents. Without the votes of the locals, he probably wouldn't stand a chance of winning against the long-term house congressman running against him.

If that wasn't enough to leave every nerve ending frazzled, his daughter would be in the audience. He wanted Lizzie to be proud of him, to recognize him as one of the good guys, a politician who truly cared. And then there was Alex, the woman he hadn't been able to stop thinking about since the horrible breakup almost two weeks ago.

He hadn't stopped caring about Alex. He hadn't stopped loving her. But the moment he realized that Lizzie was his daughter, when the similarities between her and his mother were so obvious, he hadn't been able to *unfeel* the hurt. Did the pain go so deep that he could never trust Alex again? If she hadn't trusted him then, would there come a time when she didn't trust him again? A relationship that wasn't built on trust didn't have a chance.

What if she was here tonight? How would he react if he saw her in the audience? As much as he wanted to test his feelings, as much as he wanted her to be here to show support, he hoped she wouldn't come. If he saw her, he didn't know what he would do. So many days had passed. Almost two weeks. She hadn't called except to tell him that Lizzie was home. He hadn't called her with the exception of those brief communications to check on Lizzie. Was it too late for them? But what if he never found that kind of love again? He'd found Alex twice, and that was testing fate.

Daniel remained backstage until Greenfield's mayor introduced him.

"Our own native son, a man who has made us all proud to be Greenfielders, the politician with a heart, Daniel Chandler."

A bit over the top, Daniel thought as he came on stage. True, he was a native Greenfielder, but his heart? He didn't even know what his heart was telling him anymore.

As he took the podium, Daniel scanned the crowd. He picked Lizzie out in the first row immediately and gave her a special smile. She sat with his father. He recognized many folks in the crowd, neighbors, customers of the hardware store, people whose businesses he'd frequented for years when he was growing up. The second row was reserved for reporters. Not all those faces were welcoming. Some were downright challenging.

As he started to speak, he noticed movement at the rear of the auditorium. Two women moved among the crowd, choosing seats in one of the last rows. But the auditorium wasn't that large, and the houselights were on. And so he saw her. Alex, with the owner of Fox Creek's newest bed-and-breakfast.

Why hadn't she come with their daughter? Did she not want him to see her? Was she here to support him or just because she was curious?

His reaction was instantaneous. His heartbeat accelerated. His palms grew moist. His eyes burned just enough to signal an attraction that definitely hadn't died. And then, as she sat down, he felt a calm settle over him. Maybe deep down, he knew he had at least one friend in the audience. Remembering the rules from his college speech class, he decided to speak directly to her. Maybe he wouldn't have to try to win her over as he might the others in attendance. Or maybe she would be the toughest one to convince. The judgment was still out on that.

"Ladies and gentlemen, Mayor Duncan, friends, neighbors—" he glanced at the first row "—family members, thanks for taking time from your busy schedules to come out tonight."

Effortlessly, he launched into his newly revised speech, the one in which he outlined his vision for the district, and now the nation. He thanked those who had helped him along the way. And he followed with a detailed description of what he'd like the national government to do for the people of Ohio.

He ended by expressing his confidence that he would be the right man to implement the changes he envisioned for his home state. Several times he was interrupted by applause but none as energetic as the cheers that went up when he announced his candidacy for US Senate. In the back, Alex cheered with the rest. She was smiling. His heart kicked back in his chest and swelled. She had a beautiful smile.

"I can't do it alone," he said to conclude. "I will need your help and support. I invite each of you to contact me at my email address or my office to tell me your concerns or to offer advice. I assure you, I'm always ready to listen. I'm here to serve you."

He took a deep breath. "And now I will take a few questions."

Each reporter who had a question identified himself and the paper or blog site for which he worked. The questions were general, restricted to Daniel's record in the Ohio Senate, his beliefs on different topics, his possible choice for campaign director and so on. Since he was familiar with nearly all the local media, Daniel answered each query with ease.

Until an unknown reporter caught his attention.

"Yes, go ahead," Daniel said.

"Leonard Marshall, *Integrity in Politics* blogger."

Daniel recalled the website and its connection to his opponent, a man who used the site to convey his opinions.

"What is your question?" Daniel asked.

"In light of the number of voters who have become disenchanted with politics these days, Senator, I'm wondering… How important is integrity in politics in the modern era?"

Daniel cleared his throat. "Is that a trick question, Leonard?"

A few chuckles rose from the crowd.

"Obviously, a man's character is still of utmost importance," Daniel said. "His integrity should never be called into question."

"And your background, Daniel? Squeaky-clean?"

"I like to think that I haven't committed any blunders that might follow me on the campaign trail," Daniel said. "I've always tried to be honest with my constituents."

"Then Senator, how do you explain keeping such a secret as an illegitimate child you fathered eighteen years ago?"

Daniel took a second to compose himself. He glanced at Lizzie and his father. Their faces reflected shock and uncertainty. In the back row, Alex had started to stand but took her seat again.

"This is not the time or the forum to address your accusation," Daniel said. "You have clearly crossed the line between my public life and my private."

"Pardon me, Senator, but this is exactly the right time. You are asking the people to give you their most sacred right in a democratic government, their vote. So in the interest of openness and honesty, I ask you, are you denying the existence of this child?"

"I'm not denying anything."

A low rumble rippled through the crowd.

"The voting public knows you are a single man, never married," the reporter said. "And yet you are the father of a seventeen-year-old girl, one who, according to my records, was raised without benefit of a penny from your own bank account. Is this true?"

"This has nothing to do with my record as

a public servant," Daniel said. "If you have another question, one that pertains to the issues in this campaign, I will happily address it." Suddenly, Daniel felt sleazy, like so many of those in Washington who'd had their pasts called into question.

"Then integrity, personal morality, isn't important to you, Senator? You don't think the public has a right to know about past indiscretions, especially one that puts you in a light of ignoring personal responsibility?"

Daniel was teetering on a precarious beam. On the one hand, he wanted to protect his reputation. On the other, he needed to protect Lizzie. And Alex. He cleared his throat. "I will address anyone's concern over this matter on a one-to-one basis. Any of my constituents is welcome to call me during the week." Daniel tugged on his jacket, pulled at his cuffs. He gathered up his notes. "If that is all…"

"You're dodging, Senator," the reporter said. "And we all know it."

The crowd was deathly silent, the room as still as a tomb. And then one woman stood up near the back of the auditorium. At first she seemed unsteady on her feet, but she quickly regained her composure. "Excuse me," she said. Her voice was strong and clear without benefit of a microphone.

"My name is Alexis Foster Pope. Many of you know me, know my family. We have been residents of this area of Ohio for three generations. I would like to address the topic, if I may."

All eyes turned to the back of the room. Alexis took a long, deep breath, twined her fingers in front of her abdomen. "Eighteen years ago," she began, "when I was just a teenager, I fell in love with the most honorable, kind, considerate man I'd ever met. His name is Daniel Chandler, and he is your candidate for US Senate."

Daniel forced himself to breathe. His admiration for Alex was only outweighed by his fear for what her next words might cost her. He ached for her, wished he could take her away from this scene, save her from the emotional turmoil she must be suffering. He was a public person, but she certainly wasn't. He held his breath and waited for what was to come.

"Daniel and I were young," she said. "And like many of us finding our pathways into adulthood, we were sometimes foolish. The result of my admiration and love for Daniel resulted in our beautiful, talented, intelligent daughter, Elizabeth."

Lizzie stood, turned around, smiled and waved to the crowd, exactly what Daniel would have done if he had been in her shoes. He could have jumped off the stage and hugged her right then and there.

"My mistake was not that I had my Lizzie," Alex continued. "My mistake was not telling Daniel I was pregnant. I had my reasons, and I won't go into them now. Daniel, the man he was then, and the man he is now, would have stood by me, but I didn't give him the chance. He has only known about his relationship to our daughter for a few days. My daughter has taken him into her heart as he has taken her into his.

"If this is a question of fault, then I assume the entire blame. I ask you all to hold me responsible, not Daniel Chandler. But the truth is, I don't see the miracle that has transpired in the last few days as a matter of blame or fault. The overdue meeting between these two special people in my life is cause for joy, not shame.

"These are the facts, the truth with nothing

hidden. Please judge the man before you on his merits as a public servant, not as a man who should be held accountable for something he knew nothing about." She looked at Daniel. She looked at Aurora. And she smiled. "Thank you."

Daniel had never felt more humbled. What it must have taken for Alex to strip herself bare in front of this crowd, her neighbors, her friends. He leaned into the microphone. "Thank you again for coming. This concludes the town hall meeting."

ALEX AND AURORA were among the first to leave the auditorium. Arriving late and getting the worst seats had its advantages. Alex was trembling so violently, she had to grab on to Aurora's elbow for support. "I can't believe I just did that," Alex said.

Aurora pumped her small fist in the air. "You were marvelous, Alex. You could have heard a pin drop in that meeting. I'm so proud of you."

Alex emitted a near-hysterical burst of laughter. Imagine this little woman, whose strength belied her small stature, a woman practically a stranger to Alex, saying she was proud of her.

Yet, to Alex, who couldn't stop shaking, it was high praise.

"Well, I had to do something, didn't I?" Alex said. "I couldn't let that idiot reporter railroad Daniel into saying something gallant or courageous to save Lizzie's feelings and mine." *Unfortunately, I might have driven an even greater wedge between us.* She prayed Daniel didn't resent her interference.

"You told the truth, sweetie," Aurora said. "That can almost never be a bad thing."

The two women hurried across the parking lot and got in Alex's car. "I'm glad I don't have to wait for Lizzie," Alex said. "Daniel will bring her home."

As much as she wanted to know what was going on inside the building, Alex was grateful that hers was the first car to leave the high school.

DANIEL SPOKE TO everyone who wanted to ask him a question. Most of the questions were about policy, his campaign, how his father was feeling. No one asked about his daughter, but several of his neighbors came up to Lizzie and introduced themselves. By the end of the night, Daniel figured Lizzie had become an honorary Greenfielder and a very worthy sidekick.

As soon as he got a chance to leave the stage, Daniel walked up to her. "Where's your mother?" he asked.

"I guess she went home," Lizzie said. "I saw her leave the auditorium with Aurora, and I haven't seen her since." Lizzie smiled at him. "Why do you want to know?"

He recognized the now-familiar smugness in his daughter's grin. "Wouldn't you like to know," he said.

"She was pretty cool tonight, wasn't she?"

"The coolest," Daniel said. "I need to thank her."

When they got to Dancing Falls, all the lights were dimmed except for the porch light. Daniel walked Lizzie to the door. "Do you think I should bother her tonight?" he asked.

"Probably not. If I know my mother, she's still throwing up."

"Nice."

"Come over in the morning, Daniel. You can see her before we leave for Chicago."

"Thanks for handling everything like a

champ tonight, Lizzie," he said. "And you can count on it. I'll be here in the morning."

And he was. But Alex and Lizzie had already left.

CHAPTER TWENTY-THREE

AFTER BREAKFAST AND saying a brief good-bye to his daughter and granddaughter, Martin made his morning visit back to his wife's room. He picked up Maggie's hand. "Listen to this, Maggie-mine," he said, flipping open the newspaper. "Our daughter is a headliner because of last night's town hall meeting."

He read the lead article in the local paper, his voice booming with pride. This was the third time he'd read it, including rushing through it for Lizzie and Alexis before they got in their car.

"She stood right up to that newshound and gave him all she's got. Our reserved, elegant Alexis stood in the middle of that ring and symbolically punched that guy in the nose." He leaned over and kissed Maggie's forehead. "We raised a fine young lady, Maggie, and I told her so when she left."

He coughed to clear his throat of a rush of

emotion. "That's all I came to say now, Maggie. I'm going to the office. But if you don't mind, I may read this one more time to one more person. Her name is Aurora, and she was there last night alongside our Alexis." Martin stroked Maggie's hair. "You'd like her, honey. You two are alike in here—" He rested his finger on Maggie's heart. "Where it counts."

AN HOUR INTO the drive to Chicago, Alex recognized the uncanny similarity between their drive to Dancing Falls weeks ago and the one to Chicago now. Lizzie had been silent for most of both trips. Unable to stand the quiet anymore, Alex said, "I know something is bothering you. Why don't you tell me what it is?"

"Gee, Mom, the sun hasn't even been up an hour, and you're wondering why I'm not chatting away? Maybe I'm not a morning person."

Alex sighed. "I know I got you up early, but…"

"Early? I felt like I'd just gotten to sleep when you came in with your cheery 'rise and shine.' Excuse me if I don't exactly feel like shining."

"Look, getting an early start puts us in Chicago around four this afternoon. The day isn't lost. We can begin packing for college."

"I could pack for college in an hour if I had to, Mom."

Alex knew that was absolutely not true. In an hour, Lizzie would have only sorted her T-shirts.

"I know why you wanted to leave at the crack of dawn," Lizzie said.

Alex debated her choices and settled on the most obvious one. "You're assuming this has something to do with Daniel, right?"

"You got it. I told you he was coming over, but you left before giving him a chance."

"I didn't want to put either one of us in an awkward position," Alex said. "I don't know how Daniel felt about my little speech last night."

"I told you how he felt!" Suddenly, Lizzie was animated. "He looked for you after the town hall. He wanted to thank you."

"That's what he told you," Alex said.

"So he was lying to me? I don't think so. He appreciated what you did. So did Grandpa. We all thought you did the most courageous thing."

"I hope that's true, but I wasn't ready to face him. My little speech will be all over the state before noon."

"And once everybody has talked about it, so what? They'll either forget or build you a statue. You don't have to take my word for it. Grandpa wasn't upset."

Thank goodness for her father. "No, but that's Grandpa. He tries to take the messes his daughters get into in his stride."

"Mom, I don't understand. You didn't even wait for Daniel to show up. You love him! At least I think you do. If you love someone, you keep the lines of communication open. You don't shut down. How many times have you told me this?"

Alex expelled a long breath. "I can't explain this to you, Lizzie…" How could she tell her daughter that she was flat-out terrified to face Daniel again? That she was guarding her heart, protecting her fragile ego. She tried to make some sense of her behavior. "Daniel and I… If you'd seen him when he found out about you, what I'd done."

"I did see him! I came onto the patio, remember? He was upset, sure, but he maintained his cool. That's more than I can say for myself, and you're still talking to me."

Alex smiled. "Here's the thing, Lizzie. It's enough for me to work on reestablishing what you and I had. I don't think I can take on Daniel right now. It's entirely possible that his feelings for me aren't as generous as you believe them to be. Just because I made that speech last night…" She stopped to take a long breath. "I hurt him, honey. He may never get over it. Once you and I are on solid ground again, I'll consider contacting him, but for now you are my top priority."

"News flash, Mom. You're going to see him in a little over a week anyway."

"What?" Alex blinked, stared at her daughter.

"He's coming to OSU to see me when I get there for fall semester. He's only a few miles away."

Naturally, Daniel would be there. Alex should have thought of that. Well, she'd have to deal with his presence the best she could. Lizzie was what mattered at the moment, and Alex would see her settled in her dorm. If she ran into Daniel, she'd handle it. She had a week to prepare.

"Well, sure," she said. "I figured he'd be there." She hoped Lizzie didn't see the flush creep up her neck. "I'll see Daniel then and I'll reevaluate our relationship."

"Mom, you're sounding like this is a clinical decision. It's not. It's emotional. You should act like your heart tells you to."

"Okay, Lizzie, I get it." She'd be polite. They'd talk about Lizzie, the coming semester. And then it would be over.

She didn't think her heart could take another blow. Not that Daniel wouldn't be a gentleman. He would be. But who knew what ramifications might have resulted from the announcement last night? Sure, her dad, Lizzie and Aurora thought she'd done the right thing, but in the next week the media might not drop the story. His opponent could play up the fact that Daniel had fathered a child outside of marriage, making him seem irresponsible. Maybe his career was ruined. Maybe he would have even more reason to hate her than just the secret she'd kept from him all those years ago.

ONE WEEK LATER, after spending Friday night in a nearby Columbus motel and armed with a detailed map of the extremely large OSU campus, Alex and Lizzie arrived at the dormitory, which would be Lizzie's new home. An air of expectancy permeated the atmosphere. Excited freshmen helped nervous parents unload minivans and SUVs. Wheels on overused dollies rumbled along sidewalks. Volunteers watched for any new student who looked lost, and offered to help.

In a way, the energy and anticipation reminded Alex of the day she'd arrived at Birch Shore so many years ago. Her life had seemed about to change that day, similarly as Lizzie's did now. She'd experienced her first taste of freedom then, and Lizzie was ready, she admitted, to begin her own life as an adult, making her own decisions.

"I hope my roommate is here," Lizzie said, as she transferred a box of electronics from the car to the dolly. "We're planning to walk over to the theater department this afternoon." She scanned the huge campus and laughed. "Or maybe take a bus."

Next onto the dolly went the crates of Lizzie's new linens and hair and skin products, followed by a box of her cherished stuffed animals. When the dolly was full, Alex locked the car until they could get back for the next load, Lizzie's clothes. The women struggled with the cart, attempting to turn it around, when a voice from behind them said, "Can I give you ladies a hand?"

Alex's heart jumped into her throat.

Lizzie squealed, "Daniel! You're here. I only called you fifteen minutes ago."

Without telling her mother.

"Of course I'm here," he said, giving her a quick hug. "I couldn't let you begin at my alma mater without my blessing." He looked around the campus with a wistful expression and pretended to be concerned when he said, "Lizzie Pope has arrived. Ohio State will never be the same."

Then he turned to look at Alex. Her hand went involuntarily to her hair, which whipped around her face in a stiff breeze. The stylish braid she'd fashioned that morning was ruined. Dirt smudges dotted her white jeans. And she was quite certain her expression reflected abject terror.

Meanwhile, Daniel, Mr. Calm, Cool and Casual, could almost have passed for a university student himself in blue jeans and a neat button-down shirt. Anticipating the windy weather, he'd crunched an OSU ball cap over his hair and donned a pair of aviator sunglasses. He smiled at Alex, that natural, easy smile that could melt ice—and her heart.

"How are you, Mom?" he said. "Handling this okay?"

She tried to smile, but her lips felt like plastic. "I'm pretty sure I started experiencing separation anxiety before I got out of bed this morning," she finally managed to say.

Daniel took the handle of the dolly and effortlessly guided it toward the dorm. "I'm following you gals, so lead the way."

Thankfully, Lizzie chattered nonstop through the dorm lobby and up the elevator. Several times Daniel glanced in Alex's direction, giving her a knowing grin. How easily he'd slipped into parent mode, as if he was born to do the job. When they exited the elevator and Lizzie ran off to find her room number, he said, "Reminds me of another girl eighteen years ago."

Alex nodded, certain his thoughts mirrored her own. "But I was anxious that day, too," she said. *Until you showed up and made everything right.* "Lizzie is only a ball of excited energy." She smiled. "This was definitely the right decision."

He gave her a sympathetic grin. "All too often the right choice is the difficult one," he said. "I'm proud of you, Alex, for allowing her to follow her dream."

"You'll find out, Daniel. Just wait. She can be very persuasive. I didn't so much *allow* as give in. Something you'll understand soon enough."

He stopped pushing the cart and stared at her. "Do you know what you just did?"

"No. What?"

"You indicated that my relationship with Lizzie is for the long run."

"Hmm..." She had subconsciously done that. *You'll find out, Daniel.* Actually, he would be geographically closer to Lizzie than she would be for the next four years. And it was okay. He'd already been a mentor to their daughter. Now he was taking a step up. "You're her father, Daniel," she said. "It's a lifetime run, not a long one."

He touched her arm, and she felt an instant reaction of warmth and comfort. Unfortunately, his touch only made her want more— a kiss, an embrace, a comforting arm around her shoulders. She recalled the day at the covered bridge and nearly sighed out loud. There would never be enough Daniel in her life.

"I'll try not to blow it," he said. "I don't want to disappoint either one of you."

"You won't," she said. *You couldn't.*

DANIEL WENT BACK for the last load while Alex and Lizzie began unpacking. This fatherhood stuff was so new, but he found himself wondering how he'd ever gotten along without it. Sure, having a kid was a major responsibility, but to his way of thinking, not having a kid was a major void. He prayed his connection to Lizzie would grow and develop into something wonderful. He'd never thought of himself as a nurturer, but if that was what the job demanded, he'd give it his best shot.

For days after learning he was Lizzie's father, he focused on the negative—the time he'd missed with her, the things he'd never see her do for the first time, the way Alex had chosen to leave him out of her life. Now that his attitude had mellowed and his anger had subsided, his expectations had steadily grown. He was a young man. He would have lots of time to see his daughter become what fate and determination would make her.

Was this new Daniel ready to forgive Alex? Maybe he was already on the path to doing that. But he knew one thing for sure. He missed her. She'd become a part of his life as quickly and with the same emotional punch as she had back at Birch Shore. He'd seen her that day eighteen years ago looking lost, yet expectant, and he'd known there was something special about her, something he needed to explore. And he'd seen her from across the parking lot today, looking the exact same way—a young woman lost and expectant, and his heart felt full again.

What she'd done back then was unforgivable. No one would deny that. He'd been cheated, robbed of years with his daughter. And yet, seeing Alex today, he knew she didn't have an ounce of malice in her heart. She'd had her reasons for what she'd done, and she thought she'd been doing the right thing. Could he cross that line and totally believe in her? That remained to be seen. Would she let him cross it, or would her guilt keep them apart forever? That too was still a question for the universe.

Daniel piled two large suitcases and a duffel bag on the dolly. Next to them, he stacked three large boxes. One of the boxes opened and a fresh, flowery scent drifted to his nostrils. A sweet, natural scent, perhaps Lizzie's shampoo. So this was what it smelled like to be a father of a girl, he thought. He closed the box again and headed back to the dorm, and realized that the last emotion he was feeling right now was anger.

WHEN MOST OF the boxes and cases were unpacked, and Daniel had stuck posters and mementos to the walls, Lizzie answered her cell phone. After a short conversation, she ended the call and told her parents, "That was my roommate. She'll be here in an hour. I can't wait to meet her."

Daniel looked at his watch. "Good. Just enough time for lunch. Let me take you ladies to the student union for burgers."

"That would be great," Lizzie said, getting out her map. "I think it's within walking distance." She laughed. "Probably the only thing that is on this campus."

Daniel looked at Alex. "Okay with you?"

Alex's plan to escape to her car and head out of town was ruined. She couldn't disappoint Lizzie. "Sure. Sounds good. A burger is just what I wanted."

They walked to the student union while Lizzie consulted her map and pointed out buildings of interest. Daniel stood in line to order and brought the burgers to the table. Alex managed to not focus on Daniel. She even ate her food, probably because she was famished. Lizzie downed a hamburger, an order of fries and a chocolate milk shake.

"I read in a magazine that college freshmen tend to gain an average of ten pounds their first year," Lizzie said. Staring forlornly at her empty food basket, she added, "I'm going to have to watch that."

They walked over to the dorm together, and Daniel announced that he had to get back to his office. The past hour had been pleasant but awkward, like strangers reconnecting after many years. Both adults had carried on polite exchanges. Alex wondered if that was because they were feeling connected again, even to a small degree. Or were they acting to keep up a front with Lizzie? What would she and Daniel be like alone? Would they be more natural? Would the tension be even greater? She couldn't answer that question.

"Mom, you might as well go, too," Lizzie

said. "Ashley will be here any minute, and we'll want to go exploring."

The sting of dismissal brought tears to Alex's eyes, but she was determined not to let Lizzie see them. The separation of mother and child was a natural phenomenon, and going through it was a part of growing up and letting go for nearly every species. Oh, but how empty that apartment in Chicago would feel from now on.

"I'll walk you to your car, Alex," Daniel said.

She nodded, not trusting herself to speak. She hugged Lizzie, told her to study hard and hugged her again.

"Mom, I'll be fine. I'll call you tonight. If you get tired, stop at a motel. Don't try to drive all the way."

Now who was being the mother? "I will," she promised. She pointed vaguely at the hallway. "Daniel, I'll wait for you out…"

He smiled at her. "I know. I'll just be a minute."

She went into the hall but stayed close to the open door. Voices carried from the room. Lizzie thanked Daniel for helping out. Daniel made her promise to call if she needed anything, and then he amended the order to include, "Just call, okay? I'll want to hear from you."

Lizzie protested in the little-girl way that still made her seem like Alex's baby. "Daniel, I'll be okay, but yes, I'll call."

And then Daniel was in the hallway. He put his arm around Alex's shoulders and led her to the elevator. Without his support, she feared she might have run back into Lizzie's room for one more hug.

The elevator doors opened, and thankfully, they were alone. Daniel kept his arm around her and said softly, "You did one heck of a job raising her. She's strong and bright. She'll be fine."

"I kn…know she will be, but I'm not sure about me."

His arm tightened, and her head fell to his chest. He rubbed her arm as she tried to control her sobs. "If anyone sees me like this…"

"They'll be seeing you and nearly all the other mothers," he said, his voice tight. "And a few of the dads."

She laughed through a sob. "Daniel, I'm sorry…"

"Stop it," he said. "Now is not the time for

apologies. Besides, you've already given me enough to last a lifetime."

The elevator doors opened and they quickly walked through the dorm lobby. Daniel kept his hand on her elbow as he led her to her car. "Are you going to try and drive the whole way?" he asked.

"I don't know. Maybe I'll get in a zone and just keep going."

"Remember what Lizzie said."

She got in her car. "Daniel..."

"Yes?"

The words she wanted to say became jumbled in her mind. Her emotions were swirling in her head until she couldn't separate one from the other. Sorrow, guilt, love... She felt dizzy. Apologies mixed with longing, mixed with the loss of her other half. She didn't know how to express what she wanted to say. "Maybe someday, you and I..." She stopped, suddenly exhausted and frightened of saying too much too soon.

His knuckles brushed her cheek, a feather-soft, sweet caress. "Maybe, Alex. Maybe someday."

She started her car and drove toward the highway that would take her to Chicago, the last place she wanted to be. But when the traffic sign pointed west, she took an entirely different direction. She drove onto the ramp that would take her north. And she headed into the waning horizon.

CHAPTER TWENTY-FOUR

THE WIND BLEW strong across the causeway that connected the mainland of Ohio to Birch Shore. Alex gripped the wheel and kept going even though she knew many parts of the resort would be closed. Except for the hotel, everything always shut the day after Labor Day.

In the growing dusk, she recognized silhouettes. The track of the roller coaster, the Ferris wheel, the gabled roof of the grand hotel where Daniel had made most of his tips. None of the rides were running tonight, and only a few rooms in the hotel glowed with light.

Some people probably preferred to stay in the resort at this time of year—older couples or young marrieds grabbing a last weekend before the cold weather set in. School was back in session. The Midway, always dazzling during the season, was quiet, the beach empty. Even the food concessions were closed, leaving the few guests there to pay top dollar in the hotel restaurant or drive onto the mainland for a meal.

When she reached the entrance to the hotel, Alex was stopped by a locked gate. She didn't recall the gate ever being locked during the summer season. She drove up next to an intercom and pressed a call button.

"Can I help you?" came a practiced female voice.

"Yes. I'd like to come in and see a room."

"Certainly. So you don't have a reservation?"

"No." Alex glanced at the darkened rooms. "Do I need one?"

The woman chuckled. "You do not. I'll buzz you in."

The gate swung wide and Alex parked in a spot close to the main double doors. She had no intention of renting a room, but perhaps she would go inside later and order a cup of coffee. For now, it suited her purpose to park, get out and wander, letting her mind crisscross the planes of her memory.

She went around the hotel, stopping to glance in the dining room window. About a quarter of the tables were occupied, mostly by couples. The lighting was low, romantic, and Alex sighed.

She walked to the dormitory where she and the other teens had stayed. Pelican House was still there, but it was obviously not used for the same purpose. Trucks occupied the front parking spaces, flanked by utilitarian golf carts. Perhaps the building was used for storage now.

As she stood at the plain front door of Pelican House, she imagined the times she'd gone in at night, tired but filled with the wonder of being in love for the first time. In her mind, she traced her steps to her room, pictured herself going inside, greeting her roommate, talking until one in the morning. And then sleeping soundly, anxious for tomorrow to come so she could be with Daniel again.

She strolled along the building's exterior until she came to the window of her room. Curtains and height kept her from seeing inside, but that was okay. She knew it wouldn't be the same. Very little ever was. She turned up the collar of her long-sleeved blouse to protect her nape from the wind and stayed where she was, outside her room, for a while, trying to decide if this journey to the past was making her sad or happy. Probably both, she acknowledged. One fact was certain. She was alive again, the numbness of the past weeks at last leaving her body.

And then she followed a familiar path between the birch trees to the shore. The canvas cabanas were stacked against the lifeguard stands. Deck chairs and lounges had been pulled back to the tree line and covered with tarps. For Birch Shore it was the end of a season. For Alexis Pope, it was the end of an era.

A pain sliced into her chest when she saw the rugged form of the old wooden pier sticking up from the water, bathed in a rising moon. She couldn't have prevented herself from going down there if she'd wanted to. And she didn't. Despite the wind, the cold, the waves rushing a bit crazily to the shore, she kicked off her shoes and walked through the sand.

DANIEL DIDN'T UNDERSTAND what had gotten into him. He was supposed to attend a dinner for a Columbus circuit judge tonight, a stuffy affair where too many people would drink too much, and he would try to leave early. But he didn't go to his apartment to change. Instead, he followed a sappy instinct to connect with his past and drove north to Lake Erie.

On the way he called his father. "How're you feeling, Pop?"

"Pretty good," Gus said. "I talked to Margaret this afternoon, and we're planning our trip to the West."

"When do you think you might leave?"

"Next Monday," Gus said. "Taking a bus tour with a travel company. We'll go through the central plains and into Montana and Wyoming. Margaret's making all the reservations we'll need. Should be gone about three weeks."

"Sounds great, Pop." He hated to ask, but the question was vital. "Have you talked to the doctor about this?"

"I did. He told me to go with his blessing. I'll be back, son. You don't need to worry."

As if it was possible not to worry. Daniel disconnected and thought about his dad. Gus, a dying man, had something like this trip to look forward to. Daniel rolled down his window and let the cool air blast his face. *Shake it off, Daniel*, he said to himself. *Take a lesson from your father, who is living every day to its fullest while you can't seem to think about getting through tomorrow.*

In the past week Daniel had taken to counting his blessings. And there were many. He had a job he loved. His future in politics looked bright. And, best of all, he had a daughter. Any one of these should leave a man grateful to be alive. And yet he couldn't stop thinking about the one thing he didn't have. Alex.

He knew he'd disappointed her, taken liberties by discussing things with Lizzie without her, like the talk they'd had about colleges. Perhaps she still resented his interference. But Alex had disappointed him, as well. She'd adapted the past to suit herself and gone on with her life as if he didn't exist. They'd both made mistakes, and was it really so important to weigh whose were the worst?

He reached Birch Shore and was surprised that the gate was open. Usually after the Midway closed, the gate was kept locked. Maybe someone had just driven in, and the front desk attendant at the hotel had forgotten to close it. He entered and drove to the front of the building.

He'd been back to the resort several times, sometimes because political conferences were held there, sometimes for a quick getaway, once in a while just following a sentimental journey. Tonight he was here hoping to heal the part of himself that still didn't have answers.

He left his car and wandered down to the shore. The breeze was crisp and strong. Whitecaps rolled on the horizon where low clouds hinted of coming rain. He thought of the last time he'd been caught in a rainstorm. A covered bridge, a picnic, Alex in his arms and a kiss that had left him breathless. Could they get those feelings back? Could they go on from here, as a man and woman, as a family united after all that had happened?

Maybe. Like his father, he needed his trip to the West. He needed something to believe in. He needed Alex.

And then he saw her. A lone figure seated on a boulder near the pier. She sat cross-legged, her collar turned up, her hair wild in the wind. The nearest dock light reflected off her blond hair, and Daniel knew instantly that it was her.

His heart pounded. His blood flowed like melted silver through his veins and thrummed in his temples. He should have been surprised to see her, but he wasn't. In the dark, at the end of a special day with their daughter, at this special place, they should meet again where they met the first time. She was here. He was here. Being together seemed as natural as the waves washing on shore.

He walked quietly up to the rock where she sat. With a light hand, he touched her shoulder. She started but did not make a sound, as if fear was the furthest thing from her mind. She turned and looked into his eyes. "Daniel... How? What?"

He glanced down at the small space next to her on the rock. "Is this seat taken?"

"No." She made room for him.

He settled next to her and took her hand. "It's been a crazy day, hasn't it?"

"Yes, and the craziest part of it is happening right now. I can't believe you're here."

"I didn't think about it," he said. "I left the campus, started driving and ended up here at Birch Shore."

"The same thing happened to me. I should be halfway to Chicago by now."

He threaded his fingers with hers and brought her hand to his lips. He kissed each knuckle, opened her palm and kissed her there. He'd never seen an image as beautiful as Alex on this cold end-of-summer night, her hair blowing about her face as free as his heart felt now. Her blue eyes held his with a force more powerful than any he'd ever known. He couldn't have looked away if he'd tried.

"I guess I came here because I have something to say to you," he said. "And maybe you're here because you had to hear it."

"All right," she whispered. "What do you want to say?" Her voice trembled, hinted of her uncertainty.

He held her hand more tightly. "I love you, Alex," he said. "I suppose I always have. That's why I've never married. No one ever measured up to that sweet, bright, innocent girl from Fox Creek who stole my heart on the sidewalk in front of Pelican House."

She swallowed, blinked hard. "Even after…" She stopped, swallowed again, unable to get the words out.

"Yes, even after. And now that we share Lizzie, maybe even a little *because* of all that history."

"But I lied to you about being on the pill."

"Yes, you did."

"And I kept Lizzie a secret for so long."

"Yes. That, too."

"And still you love me?"

He smiled, tucked her closed fist against his heart. "Madly, thoroughly, eternally. I'm not saying our path will be easy. We have some things to work out. But I want you by my side, Alex, through the pain that is to come, the joy that Lizzie will bring us, the trials of public life and the passion of every day together."

She bit her bottom lip to keep it from quivering.

He traced her mouth with his fingertip. "I've poured my heart out to you, Alexis. You can't just leave me sitting on this rock, not telling me how you feel."

"I think you know, Daniel. But in case there is a doubt…" She wrapped her free hand around the back of his neck and brought his mouth to hers. The kiss was worthy of philosophers and poets, lasting long and tasting sweetly of the salt from her tears. When at last they drew apart, she said, "Daniel Chandler, love of my life, you have my heart, my support in all things, my deepest trust…" She gave him an impish grin. "And my vote."

He laughed and she cried until, emotions spent, they walked back to the grand hotel where they would sit at one of the romantic candlelit tables and plan the next fifty years of their life.

EPILOGUE

MARTIN PULLED HIS shirt cuffs so a gleaming rim of white appeared at the end of his tuxedo sleeves. He glanced at the door to the private room next to the sanctuary where brides dressed for their special day. Then he checked the time on his watch. Alex was only three minutes late, but even minor tardiness was unusual for her. Her whole life she'd been on time or early.

Always in a hurry, young people today, he thought. People should slow down, appreciate what they had. Thanksgiving was a mere few days ago, only a little more than two months since Lizzie went off to Ohio State, and her mother and father were getting married already. Thanksgiving. What an affair that had been. Alex and Jude insisted on fixing the meal. Carrie, home from her woodlands wandering, had supervised and kept the appetizers and wine flowing. Aurora was there, and of course, Wesley and Daniel.

Sadly, one person wasn't at the table: Gus Chandler. He'd passed away ten days before the holiday, but Daniel said a lovely blessing for his father before the meal.

What a real shame, Martin thought.

The door to the dressing room opened and Lizzie, dressed in flowing burgundy, came out. "She's ready, Grandpa."

Jude and Carrie, in dresses that matched their niece's, held the door for their sister. Alexis appeared like an angel in white. "It's really true," Martin whispered to Lizzie. "Brides really do glow."

The ladies formed the front of the processional line, waiting for their musical cue. Alex stood by her father. "You are beautiful, sweetheart," Martin said, choking on the words.

"Thank you, Daddy, and thank you for all this." She peered into the sanctuary where family and friends waited. The ceremony would be simple and elegant, like Alexis.

"You didn't have a real wedding last time," Martin said. "I can just imagine what your mother would say if I didn't give you one now."

The processional started, and the Foster

women began their short walk down the beautifully decorated aisle. Alex looped her arm through her father's, and all heads turned.

Martin felt blessed to be able to share in his daughter's happiness. And blessed to welcome Daniel into the family. *It's all good*, he thought, and then he caught a glimpse of Liam Manning and smiled.

Jude probably wouldn't remember Liam. They'd met only once when they were children. But she was about to meet the Wharton business school graduate again today; Martin would see to it.

Ah, his stubborn, hardworking, impractical Jude. She wouldn't give in easily to working with Liam. But it was time to get his middle daughter's charities in order and maybe, at the same time, have her set her sights on her future happiness.

* * * * *

Don't miss Jude's romance coming next in
THE DAUGHTERS OF DANCING FALLS
miniseries from acclaimed author
Cynthia Thomason!

LARGER-PRINT BOOKS!

GET 2 FREE LARGER-PRINT NOVELS PLUS 2 FREE MYSTERY GIFTS

Love Inspired®

SUSPENSE
RIVETING INSPIRATIONAL ROMANCE

Larger-print novels are now available...

YES! Please send me **The Montana Mavericks Collection** in Larger Print. This collection begins with 3 FREE books and 2 FREE gifts (gifts valued at approx. $20.00 retail) in the first shipment, along with the other first 4 books from the collection! If I do not cancel, I will receive 8 monthly shipments until I have the entire 51-book Montana Mavericks collection. I will receive 2 or 3 FREE books in each shipment and I will pay just $4.99 US/ $5.89 CDN for each of the other four books in each shipment, plus $2.99 for shipping and handling per shipment.*If I decide to keep the entire collection, I'll have paid for only 32 books, because 19 books are FREE! I understand that accepting the 3 free books and gifts places me under no obligation to buy anything. I can always return a shipment and cancel at any time. My free books and gifts are mine to keep no matter what I decide.

263 HCN 2404   463 HCN 2404

Name	(PLEASE PRINT)	
Address		Apt. #
City	State/Prov.	Zip/Postal Code

Signature (if under 18, a parent or guardian must sign)

Mail to the **Reader Service:**

IN U.S.A.: P.O. Box 1867, Buffalo, NY 14240-1867
IN CANADA: P.O. Box 609, Fort Erie, Ontario L2A 5X3

* Terms and prices subject to change without notice. Prices do not include applicable taxes. Sales tax applicable in N.Y. Canadian residents will be charged applicable taxes. This offer is limited to one order per household. All orders subject to approval. Credit or debit balances in a customer's account(s) may be offset by any other outstanding balance owed by or to the customer. Please allow 4 to 6 weeks for delivery. Offer available while quantities last. Offer not available to Quebec residents.

READERSERVICE.COM

Manage your account online!

- Review your order history
- Manage your payments
- Update your address

> *We've designed the*
> *Reader Service website*
> *just for you.*

Enjoy all the features!

- Discover new series available to you, and read excerpts from any series.
- Respond to mailings and special monthly offers.
- Connect with favorite authors at the blog.
- Browse the Bonus Bucks catalog and online-only exculsives.
- Share your feedback.

Visit us at:

ReaderService.com